MW01224040

To Janene
My best editor ever

SUMMERS RUN

AN AMERICAN BOYHOOD

JAMES COTTON

IUNIVERSE, INC.
NEW YORK   BLOOMINGTON

Summers Run
An American Boyhood

This is a work of fiction. All of the characters, names, incidents, organizations, and dialogue in this novel are either the products of the author's imagination or are used fictitiously.

Cover painting by Brent Cotton, www.cottonfinearts.com

iUniverse books may be ordered through booksellers or by contacting:

iUniverse
1663 Liberty Drive
Bloomington, IN 47403
www.iuniverse.com
1-800-Authors (1-800-288-4677)

ISBN: 978-1-4401-7361-5 (sc)
ISBN: 978-1-4401-7363-9 (dj)
ISBN: 978-1-4401-7362-2 (ebk)

Printed in the United States of America

iUniverse rev. date: 10/8/2009

CONTENTS

Chapter 1   A Farm in Pennsylvania. 1

Chapter 2   The Stranger. 7

Chapter 3   Off to See The Rooster 13

Chapter 4   The Sow's Ear 19

Chapter 5   Peepers and Panthers 26

Chapter 6   Like Father, Like Son 34

Chapter 7   The Sacred Forest 41

Chapter 8   When Blake Shot his Pontiac 47

Chapter 9   Boys Raised in The South 55

Chapter 10   Revelations 58

Chapter 11   The Surprise. 67

Chapter 12   Dear Hearts and Gentle People 73

Chapter 13   Mr. Standing Ovation. 79

Chapter 14   Mellow as a Cello 86

Chapter 15   Silver Nights, Golden Mornings 93

Chapter 16   No Abfustication Permitted 100

Chapter 17   Finding Our Boyhoods 107

Chapter 18   The Filmography of Nathean Hale
             Summers 113

Chapter 19   The Little Winchester. 123

Chapter 20   The Bearcat 130

Chapter 21   Nicknames 137

Chapter 22   The Homestead Room 145

Chapter 23   The Candle's Wick. 153

Chapter 24   The Neighborhood. 159

Chapter 25   Meeting Tim. 169

Chapter 26   Las Vegas on the Line 179

Chapter 27   Load and Flow. 189

Chapter 28   The Snot-nosed Adolescent 199

Chapter 29   The Cornerstone Homecoming 207

Chapter 30   The Panthers' Prayer 214

Chapter 31   The Four Horsemen of the Outfield. . . 224

Chapter 32   The Short Game. 232

Chapter 33   A Bushel and A Peck 239

Chapter 34   A Day of Pleasant Bread 248

Chapter 35   The Embarassing Home Run. 253

Chapter 36   This Matter of Adoption 262

Chapter 37   On the Oregon Trail. 268

Chapter 38   Planning and Providence 276

Chapter 39   Chase Around Brown. 282

Chapter 40   Harry the Ferguson 287

Chapter 41   The Crevices of Memory. 292

CHAPTER 1

A Farm in Pennsylvania

Back then, I took notice of how families were called to dinner. It became a curious matter to me and remains so to this very day.

Thus far, I've collected: "It's ready. . . . We're eating, you guys. . . . Dinner's (or supper's) on. . . . Come an' eat. . . . Let's eat. . . . Wash up. . . . Are we eating here or in front of the TV? . . . It's on. . . . It's getting cold. . . . Let's go, family. . . . Hurry an' eat or we'll be late."

My maternal grandmother Ronnie would call out—"Sgt. Ceee Jaay! Front and center or I'll throw it to the dogs and then to the hogs." Uncle Albert Summers' favorite seemed "take it or leave it, like it or lump it." Occasionally, he'd announce, "It's road kill garnished with a few leftovers. So grab it and growl." He was a fine cook, though a widower, who lived alone until his son moved back home. Albert and I became kindred spirits, for when I first placed my feet under his table, I was alone as well.

I'd become an orphan of sorts, beginning a journey of my own on my own. More or less.

In truth, I had a mother but she'd recently fallen for a club and casino owner from Nevada. She was hitching her "wagon to a star," she told me.

Apparently such was a one-horse cart without room for me. The arrangement began just fine. Of my two options available, downtown Las Vegas where my mother would park her wagon held little interest for me.

Instead, I ended up on a farm in rural Pennsylvania, and there began a life most boys age eleven would envy with all the considerable yearning we eleven year olds could muster.

*   *   *

The year was 1992, the month of early March, and it had been decided.

"Claude." My mother had me sit beside her, snapping off her little bedside TV, and taking both my hands in hers. This meant, *please pay close attention, son.* "You remember how much fun we had visiting the farm up in 'P.A.' and your Aunt Marguerite? When our daddy Blake went off to war? Well, we're going back to visit for a spell while I seal my mind 'bout Mister Vic. Just 'for a spell,' as Blake used to say."

"Mister Vic" was my mother's new boyfriend. Mom had been widowed in February of The Gulf War, 1991. Officially, my father had been listed as missing in action until it seemed final and hopeless. He would never return to us from the sands of Iraq. I became fatherless and she became free. Mom and Vic met in Atlantic City at an audition fair and talent search.

My mother was a vocalist and sang some on air force bases, army posts, and such. A big band song stylist, she called herself. From what little I knew about it, she sounded pretty good. Folks applauded warmly and some whistled. She drew a lot of attention at the fair, including that of Mister Vic.

After Atlantic City and meeting Mr. Ignatius "Vic" Delveccio, my mother's life had taken one crazy turn upon another it seemed to me. I hung on while she plowed into the curves, her foot to the floor, her head in the clouds, her gaze on the prize.

"The Prize" was a suave businessman whose family had made it big in Nevada decades ago. He held interests in several "establishments," as my mother described them.

2

"And do you know, hon, like I said, Vic's definitely going to help me get my musical career back on track. I'll be singing every night in one of his clubs if I want to. Isn't that exciting—your mom becoming a professional songbird! I'm gonna take some vocal lessons out there or in Los Angeles. Get the training I've never really had.

"Oh, and sweetheart, you'll be visiting when school lets out and then one day, you'll move out to Las Vegas and we'll all be back together again."

"What's Vic think about me hangin' around?" I asked.

"Oh, hon, he wants you with us soon too, but right now, he's got to get things set up so they'll be right for me, for us.

"He doesn't want us—you, me, and him—to take on too much too soon, and I can see his point. Y'see, he's never been a father before and he wants to do it right an' ease his way into it." She turned from the mirror and let the hairbrush fall slack to her lap. "I think that's best. And very wise."

I nodded my understanding if not my approval, left the bedroom, found my ball and glove, and began fielding grounders in what little backyard the army provided its married personnel. My father had served in airborne units, mainly, and at the time of his disappearance was up for promotion and if he opted, retirement. Now, as I look back, it seemed so cruel—the proverbial one last mission syndrome that claimed him and took our hopes away. The hopes I heard him voice: farm, family, the old home place. The army of course had to move on, *regrets*. It would, of course, return us to civilian life, wherever we wanted it to be.

My grandfather, Senior Master Sergeant Claude Joseph "C. J." Jarrett, USAF (Retired) had gifted me with one of those bouncy, netted things that deliver the ball back to the thrower. I'd practiced to where it would no longer return a baseball with vigor but preferred tennis balls instead. Perhaps I'd take it with me. To Pennsylvania. Like my granddad, I loved baseball and would genuinely miss my team on the fort, The Kaintucks.

Pennsylvania. We were leaving the army for "P. A.", as Aunt Marguerite called it. I bounced the tennis balls off the net as fast as I could fire them, catching some in my glove, others in my bare hand. It would seem strange to be a civilian. I'd never been anything but an army kid.

Aunt Marguerite's farm, then it is. Guess I'm going to be a farm boy. For a spell.

*　　*　　*

The US Army bade us both a formal and yet a touching farewell. My father was decorated, yes, but also highly admired and well liked in the officers' club or enlisted barracks. The honors, funeral, and memorial service had been conducted months ago, and we'd lived out our benevolent residency on Fort Campbell. Official bereavement seemed over and with our goods crated and secured on the moving van and Mom and me on a flight to Pittsburgh, we were out of the military's hair.

We wouldn't look back, I was assured. My mother bid it good riddance.

She snapped her seatbelt and gave it the strongest tug her tiny hands and thin little arms could manage. It seemed a gesture of finality. "And I declare, good bye army. The feeling is mutual, don't we think, sweetheart? I hope you'll never want to go off to war. It's the pits for those you leave at home. Thanks for some of the memories, Uncle Sam, but so long."

I had to respect her sentiments, though following my dad into the army or some branch of the service had become one of my many aspirations at age eleven. Flying jets for example; my Grandfather Jarrett championed the US Air Force. No mention of the moving about or the day-to-day life on a crowded military base, drawbacks my mom described at length as the "downside." Mother wrinkled her little nose when she called herself a "service brat," and I didn't want to be tagged thus, by myself or others.

Though I was going on twelve years of age, I knew my perceptions of some things were flawed. Yet I was not such a boy I didn't know about labels and being dismissed. Nor was I such a boy I didn't know of losing and the persistence of loss. Nor was I a stranger to those wakeful hours of the night wondering if my father ever thought of me now.

Does he know of my sorrows?

Does he share such? Or was he in a place where regrets and tears are purged from thought? A place where the views of loved ones left behind are as memories and veiled?

In 1992, I'd be twelve come August. Though I'd been told I was now the "man of the family," my father's adulthood seemed well over the horizon and his son's loneliness just around the corner.

Our flight climbed above the haze below, nosing its way into a blue and golden afternoon where we floated over the woolly overcast now beneath us. We'd been holding hands and when the sun's ray splashed across the cabin, my mother uttered a little cry, a sob, and squeezed my hand hard enough to hurt.

"Oh, hon, it's over."

*   *   *

Anne Doolittle emerged from the sea of folks swimming around as we entered the terminal. She fanned herself, breathless.

"Claude, you remember Annie, Aunt Marguerite's friend from the farm?"

"Yes, ma'am. Hello, again." I offered my hand and she pulled me into a little hug.

"Oh, you two look so good after what you've been through. Goodness, welcome home!" she choked and began to cry. The two women embraced once more.

"Oh, Annie, we're moving on, me an' Claude. We've got to."

5

"Yes," Anne sniffed into her dainty little handkerchief. "Yes, of course you must." She dabbed at her eyes and told us, oh, look at me.

"I dug this out of what's left of my hope chest," she laughed. She meant the handkerchief. "I knew I'd blubber—that's my role. Let's get down to baggage claim."

"Marguerite couldn't come?" my mother asked. Anne stopped in mid-stride and we all dodged a cart streaming by and beeping for us to make way for its load of senior citizens.

Anne touched Mom's arm again. "Grandma Bea took a spill this morning—"

"Oh, poor Granny Kinkade!"

"Nothing serious—she jiggered her back, though. She's in bed with ice packs and the heating pad. But she is farm girl strong, I'll tell the world. She stumbled off the back steps, going out to scatter scratch to her chicks. Nothing to worry about but Marguerite thought she'd better stay close by today."

At baggage claim, all pleasantries underscored by the airport's elevator music were drowned under. The sea of travelers had boiled over into a turbulent wave crashing on a shore of sinuous conveyors, foaming outcrops of luggage threatening to topple, families shuffling together like penguins, and frowning businessmen plucking suit bags and cases from the backwash, survivors rescuing flotsam. Suddenly, all were unlovely humans bent on getting this over with.

"Holy crow, get me back to the farm and gentle folk," said Anne over the tumult. "Anyways, Daisy, Granny's mishap allowed us to cook up something special for your homecoming."

"Oh, my. A surprise?" Mom relished surprises.

"You'll see shortly." Anne patted my mother's arm and smiled like the schoolgirl with a secret she'd been decades ago. Apparently, Anne was an arm-patter. I liked her for that.

*   *   *

6

CHAPTER 2

The Stranger

We stood guard over our luggage and watched the mob swirl out the doors to taxis and rental car vans like schools of fish following each other and plunging forward, either panicked or purposeful.

"Holy crow," said Anne. "I've never seen it so jammed up and this crazy before. Not used to all this noise." She turned to Mom. "I hope you'll find it so quiet on the farm, you can get things nice and settled." Mom simply nodded *yes*. Anne—not being family—didn't have much say in the matter. But she and my Aunt Marguerite might not approve of Mom's choice in husbands or the move to Las Vegas and leaving me behind.

Such would be my guess. They were older, seasoned in the ways of wives and husbands. *Life.*

The baggage conveyors continued their ebb and flow, carrying only forlorn and unclaimed stragglers. Then a man emerged through the last of the crowd, striding toward us and smiling. Something in his manner or the walk looked familiar. So very familiar.

"What a madhouse," he laughed. "Bad weather over east so they diverted a bunch of flights this way." His voice held a timbre developed from confidence, practice, and being at ease with himself. This stranger seemed not a stranger at all. Rather, someone I ought to recognize or remember. But, who should I know outside my young and sheltered life?

"Well, here's our chauffeur." Anne took Stranger by the sleeve of his linen safari jacket and blushed as if she might pop.

"Daisy, Claude—I don't think you've ever met Nathe . . . but this is Nathean Summers, your cousin Nathe—"

Mom gasped and began a goofy litany of "Oh my . . . this is just wonderful to meet—what a—this is so unexpected, such a treat—Anne if I can't find a tissue, I might need to borrow your hanky—I'm so touched to see, that you came down—"

Nathe Summers took Mom's hands in both of his and told her, "Welcome to Pennsylvania. For a spell, at least." Then he turned to me and we shook hands while Mom fluttered her way through an introduction. Summers nodded.

"That's right. Your father and I were cousins so I think that makes us second cousins. Anne, you might not know this but Claude and I are connected through the Forsythes as well as the Kinkades."

"Oh, one of those once or twice removed things, maybe?"

"I'd guess." Nathe stuck one hand in the pocket of that jacket I admired. The other adjusted his tie. He wore what I learned later was an ascot. "Let's see, my father's uncle Grant Summers married a cousin of Opal Forsythe who was Claude's great grandmother, and the mother of his grandmother Beatrice Kinkade. Of course, my dad married Margaret Kinkade—"Peg"—Grandma Bea's sister."

"Sounds like we're climbing the family tree," my mother blurted.

"Oh, indeed." Nathe seemed to smile and laugh easily, putting us at ease. "Taking a couple turns around the trunk and up the branches. Need to draw it out on paper perhaps." He pulled his hand from the jacket pocket and offered us each a mint. "Ready to roll?"

*   *   *

Here he was. He seemed tall enough, not towering as I pictured. But here he stood in the flesh. Within spitting distance—the family's Golden Boy. The stuff of our legends and my speculations. At last we met. Secretly, I nursed the hope we would within the new life where Mom and I found ourselves. Such seemed possible. And now here, today, sooner than later.

We gathered up our goods and swam into the crowds outside, Nathe telling us we've a walk.

Mom became so silly with all this, as giddy as I'd ever witnessed. She asked if we might be hounded by autograph seekers. To my relief, Nathe laughed, genuinely amused, I decided.

"Those days are over, Daisy." He popped the trunk lid of his car. "No paparazzi tagging after me anymore."

He wedged our biggest cases in and found to his relief they barely fit. "Looks like the smaller things will have to ride up front. I debated leaving the spare at home and then I thought that's sure gonna look foolish if we have a flat." He closed and locked the lid.

"Oh, now and then someone comes up and says, 'Pardon me, but aren't you . . .' and sometimes they mix the name or face, confusing me with that other guy. It's all right."

Nathe held the door open for the ladies and Mom said, "Oh my," as she climbed in the back.

I marveled. This car was made of wood.

At least some of it. The hood and fenders were painted a forest green so deep and rich it looked as if I could plunge my arm down clear to my shoulder.

The rest was fashioned of maple and mahogany, said Nathe. "I'd been looking for one of these in decent shape for years. And as luck would have it, about the time I quit, up popped two for sale the same week.

"One in excellent condition. All original. A little leather work, a new top, refinished the wood and I sold it to a guy who wanted it worse'n me. Got a nice price and went to work on this one.

"She's nowhere near original, Claude. Totally modern power train. Power steering, disc brakes, windows and locks and so on. Just the shell is restored. All the mechanicals are bogus, imports, nothing factory about it. Such cuts its value to the collectors." He acted apologetic. "But . . . today we can't do without automatic tranny, turn signals, or cassette players, can we?"

I nodded. "What kind is it?"

"A Chrysler Town and Country."

We hopped in the front and I sank into a cushiony couch of sumptuous leather. I looked back at Mom who was flushed and glistening. "Smells good," I told her.

She nodded and we exchanged our *can-you-believe-this* glance.

"Hon, we're riding in style."

"And . . ." Nathe ushered the big hood toward an exit. "We should beat the rush hour if I don't get us lost," he laughed.

I decided I might like this Nathe Summers, my illustrious cousin.

*   *   *

His film career began in 1954 at the age of eight. A studio publicist wrote glowingly: "Audiences find the earnest and convincing performance of newcomer Nathean Summers so engaging, young and old alike are demanding more appearances of this talented youngster." A critic blessed the casting agency, calling Nathe "a brilliant choice. Young Summers might become filmdom's quintessential farm kid or everyone's favorite young prairie pioneer."

As it happened, the writer proved prescient. First impressions stick in Hollywood and Nathe went on to play the plucky son of Russian émigrés trapped by avalanches and a ravenous pack of movie dogs in *The Wolves of Wind*

River. Then, he helped turn the tables on gun runners as the son of a Scottish freighter in *The Remington Rifles*. In *Where the Sun Now Stands*, he tagged along with the Nez Perce in their desperate flight to Canada, his blond mop backlit against the somber evergreens on location and contrasting with his swarthy companions. He became the tribe's good luck symbol and the envy of every young boy in 1950s America.

Wrote one reviewer: "The shocking death of the film's narrator and lead character, Daniel—played to perfection by 12-year-old Nathe Summers—at the Bear Paw Mountain Surrender is a performance worthy of the Academy's attention. I'd wager there wasn't a dry eye in my theater, at least, when Daniel dropped to his knees and pled for the life of his red-skinned friend. A Juvenile Oscar, perhaps?"

In all, he played in more than a dozen full-length features, paired with the likes of Joel McCrea, Randolph Scott, Robert Taylor, Gregory Peck, James Stewart, Richard Farnsworth, Richard Widmark, Gloria Grahame, Myrna Dell, Loretta Young, Myrna Loy, Greer Garson, Colleen Dewhurst, Lillian Gish, Marjorie Main, and Jane Darwell. His drawing power was sufficient to earn him a spot on lobby cards and posters and his name in the second tier of billing.

A fan club started up and after *Where the Sun Now Stands* was released, Nathe was tapped to play Jacob Hogan on *Children of the Oregon Trail*, a Saturday morning television series that aspired to be a cut above the usual kid fare, airing for ninety minutes and biweekly. It became highly anticipated and showcased Nathe's horsemanship. The schedule allowed him to continue his feature film work, and he grew into a well-respected supporting player approaching stardom. He was now barely fourteen years of age.

I knew all this. Steeped myself in it. When my mother married and joined the family in the late 1970s, she began collecting every scrap, jot, and tittle she could find about her husband's famous cousin. By then, though, Nathe's career had grown stagnant. He'd been in front of the cameras only once in ten years. Westerns had fallen from favor. And he became perceived as hard to cast, passed over for the more hip, young performers moviegoers paid to see in car chases and glamorous surroundings. Still, the industry cherished him as an icon of that era, the golden-haired symbol of the wholesome good it brought to the screen and into American homes back in the Fifties and Sixties.

It wanted him to remain . . . the cowboy kid who could drive a six-up hitch and yet wring a tear from the toughest curmudgeon around. Whether Lionel Barrymore on celluloid or your crusty uncle, the truck driver who hadn't cried since his dog died.

The quintessential rustic and utterly endearing boy of the frontier faded quietly. Like the prairie breezes that spawned his beginning, he slipped over the dusky horizon and was gone. He started as Lars, the little Swedish guy who found the Indian babe left behind in the wheatgrass. Lars, the darling of the pioneer band, Lars who lay mortally ill in the covered wagon, touching the cheek of his father, both smiling through their tears:

"Papa . . . I know . . . I shan't see the ocean. Will you skip a stone across the water for me?"

*   *   *

CHAPTER 3

Off to See The Rooster

"First, I blew the top off the blender and that slopped over into the salad fixin's. Right about then, Bethany called . . . with her tail of woe—"

"Things are no better?" Anne asked.

Marguerite shook her head. "She's been talking to her father and the kids are in a state. Looks like she's going to move out for a spell. Back here.

"So, I got wrapped up in all that and forgot to set the timer on the cornbread," she laughed "So welcome back you two, back home to chaos and crisis!" she cried and hugged Mom and me together. She smelled of cinnamon and nutmeg, I guessed.

"My chili supper's a wreck and I so wanted it nice for Daisy and Claude and wouldn't y' know, it's a calamity instead of a homecoming." Aunt Marguerite thanked Nathe for meeting us at the airport, and he suggested we rescue dinner by going for pizza.

"Let's order and Claude and I'll drive up to The Shack and get a couple. Maybe the cornbread's all right—I like a crispy edge to it."

"Oh, cousin, I think not. I'm throwing it out. Even the birds will bend their beaks, it's too tough and charred."

*   *   *

We put the top down on the Town and Country for the drive over the back roads up to US 98, what the locals called "The Highway." I knew from watching old movies on television that woody convertibles or flare-fendered roadsters were driven like this: with casual elegance and deference to the dignity of both the car and the country it passed through. One should loll one's way around the gentle curves of the lane, go slowly enough to count the posts of the white fences passing by, follow the contours of the rolling green pastures where the mares and their foals watched as we drew abreast. Nathe pressed the horn ring and the Chrysler trumpeted our presence. The horses looked up and the young ones either gave chase or bolted away, bucking or crow-hopping.

"Starting to look like the hunt country of Maryland or Virginia hereabouts. Changed a mite since I grew up on this road. That place over there . . . used to be an old house that never knew a coat of paint, a herd of bony dairy cows, and every field and ditch bank full of Canadian thistles. Now it's a showplace. Still have some eyesores here and there, though."

I felt like some country gentleman sporting a moustache, smoking one of those elegant Meerschaums and wearing a shooting jacket, whisking along in my elegant motorcar, mildly praising my responsible tenants, and quite assured of my position as squire of the village, swelling into my destiny.

The girl at The Shack brought me back to earth. She leveled a skeptical appraisal on us both, more curious than annoyed. Nathe blessed her with that magnetic smile, and she blinked, perplexed why she couldn't quite connect a name and face. I followed him out but not before she asked me, "You'uns visiting hereabouts?"

I nodded. "Sort of. For a spell."

"Thought so. From California, maybe. Enjoy your pizzas."

I said thanks and considered correcting her but was too shy. I noted her and her co-workers, a guy and another girl, discussing us—or the car—as we climbed in, placing the boxes between us.

"We'll stop by the place and pick up Dad. He wants to check on your Gram . . . and he loves pizza."

The Summers Farm was not as imposing as Aunt Marguerite's Shadeland. Yes, both homes shared the tree-lined drive but the Summers place was smaller and painted white, typical of its day and age. The lawns surrounding it looked freshly clipped, though the trees were graced by tall grassy collars that had escaped the mower.

"Dad sticks to the old gang reel mowers. Won't change to a rotary—claims they're hard on the grass. Some things never change. You've never been here, I suspect." We pulled up to a brick walk that looked freshly placed.

"Umm, yes, I have actually. We came over for a birthday party . . . just before Dad left for overseas. Mr. Summers told m' dad just old men should go to war. He said, 'both sides will see we're too pitiful to fight, so let's play pinochle instead.'"

When I stumbled through this account, Nathe laughed to my relief. "Sounds like my pop, all right. He always had a quip for the location crews—they loved him. Pretty good sense of humor, not the stodgy . . . miserly accountant they expected."

Before we could dislodge ourselves from the car, a white-haired gentleman with silver mutton shops shining in the sun came weaving his way down the walk toward us.

He paused at the gate and surveyed us. "Well, there's a pair to draw to. What a gorgeous night for the top down. Let's go to town, what say, Claude? Cruise Main." He shook my hand as I opened the door and stood next to him. Then he gripped me on the shoulder and tilted his head back to look me over. Another appraisal but more benevolent than the girl's at The Shack.

"One day soon, we'll have to start looking you in the eye. You're shining fine. Welcome back to P.A."

"Yes sir. Good to be back."

"Glad you're here. Perhaps this time you can stay with us for a spell."

I took to the back seat while Mr. Albert Summers settled himself up front. "Gots to get over and give that gram of yours a scolding for such imprudence. She doesn't let herself go down very often—might be a sight worth seein'."

"Marguerite's says the phone's been on the ring all day long," Nathe said. "News speeds along on the church and the garden group grapevines, you can guess. Plus her book club gal pals are all a-twitter."

"And the gossip," Mr. Summers added. "Worse when we had party lines," he laughed. "Claude here's too young to remember when we dialed Central and later, we got party lines with different rings for each family. We had six on our line at first, then down to four.

"My mother loved what she called, 'the Bell'. She'd listen in and when we'd chide her for eavesdropping, she'd say, 'Well, it's a good way to keep up with who's who and what's what around here.' Never did correct her of that habit."

"When I moved back here to go to school, Claude, Gram Summers used to monitor the girls phoning or being phoned," said Nathe. "Then she'd hold an inquest later, and I'd get the lowdown on the young lady's family. Used to annoy me at first. Then I'd get amused and cook up some devilish yarn about us getting engaged or eloping. Gram caught on and quit snooping about."

"Yup, she was just enough Forsythe that blood will tell. Forsythes could be busybodies. Guess you know the clan's stirring up new trouble for Marguerite?"

"Heard tell."

"Can't let the old wounds heal." Mr. Summers shifted around to look back at me. "There's always been a little bad blood, Claude, between the Kinkades and the Forsythes. Stems from back when Shadeland passed out of Forsythe hands into Kinkade's."

"Oh?" I asked. "A family feud then?"

"Y' could say. Worse'n the Hatfields and McCoys down in West Virginia. Even to this day, folks keep their .30-30s loaded an' behind the door where they can get to 'em, quick-like."

"Balderdash—Claude, don't swallow too much of what y' hear about this. Everyone's on terms for the most part."

"Umm, 'fraid not with Eugene, son. He's mounting a charge, says they found a codicil to the old will written by Old Billy himself reinstating the original Forsythe heir, Young Billy. And that the will was supposed to be changed, that it can be contested and the like. Marguerite's worried."

*   *   *

My Grandmother Beatrice Kinkade took her pizza in bed and complained about it.

"Doctor Strickland was indeed very 'strict' indeed. I'm to stay off my feet. So I'll be a meek little lamb and do as I'm told for a change. How are you, Claude? You've grown, of course." I approached her bedside and bestowed a little peck on her forehead. "I'm fine, Grandma. But, how you doing?"

"Well, I'm embarrassed and a little peevish with myself. I was thinking about Nathe and Blake after my fall. The 'twins' we called them, since they could pass for brothers. Don't expect you knew that. Twins they were, even though they were two years apart. They usually came as a pair, almost inseparable. Find one and there'd be the other.

"Anyway, we were re-roofing the barn . . . summer of 1951 after that bad storm we had. Nathe, being the oldest, was allowed to help a little. Your Grandfather David told him he could run one of the bucket pulleys—wasn't a big job—but that he was to stay on the bottom planks of the first scaffold, no higher.

"Well, Blake—so like your father—decided he could help too and that little pill not only climbed up to the first scaffolding, but he went on up the next one, and then he climbed the ladder to the very peak behind the maw where we had the weathervane situated.

"Fortunately, we had this courageous neighbor boy helping us. He was daring and he crawled out there and brought him down to me. I became so frightened—shaking to my bones and while I didn't believe in spanking my children, I felt sorely tempted that day. I hugged his little body and cried my eyes out and he pushed away from me, and said, rather petulantly, 'Mahter, no be sad. God see me.'

"Oh, my stars," she now laughed through her tears. "Here, I take a two-foot tumble and your daddy could have plunged thirty feet. He wasn't three years old at the time."

"I never heard this story." I hadn't. It supported my perception of Dad, the Airborne instructor, so self-assured, the warrior leading by example, bravery personified.

"Here I am blubbering into this nice pizza you brought me. No . . ." she dabbed at her eyes. "I suspect you hadn't heard about the fright of my life. It's a story I don't tell easily. But," she smiled, "I wish he were sitting beside us here tonight so he could hear it too."

"Yes, ma'am."

"Of course, he'd heard it a dozen times but wouldn't it be special? He told us back then he was 'going up to see the rooster.' You know, the big copper one that swings in the wind up there. It became the family slogan.

"So . . . if you ever hear any of us say, 'I'm going to see the rooster,' it means we're off on an adventure, taking a journey, going out to see the world . . . . Or, leaving to do a hard job of some kind. Like going to war."

We looked at each other and exchanged our understanding. Nothing more needed to be voiced. My father Blake David Kinkade, Major, US Army, had gone to see his rooster.

*   *   *

CHAPTER 4

The Sow's Ear

My new friends and I staggered over the grass, stumbled into each other, and giddy with the joy of seeing baseballs in flight, we laughed and fell into a three-boy heap on the damp ground.

I could smell them: the musk of young boy sweat and laundry soap, fresh from one's re-entry into spring, basking in its first warm morning. The day was filling its promise. Easter would soon be celebrated but we were experiencing a resurrection of our own known only to boys.

Boys for whom the coziness of winter's cocoon had become tiresome. Boys who longed to burst from the earth and savor the signature aromas of fresh dirt and fecundity. Boys who wanted baseballs: in their hands, swelling their hopes, sailing above their infinite horizons.

We had no words for the process. We couldn't declare our sentiments in well-turned musical phrases other than an absent-minded whistle floating over a daydream. It had to be, simply, spring. Or baseball. Or both.

We hadn't decades of springs within our instincts to tell us so. Just an ancestral bonding we could still share with the creatures that pursued chores more serious than chasing baseballs in the sky. Birds build nests while boys build dreams from grass and sand.

I watched Nathe, obviously enjoying himself. I could only imagine him speaking with the dark-skinned man standing next to him. I could only guess, but I suspect Nathe was telling him, I haven't hit flies in years. And he seemed to attack this diversion, this renewal of spring's promise with a boyish aggression that quite stunned me to behold.

For my friends and I had no sooner returned one ball for him to hit again when another fly came arcing our way. Then another, even higher than the rest. We shagged one after the other until we were on the verge of breathless.

My companion, a black boy named Jules, said: "Man, don' he slow down? I'm about to cook out here."

"You gots to get your wind back," said his twin brother. "Been cooped up inside too long. This one's mine," he called at the *ping* of the bat and the ball drifted to our left, his side of our impromptu outfield on the Summers lawn. His name was August ". . . but don't call him Auggie. He's Gus."

Nathe twirled the bat around his wrist and I watched him offer it to Mr. Alphonse, the boys' father, who declined. Then, he waved us in.

"Whew, that was fun. For me anyways."

"Man, Mr. Nathe, you hit like a big leaguer."

"Well, thanks, Jules. But I didn't usually hit like that in any game I ever played. Well . . . we must let Mr. Alphonse and you boys get on with your work." At that moment, another bright teal blue dump truck arrived with its five yards of gravel. A young man set its brakes, jumped out, and hooking his thumbs in the bib of his overalls, came strolling toward us, obviously enjoying spring's brightest day thus far.

"This is my eldest son, Lawrence. Lawrence, Mr. Summers and his son Claude."

"A pleasure, sir," said Lawrence.

We shook hands and Nathe explained we were cousins. Later, in my mind's eye, I pictured what must have been a striking contrast to any onlooker passing by or pulling into the yard.

Four black folks, skin burnished bronze by good health and working out-of-doors and two white guys, as pale as milk. For I was blond and Nathe retained much of his original flaxen hue though it was muted or enhanced, depending on the light, by streaks of platinum or spots of gray.

"You guys are good with a glove." Nathe gathered up the baseballs and wiped any dew from each one vigorously in his bare hands. "Do you have a team?"

"Nossir," the twins chorused.

"That's too bad."

"We thought about signin' 'em up for a team in town," said their father. "But, it's a ways to drive and I got a busy business to take care of. And their mother doesn't like for them to be out there on 'The Highway' all that much."

Nathe nodded. "Nothing local, I guess?"

"Not really," said Mr. Alphonse. "You know, there's a few diamonds here and there but they're set up for th' big guys. No Little League 'cept in town. I don't know why, because there's some talent in these little places. Take th' Catalino boys, who got th' vineyards, they have always been good ball players."

"Oh, yes, I remember them. My dad tells about the older Catalinos playing for the Blooming Valley Bunch, and I believe Joe Catalino went on to play Triple A somewhere. So . . . we need a team hereabouts."

"Well, I feel th' boys around here—and not just mine—are being denied an opportunity they should have. There are boys that would come out if there were a league and some supervision, I'm sure. They need to learn th' game."

"The high school boys have a Legion league," Jules said. "But they get a game going and pretty soon everyone gets in a big fight about somethin'."

"Don't have any umpires is one reason," said his brother.

"Yes, indeed . . . that is a problem. Have to have order at the plate, out in the field."

"Say, Nathean, didn't your daddy have a ball field somewhere here on the place?"

"Yes, James, he did for sure," Nathe said, pointing the bat towards the barn. "It's still out there. Just a cut or two above a cow pasture but he did put up a good backstop and an outfield fence. Our family would get up a game and what neighbors we could round up to fill out as best we could. Girls played, even my mother once."

"Sounds like your father's 'Field of Dreams'." Lawrence smiled, clearly in awe.

"Oh, indeed. Dad was ahead of his time." Nathe drew a circle in the dirt with the knob of a bat handle. "I'm thinking . . . I'm a-thinkin' maybe we make that into our Little League field. . . if there's enough interest. Could you manage a ball team, Lawrence?"

"Oh, I dunno about that. I've got no experience and let me emphasize, I surely do not have near enough experience . . . or the courage to be an umpire, that's for certain."

Mr. Alphonse nodded his approval. "Now, that's being sensible, son. On the surface. 'Course, you might like th' challenge."

"My experience with baseball is pretty scattered, just fragments here and there," said Nathe. "My folks tried to get me into Little League when we were in California, but I'd be at the studio until late, going off somewhere on locations, and missing practices and such. Some of us on location or in the lot would get a pickup game together between scenes and that was fun."

"With some of your fellow actors, then?"

"Right," Nathe laughed. "One time, Billy Whipple—I think it was he—hit this really long drive into another set where they were filming a sword fight. Now, here are these two guys slashing away at each other and in hops this baseball bouncing across the castle floor. We all got a scolding for that little trick."

"They didn't see the humor in it, then?"

"No, no indeed. The motion picture business is pretty humorless when it comes to time and money. No time for kid stuff in the movies. Or kids for that matter. Unless you were making money for the studio."

"Do you miss it, sir? I mean—man alive—being a movie star an' all. Seems like it must have been mighty fine at times."

"Oh, it *was* fine, Lawrence. I tried to keep my career going behind the cameras but I was young and no one wanted my kind of films. Even for television. *Bullitt* became the rage when I was struggling and after it came out, everyone wanted cops and car chases." Our conversation lulled to an awkward close and the Alphonse father and son started their trucks and moved into place. "Got to have this gravel ready for Banks McIntyre to spread and roll."

The first load was laid down, then the second. Lawrence drove out for another and Mr. Alphonse followed with the boys in his matching truck. I wondered what my new friends thought of my famous cousin. *I'll bet they're asking their dad about Nathe and his films right now: "Was he really a movie star? Have you seen any of his pictures? Have we, poppa?"*

*   *   *

Nathe and I watched the refreshed driveway take shape under the expert and gentle-handed guidance of Mr. Alphonse. "Folks say his materials are the best around. Everyone wondered, 'Well, why'd he buy that worn-out farm? Nothing there but rocks and sand.'

"But, James knew a gravel pit could become a gold mine. Building a good family business for his boys someday—look at those trucks. You'd think they were brand new but James said they're from the '70s." He folded his hands over the fence

23

rail and studied the ground. "I admire such." Nathe resumed the same wistfulness of a few minutes earlier, reflecting on the end of his career. "I envy such. 'J. A. Alphonse & Sons . . . Sand & Gravel.'

"Fathers and sons. Working together. Might be nice. On the other hand, perhaps nothing but a migraine, as some families go. 'The waters of a father and son run deep, boy'—an old movie line," he looked up and my way. "From *One Hundred Horses*. A character actor by the name of Glen Esterline said it to me and my line back was: 'Deep water's right, Amos. So deep it's pulling me down and under.' I think of that scene ever now and then.

"Claude . . . let's you and I . . . take a look at Dad's old baseball park."

*   *   *

I'd been on the Summers farm before but I hadn't explored it as I might Aunt Marguerite's. I had no limits on her place but this was the neighbor's. And though we all were family, a country boy, like the farm's collie, had to know his boundaries. Not everything was public. And I was about to become a country boy. So, I needed to know these things. That I'd only been in "P. A." and on the family's farms one full day seemed to open a new life and its wonders for me and my future. I wondered if I might feel a sense of something here. Perhap a belonging or the faintest stirrings of . . . home.

Plus, building Nathe's new project might open more doors yet and install me as the family's official Farm-Kid-in-Residence of both Shadeland and Summers Run Farm.

Nathe and I climbed the fence surrounding Albert's baseball diamond. Yes, it would take some labor but not a miracle.

"Dad keeps it mowed. Grass took over the infield. Those blue spruce will soon crowd the outfield fence, I'm a-thinking." Nathe pointed out. "'Course we'll move the fence in for Little

League. Two hundred feet and some, as I recollect. Yup. Trees grow when you're not watching them every day.

"We dragged the infield with an old bedspring," Nathe laughed. "Had a lot of fun building Dad's Diamond—that's what we called it. Mother called it Dad's Disaster. I got into my first real fight . . . right about there between first base and the mound. Guy called me a sissy for crying in a movie."

"Did you win the fight?"

"Yup. What do you think, Claude? Can we make this sow's ear into a silk purse?"

I told him I thought so. I told him I knew so.

*   *   *

CHAPTER 5

Peepers and Panthers

"Folks," said Nathe, hoisting his mug, "let's toast something. Claude, you're allowed a cup of coffee now and then, are you not?"

"Sure."

"There's hot chocolate there in a packet, if you'd rather," Aunt Marguerite said as she blew over her steaming mug. Then, Nathe announced: "Here's until the money runs out!"

"Lord, cousin—what an awful toast! I refuse to drink to such." Aunt Marguerite sat her coffee down and called out to my mom. "Daisy, we're out here on the sun porch."

"Mom's on the phone with Mr. Delveccio," I told them. "She could be a while." This was her first phone visit since arriving in Pennsylvania. Their conversations tended to be long-winded and whenever I eavesdropped, the topics seemed focused on his businesses, musicians he knew, the celebrities, the parties, new acts in town, and the television star who stopped in for dinner last night. "When we were back in Kentucky, Vic put Mom on the phone with Tony Rossi."

"Wow, that's the big time."

"Right an' they talked for quite awhile about songs they liked and other artists an' such."

"You're mother's right to be excited, Claude. I hope it works out."

"She said much to you?" I asked of Aunt Marguerite. "She's kinda concerned about, you know, the family approving everything an' all."

"Yes, I guessed as much. We can't sit in judgment. Lord knows I'm no expert on staying married. I fumbled mine and now here comes my daughter with hers heading for the rocks."

"When Peg and I had an issue," said Albert, "she'd say, "'Now, let's communicate here.' However, I always said communication is fine enough but compromise is the art we really need to practice. Let's not fuss it into something bigger than it needs to be, I'd say. Let's build a solution and not listen to our egos and whatever's telling us we can't lose a little. Keeps things sunnier. Now, I suspect this Vic appears—on first glance—to be one who doesn't compromise. Most highly successful folks don't. What's your take, Claude?"

"Hmm. He's . . . pretty much in charge, I think. I hope she finds she can trust him. I mean, even . . . I dunno." We fell silent. I nearly volunteered that things weren't all that swell between Mom and my soldier dad. Once when they were having one of their "discussions," I heard Mom ask: "Why can't you support my career when you know I'm good at what I do? Just as you're good at your job. I sing, I entertain. You teach, you fight—that's who we are." Just weeks before he left for Kuwait, then Iraq.

The air seemed heavy with rhythm as if thousands of nighttime critters were bouncing a squeaking toy amongst them. One of those mouse things you squeezed and it went *wheeze . . . wheeze.* "Are those crickets I'm hearing?"

"Those are peepers, Claude. Little frogs hereabouts. This time of year, they set up such a serenade this time of night, y' can hardly talk over them when they're at their peak. Marguerite's hosts a million, I suppose, and over on Swenson's farm, there are even more on account of it being more marshy in spots. The boys used to sneak out at night with their flashlights and lanterns and try to catch some but they're so shy and elusive—did you ever find a colony, son?"

"Blake tried hard enough, but no, I never saw a peeper."

"Dad," I said, "claimed he saw a black panther once, here on the place."

"Yes, I think he did. There was a scare and a couple sightings, remember Nathe, when our mothers wouldn't let us go out after dark? We were supposed to play in the yard and not go near The Enchanted Forest."

"Where's that? Sounds neat."

"It's a big grove of timber on the north end of our farm. Lots of ravines and hemlocks. And, it *was* enchanted. There's a big spring—well, there are several springs in the forest—they're the headwaters of Summers Run. And a waterfall. We'll mosey up to see it here soon." Nathe refreshed his coffee, pouring it gingerly as it was nearly dark on the porch with little light shining from the house. I shivered.

A black panther—the very words gave me a delicious chill. I wished my Dad were here to help me watch for one. Stake ourselves out in a tree and bait it in.

"Panthers and peepers. This Pennsylvania is a strange place I'm livin' in right now." They all laughed. "I've got some investigations to do, I can see."

"Claude, while you're investigating things, find out what your Aunt Marguerite puts in her coffee to give it that extra zip."

"All right. What is it, Aunt Marg?"

"Aha. If I tell, then Nathe has to tell me something. Fair is fair."

"I see. Sounds like the old days around here."

"Eggshells."

"Eggshells? I've heard that can be done. That's the secret?"

"Doctor Seaborn taught me that trick."

"Doctor Seaborn?"

"My husband, Claude. He's a professor of architecture at Yale these days. We have a 'modern' marriage, separated but not divorced. Yet."

"Oh . . . sorry. I forgot. Bethany just called him Harold."

"Oh, don't be sorry, Claude. A fine man, Yes, Beth and Harold are close. I'm glad," she smiled. "I want to stay put and he wants another world. So. . . ." I couldn't see her sit back in her chair but it *squawked* in contrast to the peepers. "Now I get to ask Nathe a question."

"Shoot."

"What more are you going to do on your place over there? My word, all that remodeling."

"Well, we're down to the short rows now. House is practically done. It's really been a joy. Place was sound to begin with so that helped. Barn next and then the fields."

"Fences are in bad shape," Albert said. "My fault. I let them go but a bookkeeper doesn't need many fences. That'll take some dollars."

"Well, we'll work on it . . . until the money runs out." Nathe hoisted his mug again.

"Oh, will you stop?" Aunt Marguerite laughed. "Money talk makes me nervous. This mortgage Harold got us into is our current beast. The day I burn it, there'll be a bonfire big enough to see clear to Chapmann, I'll tell the world as Anne would say."

Albert set his cup on the wicker table. "I probably shouldn't give us all a sleepless night—speaking of money and the like—but the word is Gene and his bunch is dickering for the Swenson place. Sale subject to the perc tests."

"Oh, uncle!"

"I know, Marguerite, unsettling news, and also, they made a handsome offer on Harvey Logan's as well, $180,000. Even the Amish wouldn't give that for it. Too small for their liking and at that price, I'm guesstimating."

"But his kids live there too, on the place."

29

"Yes, but Logans are a practical bunch. The girls may prefer the money now rather that dealing with the farm, later, someday."

"I'm thinking," Nathe said, "In fact, I'm a-bettin', Swensons won't meet the new state regs on percolation. I'm guessing the water table is too high and it's too close to the Run for a subdivision."

"Yes, could be. Mighty particular these days."

"Right, and I spoke with a fellow from the DEP just last week and he said they plan to survey the Run and that a letter was coming out to all the landholders hereabouts. Swenson's came up. Gene might run into a brick wall. Officialdom takes a jaundiced view when it comes to stream setback and water pollution. No houses, probably no golf course, I'm a-thinkin'."

"We can hope," said Albert. "The days are over when one could go off and build a house or barn near a watercourse. Remember old Fendwelder? He diverted Harper's Run so it would flow right through a corner of his new barn back then—watered his stock, kept his milk cool. Pretty neat setup. That was *way* back then, hundred years ago. Try doing that today. Wonder what Harvey would take for his place?"

"I'll find out," said Nathe. "I missed Harvey twice, said hello on the phone once. I haven't had one of Carolyn's cookies since I came back home. I need to pay a call. Claude, you'd better come along."

"Claude, your dad and Nathe would slip over to Logans, fill up on Carolyn's wonderful chocolate chips or ginger snaps and come home too full for dinner. Peg and Bea both used to get kinda irked with her. But she was such a good egg, no one griped much about her stuffing our kids full of cookies."

Aunt Marguerite sat back in the wicker rocker and once again it *squawked*. "Carolyn gave me a beautiful wooden box of her recipes so long ago, the cards are dog-eared and yellow. That was their wedding present to Harold and me. He raved.

One thing about Harold, he did appreciate my cooking. I've followed her recipes for years. Old as these chairs." She began a gentle rocking and its creaking kept in time with the peepers' undulating rise and fall. I wondered: I read that panthers would scream in the night. Suddenly she stopped rocking and jumped up.

"Oh, here come the cows! Where are they finding a hole?"

"I'll watch the garden," said Albert.

"Careful, Dad. Better let me get some lights on."

"All right."

"We'll turn 'em into the old horse pasture," said Aunt Marguerite. "That will hold them tonight and there's water in the ditch right now."

Once he shed some light from the porches surrounding Shadeland, Nathe and I eased our way to meet the herd drifting toward the house.

They loomed large in the ghostly foggy glow that threw our shadows toward them. I hoped we looked bigger and more ominous to them than they did to us. Even the calves looked dark and threatening—lithe, sleek, and sinister panthers they weren't but nonetheless, they might be emboldened by their escape from their last pasture. I suspected we were puny humans in their eyes right now, perhaps something to rush at and toss in the air.

I knew as much about cattle as I did bullfighting and I decided I'd better follow Nathe's lead. After all, he was the "quintessential country kid," not me.

"Can y' see the fence to our left, down beyond the big maple?"

I swallowed, then nodded, then managed a yes.

"There's a gate about half way. Used to be a loop there with a little latch to hold it. Swing it out in the yard and then stand off about 8-10 feet and behind it a little. I think they'll mosey off that way if they can see it. Margie's bringing a light."

I left the safety of my mentor while a huge cow and her curious calf followed my movement, not with their hooves but I could feel them tracking me with their green and gleaming, malevolent eyeballs. In the glow from the porch, I could see their breath puffing from every nostril, like steam building pressure before they blew, before they bellowed and charged. I found the fence!

I could leap behind it for safety, thank the Lord. I worked my way along the azaleas and begonia bushes there and found the gate. Now to apply any mechanical aptitude I might possess and get the thing unlocked and open as I was told. I fumbled but it came free and swung easily over the grass of a dewy night.

A flashlight's beam came bobbing along over the backs of the cattle and soon it was trained on the open gate and the dark void beyond.

Aunt Marguerite and Nathe seemed to be lost in the throng but I could hear them, visiting as they must have back in their youngest days, easing some herd toward a pasture.

"Just like old times, Marg," I heard Nathe tell his cousin.

"Nathe, remember the day you were trampled to death? I was so scared and the first thing that came to mind . . . I'd have to explain why I let us all go outside without any sunscreen." Nathe laughed and Marguerite continued. "Wonder why our mothers had such a phobia about sunburn that year? Must have read some alarmist thing in the *Reader's Digest*, I suspect. Anyway, that day, the cows all ran past or jumped over you. To my everlasting relief. I was nine, you were five."

"No worries about digging my hide out of the mud, flat as a flounder?"

"Nope, everyone said you were the rubber-bumper kid, remember? You bounced back. Fall down, bounce back. Come tumbling out of a tree, bounce back. Ran over by a herd of cows, you bounced back."

"Yup, served me well enough in films or business to boot."

*   *   *

Up the stairs I went, past the portraits of my Kinkade and other ancestors. I settled in my bed with my brain buzzing. So much to learn and so much yet to come. Baseball seemed just a part of what lay ahead for both my mother and me. Speaking of portraits, I needed to pore over all the Kinkade albums to find my father's photographs. I hoped Mom would join me if there weren't memories she'd rather not visit.

Earlier, I'd waved good night to my mother, still on the phone with Vic. I learned later Mister Vic preferred she just sing in his clubs and not around town.

"Perhaps that's okay, Claude, at the beginning, but I really do best with a big band behind me. I'm geared to that kind of setting. We'll see how it works out."

I asked if she felt disappointed with Vic and the phone call. She said no and assured me things were just right and if she were singing, she'd be fine wherever.

I wondered if Uncle Albert had it pegged, though. There'd be no compromises if they were to get married. He likely read people better than Mom did. He'd been in the tumultuous motion picture industry too, alongside Nathe. I decided it would be well for me to listen to him as someone wise in the ways of this world.

After corralling the cows, Uncle Albert told me: "Claude, you could do some growing and stretching around here, if you like." I told him such might serve me well.

CHAPTER 6

Like Father, Like Son

Long before I started college in 1998, I had $50,000 in my jeans. An anonymous donor had written a big check. I never saw it. Nor had my mother. We both, however, suspected Nathean Summers.

My grandmother Beatrice, her daughter Marguerite, Marguerite's daughter Bethany, Uncle Albert Summers, and family friend Anne Doolittle attended the memorial service held at Fort Campbell, Kentucky, held after there was no hope remaining. Officially, Nathe sent a floral tribute from Japan where he was closing a publishing deal. And we determined, he likely wrote the check establishing The Claude Kinkade Educational Trust that same day, October 28, 1991.

There was no funeral or internment; there were no remains. My father, Blake David Kinkade (1948-1991) had no final resting place we could visit. My mother and I and the rest of the Kinkades could only hope nothing would defile his earthy rest and pray the desert winds would cover the speck of earth which had become his alone.

*   *   *

I hoped, some day, to ask Nathe about his generosity. But, how to broach the matter and second, shouldn't one respect his preference for anonymity? Perhaps I could wheedle something from Aunt Marguerite. My mother and I decided the proper way to honor my unknown benefactor and the gift was to do my level best with my studies.

Knowing someone held me in high esteem and had placed confidence in my worth . . . well, it both inspired and humbled. I pledged when my freshman year finally arrived, that I'd make the family proud and do honor to the name. After all, it appeared I was the last of the Clan Kinkade. In the month of March, 1992, I was eleven and two-thirds years of age.

*   *   *

In addition to sleuthing the source of my college tuition, there was not only Shadeland to explore but also Summers Run Farm. My safaris included two farmsteads and their surrounding fields and forests. Aside from poking around outside, there were mysterious, magical attics and groaning book shelves, little tucked-away closets and curious crannies not to mention local lore and family legends. Every day promised discovery. Yes, I might start keeping a journal as my mother suggested. "These are important years for you, Claude. Important people and things happening in your life right now."

*   *   *

The next morning after the cows came up to the house, I wandered down to the gate, climbed the fence, and looked them over. They, too, regarded me. In the daylight, the cows didn't look so ominous, I decided. They seemed placid enough and I wanted their trust and friendship. I wondered if this was naïve, but surely farm boys earned a cow's faith in them and knew how to win cows over. Or was such a notion something a city kid might dream up? Nathe interrupted my reverie.

"They accept you if they decide you're not a threat." He strolled toward me, coffee cup in hand, and reading my mind.

"Did you make pets of them when you were living here?"

"Oh, yes. The herd was bigger back then, but we kids had our favorites and could move among them freely."

"So . . . how do I make friends with them? Feed them from a bucket or something like on *Lassie?*"

"You could entice the braver ones," Nathe laughed. "Or you could charm them—you can you know. Your great granddad David was the consummate stockman. A Scot, of course, and born to his trade. He told us to work in the zone between their curiosity and their acceptance.

"'Be a-knowin', lads, y' kin speak quietly to th' cows and they'll think tis in their interest to do yer biddin'.

"'Mind . . . y' dare no' harass 'em by shouting, though. Tis th' loud and grating human voice, what gets them roiled and thinkin' y' mean to do 'em harm, don' y' know.'

"'But if ye be gentle in yer manner, y'll win their trust and e'en the hearts o' a few. At times, y' need no' say a word, just pint and ask 'em if they'd kindly go to or fro.'"

"I see," I said, charmed. "It worked last night."

"'Aye, lad, it did for a fact now. I sing to 'em when it's just me an' th' cows. Hymns. They like the worshipful hymns tha' promise green pastures an' shelter from our earthly woes.'"

*   *   *

I decided years later, that Nathe's imitation of my great-grandfather was for my benefit. Rendered to lend me a flavor of the man and his brogue, surely, but also to impart a hint of what it was like to live around a persona folks in the region christened, "The Stockman o' th' Earth".

I learned it was also said that David Kinkade, Junior, followed his father's footsteps stride for stride and even clucked to the stock in the same tone; wore his hat canted to the side as did David Sr.; positioned the buckle of his belt one loop to the right just like the old man; and was never seen without a bright silk neckerchief knotted about his throat, a family trademark. Though he was second generation, he laced his speech with the same lilt if not the accent that so colored the older man's English. "He whistled much the same, loved his animals with the same devotion, and was as easily moved to tears.

"He worshipped the old man—well, we all did—"said Marguerite. "I bawled for days when Granddavey died until your Gram Bea said, 'Rest his soul, your granddad wants you to come away now, leave your sorrow and mend your heart as best you can. Your father and I need you to take up the slack, Dear.'"

Aunt Marguerite, Nathe, and I moved the cattle by foot back down Shadeland's drive. Then we turned them up the road toward the Summers Farm. I positioned myself at the turn points, trying to do as told.

The cows studied me as they passed by. I was the stranger. Mom joined us but lagged well behind. "Cows frighten me," she said. As a budding country boy, I couldn't take this approach. I wanted the cows to be the second friends I made on the farm and in the country. I planned on the Alphonse twins being my first.

On our way, we passed a dark and tangled lane on our left as we headed the cows up the hill. A sign hung from a post and it read: "Best You Not Enter Here." Another tacked below it warned: "Danger." I didn't need to ask. Aunt Marguerite read my mind.

"That's P. M. Murphy's place . . . haunt. Kind of a local eyesore, but everything's so grown over now, you can't see much from the road. I don't have any trouble from him, but he can be a thorn in the side of some around here. Eugene Forsythe won't buy him out."

"That's for certain," said Nathean. "Uncle David called him Parsimonious Mysterious Murphy. It's said he lives on a family trust and bootleg revenue. I doubt that. He came home from Korea a bit goofy, folks tell. But I've always found him cordial and sensible. He was a conscientious objector but volunteered behind the lines as a medic. He'd seen some terrible things, I think.

"He moved back to the old home place and no one sees much of him. Our mothers' used to fuss at us for snooping around his place. But Blake—"

"Who else but Blake?" said my Aunt.

"Right. Blake talked me into climbing some trees with the binoculars and we watched ol' P. M. sneak into a hut he'd built into a side hill. Steam used to rise from it and we decided it was a still all right. Then your granddad told us not to go back there. 'Yer askin' for a load o' buckshot, boys. P. M.'s got a right to privacy, illegal doin's or no'."

"Did he ever rustle a cow or anything?"

"Some guess he might take game illegally but nothing's ever been proved. I doubt such as he is very much the pacifist. Guns are not to his liking."

"Dad would offer him a few jars of canned beef now and then. Or fruit. Dad would put a note in his mailbox and he'd take a bit. Or we'd leave him a few vegetables by the post, then we'd get a note back, 'Thanks for the vittles' and he'd trade us some honey. He's a beekeeper of the first rank, and I can vouch for that. I sell his honey at the stand every year, and it's always gone within the weekend."

"Sounds spooky. I'd like to have a peek at him. Guess you keep the doors locked at night."

"Umm, not really. He's reclusive but harmless. He comes over now and then to use the phone. Maybe you'll get your gander then."

"P. M.'s an ornithologist, a bird man, Claude," said Nathe. "Amateur but highly respected."

Another secret that might require a scouting expedition. That and looking for panther tracks.

*   *   *

When we settled the cows upon the Summers pasture, we went up to the house where Uncle Albert laid out coffee and a plate of muffins. Later, we loaded up in a little cart pulled by a stout, squat tractor, gray on top, green on the bottom.

Nathe motioned me to take the wheel and we were under way after a couple lurches, a stall, and a restart.

"You'll get the hang of it. I spilled a load of pumpkins my first time, I popped the clutch so bad. Just like the cows, ease your way around it, learn to feel it engage. Think of the clutch pedal as a balloon you don't want to burst. Squeeze 'er down, float her up.

"Keep the throttle down where the paint's worn off, Claude. We're in no hurry—a tractor's not made for speed and there's no need to convince it otherwise. Remember '1' is for slow, '2' is medium, '3' is faster. Start in second gear most of the time, you will. First is for plowing, cultivating the row crops, going slow and careful-like. Third is when you're on a lane and it's safe to go faster or when you're drawing an empty wagon. I'll show you more later when we're by ourselves."

"Cool." I had never driven anything before, not even a lawn mower. "Bet this tractor was here when you were a kid."

"Well, yes and no. We bought it from Paramount Studios. It's a movie tractor. They used it on the lot and Dad dickered for it and they let him take it home. I drove it in *The Candle's Wick* and fell in love with it. He thought it would be a nice memento and we needed one here on the place. He got it for a song, but it was costly shipping the thing when we could have gone over to Stratton Implement, five miles up the road, and bought one just like it.

"But memories are worth the extra time and effort and the money. Dad was wise about such. I wouldn't sell Harry for anything."

"Harry?"

"Right, it's a Ferguson, designed by Harry Ferguson. Y' don't see many with this color combination. Turn up this lane and we'll enter. . . The Enchanted Forest, everyone," he called to Mom and Aunt Marguerite, our passengers. My aunt looked like the freckle-faced farm girl again and my mother, her pallid friend from the city, a nervous showgirl. First cows, now tractors.

*   *   *

CHAPTER 7

The Sacred Forest

I helped Mom from the cart and we all started trekking into the dark and foreboding forest ahead of us. Great evergreens stood watching these intruders enter their primeval domain. Were there lesser spirits dwelling here as well?

Nathe told us he once took a botany class in college and came out here and identified everything he could be sure of.

"Got an 'A' on that project—quite rewarding it was. Anything I questioned, I asked P. M. Left a note in the mailbox and he replied it was this or that. Same year your dad joined the army."

"Are there snakes?" my mother asked.

"Yes, but harmless, Daisy," Aunt Marguerite said. "There hasn't been a copperhead or timber rattler reported around here in years. We might smell some skunk cabbage. Look at these ferns. I gather up a bunch ever so often to go with my arrangements. What a treasure."

"Yes, nice."

Nathe and I blazed trail for the ladies. It was Spirit of the Border country, just as described by Zane Grey. Behind every trunk or thicket were Iroquois, Wyandot, and Seneca. Or their ghosts.

Suddenly, Nathe threw an arm across my chest and we stopped still. Was it a panther skulking off into the dense undergrowth?

41

Then I saw. A hulking bony figure wearing army green rose with his back to us. He straightened and one could tell he was tall and ungainly, a put-together man whose spine and joints and parts were assembled after dark, not in the light of day.

"Hello, hello," Nathe said within a tone of caution. No purpose served by startling this guy; such seemed a wise course.

The man stood, turned, and I beheld a giant whose wrath might be smoldering beneath a surface of pale skin, similar to the parchment my Grandmother Beatrice wore.

"Mr. Murphy . . . I believe. Why, I haven't seen you in years." Nathe stepped forward and offered his hand. I fell in behind, prepared to run back to Harry and place it in 3rd gear. Not a hundred yards into this wood and we had already disturbed one of its apparitions or worse.

"And here we are neighbors. Welcome to Blake's Wood." Nathe held his hand steady as a ball bat. The creature looked at it, then at Nathe, then at me and the women behind us. To my relief, he took Nathe's hand and grasped it and looked down at the two hands clasped together as if he'd not seen his linked with another human's in some time. Perhaps he hadn't experienced a handshake since the war.

"Looks like you're harvesting the fruit of the woods."

"Yes, you're Nathean Summers," the man coughed. "Haven't seen you in decades. Guess I'm trespassing on your holdings. My apologies."

"Why none needed, sir. These woods are open . . . and free. No. . . fees or penalties here. Pick what you want. I see you've gathered some ferns . . . herbs perhaps."

"Checking the progress of divine providence. Tonic material. The gifts mankind has forgotten." Mr. Murphy responded in a strikingly high pitch and in such a monotone, one might think he was announcing a bingo game. "Horehound, witch hazel, blood root."

"Yes, yes indeed. My grandparents spoke of such medications. Some are turning back to the old ways and remedies. I'm . . . hopeful."

"Possibly. Mankind is lazy and would rather pay some shyster who knows nothing of health and healing."

"Umm, true, I'm afraid."

The man surveyed us all. "I see Marguerite's here."

"Yes and this is my second cousin and that's his mother."

"Pale as a winter moon, is she not?" The man then addressed me. "Be you a Summers, a Forsythe, or a Kinkade?" I stepped forward and offered my hand. "I'm Claude Kinkade, sir." He looked down at my hand as well.

"Thought so. And a large hand. He reads true. The Forsythes were thick and earth-bound, bent to work and strong. The Kinkades, a pie-faced bunch. A round-faced people but surprisingly slim. Kinkade blood brought a Scottish mentality and they were spare, frugal to the core and yet they lent refinement and an air of grace. Up the line, the Summerses presented intelligence and creativity. All in all, a respectable blend, a worthy product."

Nathe nodded, considering the remark. "Well . . . I had not thought of that. That's from insight only an out . . . that is, an observer like yourself, would note."

"Well, I'll be off. Convey my greetings to the womenfolk." And with that, Mr. Murphy gathered his bundles and strode through the undergrowth as easily as if he were a yearling moose. Then he stopped and looked back at us, cocking an all-seeing eye while the other remained squinted.

"Be you one of they that intends to clear-cut the country, denuding it for golf courses and playgrounds for the idle rich?"

"No, indeed, Philip. I assure you." Nathe gestured grandly, sweeping his hands in an arc across the woodland. "These trees will stand until the end of time if I have anything to say about it."

"A promise to be honored. Glad to hear it. G'day."

"Yes, and you're welcome here anytime, sir."

"Kind of y'."

We watched him leave and we renewed our journey into the wood. Nathe started to chuckle. And soon he couldn't stop laughing. He put his arm on my shoulder as we walked along, then gave me a man-to-man hug. "Well, there's, there's your first encounter with the terror of Pickett Township, you . . . you pie-faced . . . product, you."

*　　*　　*

We poked about in the wood for a couple hours. Even Mom seemed to relax now that the encounter with Mr. Murphy was over and there were no snakes.

We marveled at the headwaters of Summers Run. Water in a hundred rivulets poured from a series of ledges running for nearly forty feet—by Nathe's estimate—of black shelf rock into a pool so dark it looked like ink.

We found other ledge rocks, streams, and when we turned around some huge boulders that blocked our path, we encountered a waterfall so suddenly, my mother exclaimed in spite of herself, "Oh, how lovely! Perfect place for a wedding if you could ever get everyone and the organ out here."

"Right," laughed Aunt Marguerite. "We call this the Bridal Veil. It's not spectacular or what you might see out West, but we like it. Kinda spare, like P. M. says of the Kinkades and constant, like the Kinkades, runs all year long, even in the driest summer."

"Some folks wonder if this water doesn't trace back to Lake Erie. I don't know. Marg, have they ever settled that one?"

"They'd like to. There have been geologists and hydrologists out here from the college and all over studying the grove and all this water. No one's ever been able to say yea or nay. Only Summers Run knows the answer."

Summers Run. Today I met its source. Tomorrow, I'd learn more of its secrets and of the land through which it passed.

*   *   *

We trudged our way back to the cart and tractor. I felt entranced, being a boy when anything circular of rubber, metal, or plastic lured and charmed most of us. This was my first ever experience behind the wheel, and I wanted my hands back gripping it and feeling my fingers wrapped around the knurled bakelite there.

I decided some time later, boys seem to be drawn by natural inclination to the section of geometry which dealt with spheres and circles. Baseballs and steering wheels. Planets and moons, fire rings, and fishing reels. We must have been imprinted genetically to make us thus. Some influence within the womb that made us consider roundness the king of shapes.

Nathe and I locked ourselves into a discussion of the Ferguson's apparati and basic functioning of its three point hitch.

"Harry Ferguson pioneered it," said Nathe. "Then Henry Ford applied it to his tractors. Then, over time and as the patents ran out, I guess, everyone started to bring out their own version. Ferguson's system kept a tractor from raring up if your plow hit a big rock. The hitch would release and ride over it instead of tipping backwards on the driver."

I looked back where Aunt Marguerite and Daisy were studying the woods. They were holding hands and soon my mother started to cry. They embraced and I shot a glance at Nathe. He turned and leaned on the tractor's hood.

"Blake and I spent many an hour up here. Those big rocks, those birches over there? That's where Shadeland and Summers Run Farm corner.

"This is where we'd watch planes turn on 'final' for Port Chapmann. We sit on those rocks and watch them bank and

45

lower their gear. We memorized all the 'N' numbers. We loved it here, oh Lord, how did we ever." he choked. I knew I'd return to this place often. This place where my father dreamed. Maybe, I'd catch a glimpse of him as a boy in the shady glades or even . . . perched on one of those big boulders.

Nathe named their favorites and with each one he mentioned, the tears coursed a bit further down his cheeks. "DC-3s, Convair 220s, Beech 18s, Bonanzas, all the Pipers, Cessnas, Ercoupes, Stinsons, we knew them all. This is sacred ground."

*   *   *

CHAPTER 8

When Blake Shot his Pontiac

That morning, my mother offered to borrow Aunt Marguerite's Oldsmobile and drive me to school. I declined. I needed to plunge into the deep end, not dip my toe in the wading pool. Face it alone, no escort.

Truth was, going solo might prove good practice. My mother and I were bracing ourselves. We'd never been separated during our nearly twelve years together. Dad, however, was often away on Temporary Duty here or there as a trainee or instructor. Or off on missions he could not discuss. Soon Mom would be on her way out of my day-to-day life. Mister "Vic" would be here come next week.

So, early enough, I trudged up to where we understood the bus stopped. I arrived before a gaggle of elementary and junior high kids of all stripes and sizes turned up. I was disappointed. The Alphonse twins did not live nearby, it appeared.

I "hi'd" the ones of our group that might prove important and we looked each other over with little else being said. More scrutiny on the bus. No twins in sight.

I worried they might attend a different school entirely. There were a couple or more within the district, grades one through six, holding classes in quaint old buildings refurbished or added on to meet the state codes.

Once we arrived at the schoolyard, I found a pre-school game of softball going on and there in the midst were my two black friends.

"Was your dad serious 'bout starting a league?"

"You mean my cousin?"

"Yeah, the fly ball guy."

"Yes, I think so. You interested?"

"We are. Been talking it around. Who's your teacher?"

"Uh, a Mrs. McIntyre."

"Yeah, we got her. She's good, she's cool."

At recess it seemed the new kid might be one of the more compelling things going on that day. Several classmates gathered to size me up. No one appeared hostile, no fights in the offing, just appraisal.

"You the movie star's kid?"

"No, he's a cousin."

"Where's this baseball team going to be? Y' gonna have uneeforms, right?"

"Who's the coach?"

"I heard some big league guy's going to coach."

"Yeah, I heard that too. Somebody who played for the Pirates."

"Heard it was the Indians."

"There's going to be bleachers and a scoreboard and a loudspeaker to say your name. That's what Trent Smythe said anyways."

Suddenly I was an authority on something I knew nothing about. Cousin Nathe and I needed a handle on this one quickly, or my stature with this crowd would slump before it even started.

*　　*　　*

I ran most of the way from the bus stop. To my relief, I found a dust cloud rising from behind the Summers barn. Someone was working the grounds.

I climbed the fence and passed among the cows who were enjoying the sunshine and their cuds. Most granted me a mild acknowledgment, but one calf hopped beside me and let out a little yelp that was more bark than bawl. This I learned through time and observation was "play" behavior.

I found Nathe had made a couple of rounds with a tillage tool he called a spring tooth harrow.

"Glad you're here, m' friend. How was your first day? Any homework? When you get free, maybe y' can hop on Harry here and we'll start getting things in shape."

"I'll change and be right back. Won't be a minute," I said and ran off.

"Don't wear anything good. You'll be dirty enough tonight to plug the bathtub's drain," he shouted behind me, "dry as it is."

At Shadeland, I learned it was official: Aunt Marguerite's daughter would soon be inbound from Texas with her son and daughter. Heading back home. Like Mom and me.

"Looks like it's over," said Aunt Marguerite. "Never should have started. Dad was right. She married into a clan that wouldn't let her be her. And your granddad—being a Scot—knew about clans and their expectations."

I explained my mission and was granted permission to "work till dark. Nathe says there's rain promised by Thursday and he wants the field to soak it up. . . . Sorry about Bethany, Aunt Marg. Maybe they'll get it worked out."

She poured the laundry out on the table and began sorting it. "Thank you, Claude, but I don't expect such. She was raised too independently for that bunch. The Van Strassels expect you to bend and blend. The women are as rabid as the men about being one of the team, striving, winning, showing up the competition.

"It's corn, cattle, soybeans, sports, and teams, not necessarily in that order. Compete, win, go to state, bring home a trophy. Plant more acres than last year, harvest more than the neighbor. Get bigger every year, get written up in the farm magazines, get your picture taken with the Secretary of Agriculture and your senator.

"The Van Strassels think we're quaint and old-fashioned back here. That little Ferguson tractor of Nathe's would look like a puny toy next to their giants. Poor Beth wanted a simple country life with music and art for her boy and girl. Down there, the talk is all scores and records, poor coaches, bad officiating, futures contracts, hedging, football, basketball, volleyball, the Longhorns, the Dallas Cowboys, grain prices.

"Now, of course, girls are doing sports. So different from my day," said Aunt Marguerite. "The Van Strassels brag on how they meet each other on the road to volleyball or girls basketball. Beth just didn't fit in and . . . it has to be said . . . she didn't want to and didn't want the young'ns brought up that way. That's rejection in the Van Strassel mindset. Or outright rebellion. We'll set your dinner back, Claude."

My mother was on the phone during all this, long distance to Nevada. Any report on my first day of school would have to wait. I had country things to do, my first real day of farming.

When I returned to the ball field, I found Nathe had dropped the harrow and had a big drum roller hitched to "Harry." It could be filled with water.

"We can try this filled halfway and see if we like it for breaking up these clods. Then, we've got a meadow drag we can flip over. No more bedsprings lying around these days. Heard Bethany's pulling out of Texas."

"Yes, I guess so."

"Uh huh. Moving and marriage . . . divorce and moving back . . . trying . . . change . . . re-do, re-build, start over again. Husbands, wives, and worn-out ball diamonds." He looked at me directly. "Life."

A vintage pickup pulled into the drive.

"That's Banks McIntyre, an old school chum. He's a contractor and I've got a long chat ahead with him. When you've made a few rounds with this roller, Claude, come over an' meet Banks. He's an education."

I climbed aboard "Harry" and pushed on the starter with my thumb, not forgetting to make sure I was in "N" for neutral and with the clutch depressed for an extra measure of safety.

"Keep 'er in second and make your turns wide—you'll see where you've been. Turn too sharp and the rim might dig in and leave us humps that will be a problem." The field was starting to resemble the color and texture of the buckskin Aunt Marguerite kept on the bureaus in her Montana room, the bedroom at Shadeland done in western décor. Satisfied, I shut "Harry" down and found Nathe, Albert, and Banks McIntyre on the front porch.

"Hello, Claude," said Uncle Albert. "Looks like you've been farming."

"Yessir, I've started."

"This is Banks McIntyre," he said, "an old friend of the family's. You want something done right or re-done, call Mr. J. Banks. 'Mac' McIntyre."

"But, not after 8 PM. I've fallen asleep in front of the TV by then."

We shook hands and I said, "Pleased to meet you, sir."

"Mac and I, your dad and a couple other ranahans ran things around here once," Nathe said. "Or so we thought."

"If you didn't think of it, Kiddo, Blake did," said Mr. Banks 'Mac' McIntyre.

"Don't say too much in front of Dad," Nathe laughed.

Uncle Albert smiled in my direction. "I know more about some of your escapades than you might expect."

"Well, I wasn't in on the school bus caper," Mr. McIntyre told us. "That was pure Blake."

"And Nathean," said Uncle Albert, "Your role in that nefarious scheme? Might as well let Claude in on the details."

"Banks did the scouting and was the lookout. You and that Raffter kid. I merely supplied the chain as I knew where one could be found."

"Yes, an old logging chain that hung in our barn, undisturbed for decades," Uncle Albert said.

"Anyway, some of us had taken a dislike to this particular school bus driver. He was especially strict with the little kids—"

"Sounds like a wise course to me," said Uncle Albert. "Keep them safely in their seats an' such."

"Too strict for our liking, especially Blake, who would take offense if he thought folks were being mean to other folks. So, he arranged to chain the rear axle of the bus to a big oak in the schoolyard.

"Anyway, ol' man Steiger jumped in the bus, put it in gear and thought he was on a slick spot or such, gunned it and pulled the axle loose, broke the u-joint, shackles and the like. Set up an awful racket between him shouting in German and the driveline flopping about—"

"And, what ever happened to my log chain, young man?"

"Well, Pop, it seemed to have fallen into the possession of Mr. Steiger."

"Yes, little enough compensation for the poor fellow, I'd say. The damage to the bus was quietly paid for. A check signed by Mr. David Kinkade, I'm told."

Mr. McIntyre rubbed his face and laughed. "Oh boy, it seemed worth it at the time. But ol' man Steiger got his revenge, sort of, that next Fourth of July."

"That the night Blake shot his car?"

"The very one, Kiddo."

"Understand your dad, Claude, was very particular about gun safety," said Nathe.

"Yeah, he was a nag."

"Except on this one occasion. Anyway, we'd just got a machine to throw clay pigeons and a bunch of us, Banks, myself—"

52

"Paul Raffter, Tommy Joslin, the local crowd."

"We're out shooting the heck out of a box of clay pigeons and having a good old time, betting each other, keepin' score and the like. So, what happened, Banks, how did it come about that Blake goofed up?"

"Well." Mr. McIntyre pulled his baseball cap off and scratched his ear. "We were about shot out. Nobody had many shells left and the pigeons were about gone. But anyway, we launched this last one and it must not have been set right or had a chip in it or something of the sort.

"Anyway, it took off at a crazy angle and well away from our line of fire and Blake was up to shoot and he says, 'I'll get it'. He swings over about ten o'clock, fires and forgets that he'd parked his car that general direction—BAM, out goes the back window and shatters the front, scatterin' glass all over, pings up the dashboard, fills the car full of shot, down the air vents they go, breaking gauges, rippin' up the seats and the visors and the headliner. It was a royal mess. Couldn't drive it and no one wanted to tow it ourselves as you couldn't see a thing out the windshield—it was just a spider web.

"So, Blake had to call for a tow truck and it just so happened, Steiger was driving for this body shop and came out to get it the next morning. Blake had to ride in to town with him. Never heard what they discussed or if the bus axle deal ever came up. Blake wouldn't say a word about it."

"Suitably chagrined, I would imagine. I'm sending you a bill, Nathean Summers, for my log chain."

"Fair enough, Pop."

Uncle Albert winked my way from under those bushy eyebrows, a pair of striped gray caterpillars crawling toward each other. "Been missing that thing, every day or so lately."

* * *

CHAPTER 9

Boys Raised in The South

Nathe asked Mr. McIntyre if he was still flying that cheese box he called an airplane.

"Yup. Just gave 'er a total upgrade. New turbo-charged engine, intercom system, new insulation, new interior. Let's take her up Saturday. You need to see what damage is being done to our old neck of the woods."

"Sounds serious."

"It *is* serious, Nathe. Gene Forsythe's not the only guy who has designs on the farms around here. Bring junior along. We'll see if he can operate an airplane as well as drive tractors."

Mr. McIntyre surveyed the soon-to-be-refreshed ball diamond. He nodded his head slowly as if approving the layout. Or, did he see a vision? Possibly as manager of our fledgling team? *I'll bet he's played, even ran a team, perhaps.* He had a baseball look about him.

"Well . . . this will make as good a diamond as it used to be. I'll bring a scope over and we'll shoot a line on your slope. I'd pitch that outfield just a bit so she'll drain right. Run a little ditch around the perimeter so it'll carry any runoff from the hillsides.

"Uncle Albert set the old one up nearly ideal. Natural bleachers, both sides, angled her so no one's looking into the sun. You gonna sod it or seed it?"

"Sod, Mac."

"Yeah, smart move. Cost more but it will save you a lot of time and fuss 'n' worry. Try Holland Brothers. Their bluegrass is first rate stuff."

"Where do you want your dugout?"

"My dugout? Sounds like you want me to manage the deal, Kiddo."

"You've played . . . and you've coached."

"Hah! I suppose you're gonna put a recliner in there and a little icebox to cool my fevered brow."

"If that's what it takes."

"Well, pal, I think you got yourself into a community project. I understand Claude here's the recruiter. How many y' got signed up?"

"Umm, looks like six for sure. Eight maybe—"

"Gotta name?"

"Not yet, nossir."

"You're gonna have some tough games with only eight men to field. Uniforms?"

"Umm, couldn't say, but . . . ." I looked to Nathe.

"I got some of the Amish ladies hereabouts working on that," said Nathe. Mr. McIntyre laughed and shook his head.

"Did Cousin Nathe ever tell y' about the time he took on two of the meanest ranahans that ever terrorized the county, right over there by first base? Two giants they were—one six foot four for sure and the other stood six-six."

"They were nowhere near that big."

"Weighed 250 apiece, maybe 275 on the big 'un. The first guy went down like he'd been shot, howlin' his head off and then number two waded into it and the next thing we saw was a shower of bright red and down he goes, sittin' in the blood and the dust. Y' haven't heard this?"

"Nossir. I sure want to know more about it."

"This is nowhere hear the truth, Claude."

"Sure it is. I was there. Thirty five years ago. But seems like it was just yesterday."

The two men looked at each other in a way that only they understood, across the decades and the textures of their lives as they lived them back then in that time and space. Memories and renewal, I would soon learn, would sound important twin notes through these days to come. Mr. McIntyre rubbed his ear and looked around at a little spot of earth he apparently found familiar.

"I favor this place. Some great memories here, Kiddo."

"There were."

Mister Mac addressed me. "Understand you're in Mrs. McIntyre's class."

"Yessir. I think I'm going to like it."

"You'd better. Your teacher is my long-suffering child bride. Give her any trouble and I'll come over here and slap y' silly."

"No trouble from here, sir."

He offered his hand and cradled my hand between both of his: mine soft and his coarse and calloused. "I knew your father well. He would have been a real pillar in this community . . . had he come home."

He turned to leave but before he took a step, he looked back at the future baseball field. "Don't know why we need to lose so many of the good ones." Then he looked down at me and in his eyes I saw an acceptance there I cherish to this day.

"Y' got nice manners, bud. Boys raised in the South usually do. You'll be a credit to him."

I thanked him and he walked off, waving to us without looking back.

*   *   *

CHAPTER 10

Revelations

Come Saturday, we'd be going aloft in a single-engine airplane. I hadn't told my mother. Yet.

I knew one thing for certain so far: I liked driving that tractor. And I persuaded Mom every precaution, safety-wise, had been explained to me. I even produced an old operator's manual to show her, emphasizing I'd read it through twice.

She said little, accepting my assurances without comment and then—as she did frequently these days—she began to weep.

"Oh, Claude, am I a good mother?"

"Sure you are. Don't even ask such."

"I know it makes you cross, son, but I have such doubts these days. I take them to bed and get up in the morning with the same things on my mind."

"Well, don't. Things'll work out."

"But we're going to be so far away from each other. I just have these fears. Am I doing the right thing?"

I handed her the book I'd been reading, *Children of the Oregon Trail.* "Moms, these kids, in this book? They had to deal with lots of stuff. Parents dying on the trail, moving in with strangers, losing, leaving graves behind, being lonely. Look here." I leafed to the front.

"It's autographed. On the frontispiece." There, in florid penmanship, the author, Carole Chandler Haygood, had written: *"All my very best wishes to Nathean Summers, my perfect Jacob. You brought my vision to life."* Nathe is letting me read it. His TV series was based on this book."

"Frontispiece? Such big words you're learning here these days. Frontispiece, codicil, humus—what was that streamside thing?"

"Riparian."

"Riparian. I'm not sure I understand it yet, but I am relieved I'm leaving you in a house of books and knowledge. In good hands."

"Riparian refers to streambanks. It deals with who has access or control over land that's next to a river or lake, even a small creek like Summers Run.

"Runs are like what we called branches back ho—in Kentucky. Here in the East, little branches are called brooks or runs or kills, like the Battenkill—that's a famous trout stream. Nathe says Summers Run could be re-stocked and become a fine trout stream, they tell him, like it used to be."

"Who's they?"

"The state fishing department. Some of the local folks, like the Bird and Tree Club. Come Saturday, I'll be learning airplane and flying terms an' such."

"Oh?"

"Yes, I'm going to fly around a bit with Nathe and a Mister McIntyre in his Cessna. If the weather's good, that is."

"I see. I don't suppose it would matter if I said I'd rather you didn't."

"I'm in good hands."

She sat silently for the moment, glancing at the covered wagon book and its illustrations. Yet she wasn't seeing them at all. "Vic will fly in next week. I hope you'll be glad to see him."

"I'll be glad."

She smiled at me, an expression that held both appreciation and a hint of apology. "Thank you, son."

* * *

That my mother was "going off to see the rooster" seemed quite obvious to most of us around Shadeland and Summers Run Farm. She and Aunt Marguerite were discussing the futures of all of us quietly. And politely these days. I didn't think Aunt Marguerite quite approved but she said nothing to me.

Mom told me: "We never really got acquainted back when your daddy was here. Now that I've had a few days and some heart-to-heart, I really think Marguerite's a treasure. Your aunt has her own worries these days, Claude. We mustn't add to them."

"Right."

"I know you'll be a big help, especially if Bethany and the little ones come home. Guess they're 'off to see the rooster,' like the rest of us. You know . . . the rooster story was about the first thing I heard about your father. He didn't tell me, but Grandmother Beatrice said she could finally laugh about her scare years later.

"We came through here on our honeymoon, and Blake showed me the part of the barn where he climbed to the roof. The rooster is still there, I guess."

"Still there."

"Am I doing the right thing?"

"I think you need to go off and see the rooster. Otherwise, you'll never know."

"I guess. I know I don't want to end up being lonely . . . like Aunt Marguerite."

"She's lonely? Gol, there's folks coming in an out all the time. Lotsa friends on the phone plus Anne and then Bethany and grandkids coming back, I guess."

"True, Claude, but Annie's moving down to Florida to be near her family And Aunt Margy, she says she'd like a special man in her life, someone who'll come by—like they used to say in the olden days—a beau who comes a'courtin'."

"Hmm. Guess then she and the professor might divorce. Seems something like you and Dad."

"Like us, yes, married but far apart at times, for months. She wishes I'd meet some local guy. Some kind, steady fella from around here."

"I do too, kinda."

"But, Claude, what would I do? I've always dreamt of being a professional, with a career. What singing I did in the army an' such, I liked, believe me. And folks liked me— you can't believe what it's like to wow an audience. It's . . . intoxicating.

"Now's my last chance, son. My good years are slipping away, and I don't want to end up . . . washed up or too late for anything at the end of Blake's life, wishing I'd gone to see the rooster. Understand? I know we've been over this be—"

"I understand!"

"You're still okay with this . . . an' me and Mister Vic?"

"Mom, you don't need my permission."

"But I need your approval."

"You need to go. An' you need to feel all right about me staying behind. I'll do just fine here. Only been a week and already I'm feeling this is home. I'm fitting in. It's here I wanna be."

"You have your father's iron-headed will. Once he decided something was right, that was it."

"Do you think Dad would want you to do this?"

"I truly wonder. Likely not."

"Yeah, well, you knew him better than I did, but I would hope he would say it's okay. At least, I'm here with his people and on the place where he grew up. He oughta be pleased about that."

"That's why we came back, Claude . . . to his home—"

"I know. I know—we've talked about this."

"But you don't know this. He . . . had me swear that if anything ever happened to him, I'd bring you back here and not try to go it alone. Or tag along after your Granddad C. J. and Grandma Ronnie. I wasn't going to tell you this, but your dad was dead set against me trying to live their lifestyle or farming you out to them. 'A boy needs a place to take root, not an RV park,' he said. He liked my folks but he didn't approve of them being such nomads and raising his son 'on the road,' as he called it."

"Might not be bad. I'd see a lot of country."

"Yes, hon, but they don't really have a place to live. They drive a fancy-smancy RV all right, but they rent every place they stop for a few weeks or a couple months. And, how would you get your schooling? This is best. Even if I get married to Vic and we travel some, you'll always have this as your home base. Blake would have wanted it that way. Woulda liked it that way."

* * *

These discussions about Mom's career, Ignatius Victor "Vic" Delveccio, and my future always left me "peevish"— Mom's term for such. I'd become irked and short with her—like my Dad could do—and she'd turn weepy and more befuddled, it seemed to me.

Truth be told, I'd be rather glad to see her go. Make the break and see how our separation and her likely marriage to Mister Vic might turn out. It appeared the roosters were crowing for the both of us. Beckoning us to take the next step on the ladder and climb upward, though the uppermost rungs were lost in a fog of uncertainty.

"One goofy, sad, or perfectly lovely day at a time." I learned my Aunt Marguerite lived by this. "For the most part," she would add.

* * *

Saturday morning began "gauzy," said Mr. McIntyre. "She'll burn off, according to the forecast.

"Here, bud, take the yoke. Rock it a little, get the feel. Now apply a little pressure with your right toes. . . . Good, now ease off and straighten your wing. All right. You just made a turn. Fundamental stuff. Just keep your eye on the ball, just like when you're in the batters' box.

"Now . . . left rudder—feel it slip? You're flying sideways. Now dip your left wing, keep the ball in the little pocket . . . that's it. Now you're turning left. Okie-doaky, straighten her out, level your wing hold her on this course, keep that needle right there and head toward that big silo on the slope ahead. All right. Now me an' Cousin Nathe can do our sightseeing relaxed and leisurely while you steer the thing.

"There's a barf bag in the seat pocket. Puke in it, seal it up, then open the door and toss it. Then, hold the door open while I kick y' out, understood?" I nodded behind my smile.

Nathe then asked, "What if I get pukey back here?"

"You're sitting in my mother-in-law ejection seat. I pull this lever . . . and down the hatch and out you go."

"This is a well-equipped airplane, all right."

"I thought of everything, Kiddo, this time around. All right. We're coming up on what I wanted to show y'. Look over there, eleven o'clock, red silo."

"That's the Porter place."

"Right. *Used* to be the Porter place. Remember that pasture where he ran his ewes and new lambs? Well, look at it now."

"Uh-oh."

"I'll say 'uh-oh.' Perc tests. I counted twenty of 'em the other day. They're five-acre plots. And . . . as soon as we get past this shelter belt . . . lookee there."

"Looks like bigger acreages, maybe."

"Right again. Those are twenty-acre parcels. Some are thirty. It's going to be an 'equestrian park', oh *ta-ta*."

"Maybe the horsey set will be good neighbors, Mac."

"If they're responsible. Pay their bills and don't let their dogs run. But it's the taxes and special assessments that's got me worried. Those folks will want the roads paved and all the utilities underground. Plus condos and resort development, timeshares and the like will start crowdin' us who want to stay on the land.

"And everyone knows those bridges over the Run aren't up to the new state code. Township's squabbling with the county and the county's squabblin' with Harrisburg right now as to who's going to rebuild them and who's gonna pay the bill. It'll be you and me, mister, I'm thinking.

"Okay, Claude, ease her a bit towards the left. That's it, right there. See how the plane wants to fly? You just apply a little direction and guidance, and like a good bird dog, it does what you want.

"Flying an airplane's like playing baseball. Sometimes you need the power but more often than not, you just need a little finesse. Just a light touch. Just like my hero—you a Pirate's fan? You'd better be. Roberto Clemente, Claude, to my mind, the greatest all-around player ever to grace the game. You wanna be a good player and a good human being, bud, you model after Roberto Clemente. Gold Glover—Tim McCarver said he had an arm like a howitzer. Roberto Clemente . . . owned right field, outright owned it.

"Three thousand hits—there's a milestone—exactly three thousand before he got killed. There's another shame. We lost another good one before his time, just like your dad.

"All right . . . we're about to pass over my place. See what I've got to deal with? Look at that eyesore of a butcher job that used to be a grand woodlot. Old man Johnson should be whirling in his grave. Didja ever see such a mess? Wish I woulda bought that before his kids sold it off."

"Are they taking all the timber?"

"Took some great old seed trees and some nice younger stuff both. Took enough to carve out a nine holes of an 18-hole golf course and a resort hotel. Trying to make it into a weekend spa and rustic golfing lodge—destination deal with an Adirondack-Sun Valley flair. Cross-country skiing in the winter with a rink and cozy fireplaces in your room and the lobbies, the works. Catering to the carriage trade from Cleveland and Pittsburgh. Even talking about a charter flight set-up or passenger rail service. Thirty-six hole course, if they can get enough ground. Gonna take a lot of acres to get that done—there's my house. Look where I am."

"Right in the middle."

"Between the horse apples and the golf balls. That's my buffer right below us—the woodlot and the hay pasture."

"Used to produce the best timothy in the township."

"Still does. At least I'll have a steady market."

"Timothy's a grass, Claude, considered the best hay for horses."

"Do you know how many opportunities I've had to sell that field in the last year?"

"Well, hey, Mac. There's your ticket to Cancun."

"Hah! My ticket to the doghouse, you mean, Kiddo. My bride would have me by the neck until dead if I even slightly considered an offer. That's her favorite view out the dining room window. Sits there and paints. Sunsets, sunrises—she's done all four seasons."

I found my image of "Mac" lying in the doghouse, head resting on his paws and with a choke chain around his neck amusing. And I couldn't hold it.

"Well, look at this here gigglepuss. Claude must find his elders entertaining."

"We likely are."

"Tip 'er over and point your nose towards that grain elevator, see it? Can you manage that without laughin' your head off and putting us into a death spiral?"

"Yessir," I managed.

"The help y' get nowadays."

*   *   *

64

CHAPTER 11

The Surprise

"Chapmann Tower . . . 863 Charlie Papa. . . . Seven miles north, two thousand-five hundred with information Foxtrot. We'd like to circle over the monument rocks for some photographs and then land full stop."

"Eight-six-three Charlie Papa, Chapmann Tower, approved as requested. Traffic will be a Citation entering the right downwind for two-niner. Cross mid-field and remain south of the two-niner extended centerline, advise when you're finished with your photos."

"Roger, tower, we'll be watching. . . . Okay, bud, nice job. We're getting closer to traffic so I'll take it on home. We'll head toward Summers Run and Marguerite's."

I sat back and watched the scenery slide below my window. Everything looked neat, orderly, and calm from up here. I pondered how many of those sturdy roofs were actually huffing and puffing at their eaves with family problems and domestic disputes.

"Now . . . we're going to drift between Marguerite's and Nathe's place. There's your woodlot, Kiddo."

"Looks huge from here," I noted. Nate reminded me this was The Enchanted Forest.

"It *is* huge, sprout. 'Bout the last of the really large wooded areas left. But lookee there, Nathe. Only Harvey Logan's between you and Gene's development."

"This Gene's work we're coming up on then?"

"Right, the old Swenson farm. He has 16 parcels there and eight across the road he bought from the Meyers Family Trust at the bank. If he gets the Logan place, he'll butt up against your forest land and the headwaters of the Run.

"So, he's got you and Parsimonious flanked on the north and west and will be bordering Marguerite on her north and east."

"We're going to be islands."

"That's the size of it, because the horse park and part of the golf course will be wrapping around your south and east between you and the airport. We're surrounded, pal, you, me, Harvey, and Marguerite."

"Should we run up the white flag?"

"Not on your life, Kiddo. Like your dad says, 'They're not getting it until they take me out feet first.' Here's your corner."

We glided over the spot where the big rocks loomed among the white trunks of the birch grove. Not far from where we met Parsimonious Murphy. It looked like a modern monolith from the air, something one might see in a manicured park.

I wondered if the spirit of my dad was watching us from those rocky heights.

"Chapmann Tower . . . 863 Charlie Papa. Can you advise on the Citation?"

"Eight-six-three Charlie Papa, Citation is turning on final."

"Eight-six-three Charlie Papa. We have the Citation in sight. . . . There y' go in style, bud. You think this airplane is first class, take a look at that piece of work. She's leaving hundred dollar bills in her contrail."

The twin engine jet below and to the left of us swept by, a white and silver swan heading for its placid pond.

"Eight-six-three Charlie Papa. . . . Okay, you photographers, now's when you get your shots. We're passing over the legendary Shadeland and Summers Run Farm, two of the finest agricultural enterprises of any kind in the country and of the past century."

Both Nathe and I began taking our snaps, my camera less expensive than his Canon with the heavy lens. From the air, both places looked grand and peaceful enough to grace a chamber of commerce brochure. Their roofs solid and serene, belying the less-than-settled situations beneath their rafters: the land, the heirs, the wills, divorce and separations, unspoken hopes, fears in the night, dreams, the journeys yet to be taken, the . . . loss.

"Chapmann . . . Cessna 863 Charlie Papa, permission to turn left base for runway two-niner."

"Eight-six-three Charlie Papa, cleared for left turn, runway two-niner. Winds two-seven-zero at seven."

"Eight-six-three Charlie Papa. Cleared to runway two-niner."

*   *   *

Mr. McIntyre "greased" the landing and as we taxied in, he patted the Cessna on the top of its instrument panel as one would a smiling Labrador or Golden Retriever. "Nice job, ol' girl. Y' even made the kid look good. Despite him being disrespectful of the aged and decrepit oldsters in his midst."

"Sorry about the giggles, Mister Mac—couldn't get something outa my mind. That is, the doghouse . . . thing."

"Y' better come over an' see my doghouse if you think it's so silly, speaking of first class. It's insulated. Heated with an automatic waterer even. I *could* live out there, you bet."

*   *   *

The Citation had parked. I watched its door ramp descend and a crew member climb down. Then a tanned figure emerged

67

wearing sunglasses with a sport coat draped over his arm. He did indeed look "well heeled" as Mr. McIntyre suggested.

"Probably a swell from down yonder or over Cleveland way. Flew in to pick out his daughter's horse farm."

"Or he's one of Gene's cohorts. Maybe his banker," Nathe said. "Where's Gene getting all the spondoolicks anyway?" I later learned "spondoolicks" was a family term for money, especially if one needed a lot.

"Gene's an attorney, don't y' know. Made it big in the dairy buyout back in the Eighties. Been getting richer ever since then. The last of the Forsythe's to amount to anything. Well . . . you're buying me lunch, Kiddo. It's the least you can do for the ride and . . . and for me putting up with the sprout here."

"You're on, buddy. What do you recommend?"

"The lasagne. Hands down, best around. Nancy and I come out for it special, Friday and Saturday nights."

*   *   *

Something about the guy walking in from the Citation looked familiar. I was the last to return to our table from the restroom and when I entered the lobby, Citation Guy turned out to be Mr. Vic Delveccio. We both stopped in our tracks as recognition took hold.

"Claude!" Mister Vic flashed his commanding smile and we shook hands. I was stunned.

"Wow, ah, we heard you were, ah, coming . . . next week, some time."

"Right, but I left Vegas early, got my business done in Atlantic City, and going home sooner than planned. So, I decided to drop in. How are things going up here for you and Daisy?"

"Uh, real, really good, I think. An' Mom's feeling better about things an' all."

"Well, last night, she said you would be flying today."

"We just got down."

"I need to call her but I'd kinda like to surprise her too. Think I should? Or what?"

"I could phone her." I gestured to the phone on the wall. "Tell her to meet us out here for lunch. She likes surprises."

"Think so? Okay, I'll trust you on this."

"You can join us."

I escorted Mister Vic to our table. "This is my cousin, Nathe Summers and our friend, Mr. McIntyre. His plane followed your jet in."

"Delveccio?" Mac asked. "One of my very good coast guard buddies was Joe Delveccio. From Toms River in Jersey."

"Oh yeah? That's about thirty minutes from where I started out. There's a swarm of us in that area. We're prob'ly connected."

"Joe built custom furniture. We have some of his pieces at the house. He helped me build my canine castle, Claude."

"Now I need to see it for sure."

It was agreed I'd call Mom and insist she come to lunch right now. "Tell her to take the Town and Country if Marguerite's got the Olds," Nathe told me. "Keys are in it."

Mom resisted the idea of taking the big Chrysler. "Well, if Aunt Marg isn't here by one, I'll do it. You're sure it's okay with Nathe? Is it that important, Claude?"

"Yes, ma'am, yes it is. Nathe and I want you to see Mac's airplane and some other neat stuff out here. They're having a model plane show and radio-controlled things you can't believe. Old trucks and bi-planes. Hurry. We'll order lunch."

"Well, all right, hon, but don't order for me. I've had a snack. But I still don't feel right about driving Nathe's car. What if I do something?"

"He insisted. It's not that far, Moms, and it's all backroads."

Some of what I said bordered on the truth. There *was* a display case of old WWII model bombers and fighters. And a huge radio-controlled Cessna hung in the restaurant over the diners. Plus Mac's truck was vintage. There was a bi-plane sitting in a hangar, but a modern crop duster, not an antique. But Mom relished surprises and I rather liked them too, I thought. I hoped. Besides, I wanted to see how she and Vic handled this chance meeting. Curiosity in command.

"Mom says to go ahead and order but nothing for her. She'll be along. She doesn't eat much at noon anyways."

"All right, lasagne all around then," Nathe told our waitress.

*　　*　　*

CHAPTER 12

Dear Hearts and Gentle People

During our lunch, I kept a vigil concerning the gigantic Cessna swaying gently overhead. Plus there were other model planes—mostly smaller—that drew my attention. And speculation. Helicopters lifting off, gliders banking at precarious angles, a P-40 Warhawk baring its fangs framed in red, yellow, and black. A Mustang strafing unsuspecting diners below.

All appeared fastened to the ceiling by what looked like delicate monofilament fishing line. Could that stuff actually decay over time?

I had to smile. The thought of the big Cessna plop—

"I know what's on your mind, bub." Mr. McIntyre caught me in my reverie. Trapped and netted, I had to laugh out loud. He had me fixed with that eye cocked my direction and underscored by a knowing smirk. He shook more pepper onto his salad, then looked above our table.

"You're thinking it would be plumb hilarious if that Skylane plopped itself down in the middle of our dinner right now." I was certain of it: he'd been a boy once himself.

"Yessir," I admitted and unable to contain it.

"I've considered such myself. Hope I'm here to see it happen some day or night. They've been hanging around awhile and it could break away, like that Piper Cub dive bombing into the salad bar."

71

"So . . . Claude." Vic looked down the table my way. "Daisy tells me you're driving the tractor, herding cows. Sounds like you're making a hand."

"Yessir. Trying to."

Nathe sat back in his chair. "'Making a hand' is a Westernism, Mister Delveccio, a ranching term. Where'd you pick that up?"

"Call me Vic. Oh, I worked on a Nevada spread owned by Herb Taylor, the comic? That's who got me started in the supper club business. One fine gentleman. Anyway, I finally learned enough that summer, the foreman said I'd 'made a hand'. It was a rare compliment, I learned later.

"Herb Taylor was a very generous and sincere guy. Gave a truckload of money to worthy causes. . . . And his jokes were clean. Did you ever meet him? He did a few pictures for Disney."

"No," said Nathe. "The only comedian I met of that reputation was Jack Armitage and he was crude and lewd."

"Yes, I met Jack once at a party and it wasn't ten minutes before I wanted to paste the guy. He got drunk and began insulting some ladies in their group. I always hoped he'd come into my club some night so I could throw him out. I guess you've met some bad apples in the entertainment business, Nathe. I have."

"Oh, yeah. I just try to remember the good ones."

"Such as if I may ask?"

"Well, I snuck into a movie last month and it made me think of Richard Farnsworth. Banks and Nancy were there—what did you think of it, Mac?"

"Pretty funny but the barracks language even made me blush. Nancy said it curled her toes."

"Right. That's why I thought of Farnsworth. He told me once it never hurt his career to strike any foul language in his lines. Been a stuntman for thirty years and yet his acting career started about the time mine was fading. We worked on some television stuff and hit it off right away.

"He told me, 'young man, you're good. But . . . this western thing will fade. Be prepared. You an' me and the rest of us cowboys might find ourselves out on the street one of these days. It looks like you come from a solid family—make sure you can go back to 'em because when it comes right down to it—no matter what this business dishes out to y'—if you've got the right kind of family, you're rich, you've got everything.'"

"Hmmmm. Did you find that to be true then?" Vic asked him.

"Yes, indeed. That's why I'm back here now," Nathe told us. He said after his career got short-stopped, his marriages failed, with film production, then broadcasting and the magazine business getting so nasty, he decided to bag everything and go home, back to roots and "'those dear hearts and gentle people', like the song says. I always was a homebody. Always dreaded leaving for the studio, especially. Locations were better. Outdoor work and quite the fun, despite the long hours and days. But I never forgot what Richard Farnsworth told me."

"Hmm. Yes, important stuff. I could get annoyed with Vegas and the fast lane, I find. Maybe I'll go back to Toms River and look up that cousin that makes the furniture. Think he might need an apprentice, Mac?"

Mister Mac smiled. "No, afraid not. He passed on a year ago, 'bout this time. Heart gave out. They about washed him out of the coast guard 'cause of a heart murmur he developed. But he fought to stay in—the coast guard was a family tradition. Nancy and I flew to the funeral. Lots of friends and grandkids, nieces and nephews galore. The kids all sang in a choir—very touching."

*   *   *

Lunch over, we were making our way toward the door. Mom hadn't shown up yet. She liked to be punctual. But. . . I gave her short notice.

Vic loaded his luggage (monogrammed) into the bed of Mac's Cameo pickup, hooked a finger through the loop on his jacket (leather-trimmed) and despite all the fine attire he wore and the carefully coifed haircut, he insisted on standing up in the back while the rest of us crawled into the cab.

"Hey, I haven't done this since working on Taylor's ranch."

"It's a gravel road, Vic. Be a bit dusty back there."

"A little dirt never hurt. I need to get the city outa my lungs."

We took the back road out of the airport and were soon on Summers Run Road. Mac poked along and soon he really poked his way through a band of sheep Bradshaws were moving to its new pasture.

"Hello!" Vic sang out from the back and thumped the cab. "Get a shot of this, Claude. Reminds me of the old days." He waved to the sisters driving their flock. "Hello, ladies!"

Maddy Bradshaw squinted into the sun and studied the high-spirited stranger standing up in the bed like a campaigning politician on parade. Her sister Natalie rode horseback and peered into the cab recognizing Mr. McIntyre.

"'Lo, Mac. What you'uns celebrating?"

"Life," said Vic from his perch. "A gorgeous day and two beautiful country colleens taking their wool to market."

"Are you the Hollywood star we hear about these days?" asked Maddy.

"No, he's in the cab. I'm the film's director, scouting for new talent and locations. Wanna be in my movie?"

"Not today," she said. "Come around Sunday, why don't y'? Saturday's bath night and we won't smell like sheep dip . . . more'n likely."

Mac pushed through the last of the bunch, shaking his head. "That Maddy . . . y' can't get ahead of either one of those gals. They got a slant on life. Folk and bluegrass pickers, don't y' know? Been on stage in Wheeling several times. Might go to Nashville, I hear, one of these days."

Nathe looked out the wraparound window of Mac's Chevrolet Cameo. "And Vic . . . is quite your old Vic."

"He might like it around here, Kiddo. Maybe he could beat Gene Forsythe outa the Logan Farm."

"What do you think of him, Nathe?" I asked. "I mean, first impressions an' all."

"Your granddad use to say folks are like onions. They come in layers and you have to peel a few to see if they hold true to the core."

"He must be pretty rich. Mom says he doesn't own that plane outright but a bunch of them out there lease it in a pool." I remembered that tidbit from once when Mom was ticking off his holdings and assets.

"For my two cents," said Mac, "he reminds me of Stewart Granger. Remember him? *Scaramouche?* And *The Last Hunt?* One of the best westerns ever made, my opinion."

"I agree. I devoured *The Last Hunt*, especially Russ Tamblyn's role. Just getting my movie legs under me, but I wanted every kid part in every western I knew of. I was way too young for that one."

"And too blond, I'd guess. That part was 'sposed to be a half-breed if I recall."

"Right. And I'd get my chance . . . when *Where the Sun Now Stands* came along."

"Another of the best, Kiddo." We crossed one of the bridges over the Run, took a blind turn to the left, and met the Chrysler with its top down.

"There's Mom!"

We passed her, Vic shouted "Daisy!", and I turned to my left just in time to see my mother's expression. As I turned to

75

the right, the convertible fishtailed into a bowl of dust, then disappeared over the brow of the bank.

None of us spoke while Mac skidded to a stop and whipped his pickup back to where Mom left the road. We jumped out to find the white fence down, boards scattered about, cows bucking, some just running with their tales straight out in fright.

When poking through the library at Aunt Marguerite's, I found a volume entitled, <u>Livestock Breeds of the World</u>. Under Swine, I found an image similar to what we were viewing now. The Chrysler sat on its haunches in a platter of mud, its front end enjoying the pleasant and cooling balm of Summers Run passing under its chin.

*   *   *

CHAPTER 13

Mr. Standing Ovation

Vic Delveccio certainly played the dashing swashbuckler, I decided. Very Stewart Granger-esque as he plodded through the cattails, mud, and braved the spring-fed waters of the Run, still frosty from their morning's cascade down the valley. He plucked Daisy from the car, which to all appearances seemed quite content in its situation.

Nathe assured everyone of this. "I'd say the Town and Country looks quite at home with where—"

"Oh, Nathe, I am so very sorry—"

"Daisy, you're not hurt and the car ended up just fine, no harm done."

"Oh, are you sure? Absolutely sure?"

"Yep. Just a dab of white paint on the bumper and the grill guard and nary a scratch. The water isn't even touching the oil pan."

"I feel so careless."

"Daisy, it's fine."

"It's all my fault," Vic said. "I shouldn't have shouted."

"Hey folks, everything's fine. The car's fine and you didn't hit any of Harvey's cows."

"What a rout, a stampede," said Mac. "All this excitement—they'll be talking 'bout it for weeks."

Mom stood on firm ground, rubbing her elbows, her sign for distress or the nerves. "I couldn't put the top up when I left and with all that dust, that's all I could think of and before I knew it, over I went. I feel so stupid and reckless."

"All's well that ends well and this ended pretty darn well, as Dad says." Nathe slogged through the mud, lifted the wooden trunk lid, found a little shovel, and began clearing the bumper and the undercarriage of the Chrysler. "She was begging for a waxing anyway. Claude will learn what a pain a classic can be."

"Let me drive everyone to Marguerite's," said Mac, "and we'll swing by Albert's and get the Ferguson. Harvey here sold his tractor last fall."

"The car will have to be pulled out?"

"Yup, she's bit too mired in the mud, looks like, to drive out, Vic. We'll get the Ferguson and have her out in a jiff. Claude, you might want to stay behind and keep the cows from getting out. Plus, they might take a notion to rub on the car—usually do. Especially that bull."

"I'll run 'em off."

By this time the bull, who had vacated the scene, returned with what I assumed was his owner, a sprightly looking elfin man, bristling gray on top over a florid complexion glistening with good health. He climbed off his four-wheeler.

"Well, folks, my goodness, no one hurt in this melee, I gather, ha-ha! Well, would y' look at that? An' look who's here!—ha-ha-ha!" With that, the ruddy-faced man plodded his way to Nathe, quite heedless of the mud and gave him a hearty handshake with both of his. "Well, Nathe, home at last, wonderful. The missus said you stopped by for a cookie. By golly, it's great to see you again after all these years. Missed you twice at the house but here you are today in style. And, say, you gifted me with a pretty elegant addition to my meadow here, ha-ha-ha."

Nathe again assured the man and everyone that the Chrysler suffered "only a temporary indignity, no damage—just to her pride. After all, it is a Town and *Country*."

"Good name for it. Country means nothin' can avoid cowpies and mudholes for long. Well, well, this is quite a day. The cows came a-gallopin' up toward the house—"

"And I'm so sorry, sir, about your fence."

"Oh,ho-no, Miss, that fence has been begging for attention. No harm done there. If the grass wasn't good here, I'd be worried about it. In fact, I brought some posts home yesterday 'cause I knew that bull would be taking a notion and test it out one of these days. Bulls get kinda breachy once their work's done and the grass is not to their liking."

"Harvey, this is Daisy Kinkade, Vic Delveccio from Nevada, and 'Mac' McIntyre from the local area. Harvey Logan, folks, and this young man—"

"Still the joker, Nathe, aren't y'? Hello folks, an' I've known Mac since he came up the lane on old Barnum, ha-ha-ha. Mac was about—what? Three years old?"

"I hadn't passed four yet, I know," said "Mac", scratching his ear.

"Mac's my neighbor for about fifty years or so. Anyway Mac's dad had a pair of Shires—Barnum and Bailey—an' here comes this toddler up our road, sittin' high an' mighty on Barnum as big as you please and not the least bit scared. Let the horse out of the lot, he did and—how'd you get on his back, Mac, anyhow?"

"Climbed up the fence, I guess." Mac looked at me and winked as he jostled the toothpick around his crooked mouth. I wondered: *Guess kids around here begin adventuring at a young age. Mister Mac on a work horse and my dad Blake climbing the barn to touch the rooster. I'm certain they told each other of their derring-do.*

"So here comes this little tyke trottin' up the lane, ha-ha. An' that ol' Shire stood, what sixteen hands at the withers? I couldn't see over his back!" Mr. Logan drew a line against the afternoon sun where he remembered lifting Mac to safety.

"We took him in the house and the missus fed him cookies and milk. An' then—she remembers it still—Mac said, 'Well, thanks. I gotta be going now,' and out he went to climb back on and, ha-ha-ha, continue their journey to town or wherever. But, by that time, here comes John and they all went back—rode 'im home, didn't y', Mac? What did your dad say?"

Mister Mac, doffed his ball cap, displaying his thinning hair and receding hairline. "Well, he said, 'Son, you likely ought not do that again. You stay clear of ol' Barnum and Bailey, and we'll get you a proper pony, easier to climb up and off."

"And he did—"

"And he did. Had that pony for nigh on ten years. We went everywhere. I bawled for a week when we found him dead down in the woodlot. Struck by lightning."

I noted this as something about Mac to tag in my memory bank and the journal Mom wanted me to keep. He was a boy on this very ground who felt sad about losing his pony. At thirteen years of age. Tears for boys are all right if the loss is of such importance.

"Oh yes, ha-ha. You and Commanche were quite the neighborhood attraction. Those were great old days, yessir."

"Harvey, this is Claude, Blake's son."

"Well, if it isn't indeed. It surely is. I knew Blake had a son, and well, this is remarkable, all right. Yes, such a resemblance." He shook my hand in both of his. "'Course, I could get Nathe and Blake mixed up easily enough and you boys were polite enough to not straighten me out—you looked like such a pair."

"Yes, we didn't care as long as we got our cookies. Visiting the Logans was always a treat."

"Well, it's good of you to drop in right now, ha-ha-ha! So to speak."

"Moms." I thought I'd try to get in a word and confirm Mister Mac's first impression of my good manners. "This is Mr. McIntyre, our pilot today."

"I'm known hereabouts as 'Mac', y' might have guessed." Mac touched the rim of his cap.

"Well, I'm pleased to meet you, such as I am."

"Y' had quite an adventure, little lady."

"Yes, I'm, I can feel my knees wanting to buckle."

"Why don't we get home to Marguerite's, Mac, and I'll bring the tractor back from home."

"Let's do. Think you can climb the bank, Mrs. Kinkade?"

"I'll see to that," said Vic and he swooped Mom up and charged the slope to the road.

*   *   *

I stayed behind to guard the car and watch the cows. It might become my first time solo toward 'making a hand.' Making a hand would be my focus during the days ahead, I vowed.

The bull found a dry spot along the stream bank and began pawing dust into the air and over his back. We had invaded his turf and he apparently intended to let me know more about the matter.

Then he stopped abruptly and snorted, watching the other humans leave. Then he studied me. Nathe and Vic were last seen in the bed of Mac's pickup. Mr. Logan left to get some posts and boards, he said. And I alone remained to get acquainted with an impressively ominous creature who regarded me with an eye more appraising than Mr. McIntyre's.

From where I stood I could see the bull processing the updated information: 1) There's a most intriguing new item in the pasture; 2) Left in charge is a scrawny human who it's assumed knows little about cattle; 3) The fence appears to be flat and presenting no barrier now to where new horizons beckon.

"Ah . . . good ol' bull." I managed. Then, I heard the voice of my departed ancestor, David Kinkade, echoing in the hollow of my ears. "Tis anger in yer tone and harsh words, what the cattle find unsettlin', don't y' know."

I learned from Mr. Logan his bull bore the name, "Standing Ovation."

"Well, Mr. Ovation . . . good of you all to stop by an' all.

"Ah . . . big fella, best we, ah . . ." The more I elected to speak, the closer Standing Ovation approached. Soon he entered the Run and quite deliberately, I thought, began making his way toward the gleaming and inviting chrome dental work arrayed lavishly across the bow of the Chrysler.

He stopped a few yards shy of his prize. What a good scratch he could enjoy on all those silvery bars and bumpers and knobs and projections. I stepped through the cattails and into the Run with a shock, finding it as frosty and fully refreshing as I expected.

Ovation remained standing. Then he slurped up a snootfull of the Run and let it drip off his nose. That black snout glistened in the sun like a waxy boxing glove, poised high and ready for a killer blow.

Once more he measured me. I'd drawn up beside the Chrysler's maple and mahogany door and was easing my way along the fender when I fell on the slippery footing to all fours. Standing Ovation had, in the meantime, decided his expansive rump could postpone its assault on the grill.

Perhaps that driver's side mirror might be more effective. Possibly more flexible and somehow . . . highly surgical . . . toward pinpointing and relieving that nettlesome itch. You know the one . . . just below that massive hump on that massive neck.

I fought any notion toward quick moves as I was still kneeling in the water, thinking prayer might be appropriate at this point, given my position. When I looked up, Standing Ovation stood within a coffin's width of me and the car. I held up my hand, palm open, as a sign of peace and good will. He sniffed it. Then uttered a snort from that inquisitive snout.

Suddenly, a tongue as big as a round steak slapped across my hand, my chin and brow.

I stood slowly. Standing Ovation then found my new wide and tooled leather belt of considerable interest and drew in a mighty draught, savoring a scent he remembered as that of some relative's possibly. He then regarded my dripping and quivering chin, clearly shivering, of course, from its dive in the Run. This too he sniffed and we exchanged breath, his heated and fragrant from the meadow grass. How mine struck him, I have no idea.

His head lolled about some, sniffing for other areas or items of interest on or about my person. Then, he spotted a cow returning to the scene. Whether his interest in her was feigned or not didn't matter. He plopped his way across the Run toward the cow and I allowed him a graceful retreat. So, we both retained our composure—an important lesson toward other areas of life, I later learned. It appeared I had 'made a hand' so far today.

And thus the afternoon ended with another encounter. I added this one to the growing list I would not speak of to my mother.

*   *   *

CHAPTER 14

Mellow as a Cello

Over the years and pondering these events I'm recording, I've made some observations, drawn down some insight.

An episode taking an unexpected twist or some incident upsetting the customary balance can prove mighty useful. My mother Daisy dunking a classic car in the Run qualified as one of those moments. Things knocked ajar, motivations exposed, a quirk perhaps or a new facet of personality unveiled . . . or unmasked . . . memories stirred . . . confessions aired. It had been a "Cornerstone Day."

First, the plane ride and aerial tour of the changes threatening to engulf the township. Next, Mom's harrowing plunge, Vic's heroics, and the unnerving prospect of broaching the question nagging me lately. *How would Nathe react?*

Most boys begin their journey toward relationships, knowing they lack skills and understanding. Eventually we wend our way forward either through bravado or befuddled bungling. With time, we replace impetuosity with caution, candor with tact, demands with compromise and diplomacy.

We mimic the adults around us. Much of what we sense from them is worth noting, practicing, or avoiding. When living on the army post, I observed adults, of course, but I was not surrounded by them as here at Shadeland and Summers Run. Life thus far in "P. A." might prove to be a study in how home folks get things done and relate to each other. "Home folks" being, apparently, the local term for neighbors, family, spiritual aunts and uncles, the members of closely bound crossroads and communities.

I sensed from these few days on the farm that I had much to draw from, the wells of family lore, experience, and wisdom running deep yet close to the surface. Take this afternoon. Mom and Mister Vic are at Shadeland, recovering from Mom's wreck. Standing Ovation is surveying his domain. Nathe and I are digging postholes for the repair of the fence Mom had scattered about. Harvey Logan is carrying some boards our way to replace those too badly damaged.

"Holes dry?" asked Mr. Logan. "Seeps here some."

"Dry thus far, Harvey."

"I see you've not forgotten the art of setting a good post, Nathe. Your Uncle David would be pleased. Young man," Mr. Logan addressed me, " 'One tamps the ground so tightly it squeaks, then he tamps it forty strokes more,' ahaha. Thus said David Kinkade."

"Yes, Uncle Dave's legendary fenceposts," Nathe added. 'Why, lads, y' want 'em to take root, don't y' know, so they'll bloom like the sapling they were in a former life, give them ha' a chance." Nathe pulled his shovel from the hole and directed me, "Give 'er forty more, son. Mighty fine dirt here, Harvey. As mellow as a cello."

"Yes, good Strathmore Loam from here to the house and on over to the hill and clear to m' border against Swenson's. Where I have timothy now is a bit more sandy—Beriwick Sandy Loam—not as chocolatey as here." The earth where I was now devoting my attention did indeed resemble cocoa ready for the cup.

Harvey Logan wiped his brow with a generous red handkerchief, more from habit than perspiration I was to learn. "I would have farmed this if the Run didn't pass through. Some of the best soil around even though, oddly, there's a gravelly layer when y' get beyond the Strathmore and the subsoil. But it makes splendid pasture, best we leave it as such, taking it as nature laid down. Better than a golf course, to my mind."

"Then, I take it, some real estate agents are snooping about, Harvey. Gene's team scouting your place? Eighteen hole setup, perhaps. Any offers?"

"The rumor mill has it right." Harvey Logan fished a card from his shirt pocket and squinted at it. "'Finn Murtaugh, Esquire, Attorney at Law'" says the card. "One hundred and eighty thousand for the lock, stock and barrel—timber, houses, and outbuildings—the works. A princely sum for us folks hereabouts. Pretty modest, though, I suppose by your California standards."

"Hmmm, yes. Some land agents out there would charge $100 for this posthole right here." I had finished my forty strokes and Nathe and I began tamping fresh loam around the post. "D'ya wanna hear my proposal?" he asked.

"If it will keep me from moving to Arizona. Carolyn—that's Mrs. Logan, Claude— you've not met her or her peanut butter cookies yet. Carolyn's sister wants us to rent a condo, try it in Sun City."

"What do the girls say?"

"Well, Laura's husband—he's the chiropractor, y' know—he's bought a practice up yonder towards Erie. And Sarah's moving out to Tempe to go to school. They want us to keep the farm in the family but Lord knows, there's more taxes and expense than income these days on a place this small. A man could hobby farm and break even maybe. The girls know the missus and me want them to have it but not if it's a burden.

"Their memories are here but the money's elsewhere."

Mr. Logan told us he had sold most of his farming implements. "I sold the tractor last fall. What I do around the place now, I can manage with this ATV. Guess I'm a hobby farmer myself by the looks of things and another one of those railroad pensioners. If one of the girls, now, had a son or we ourselves had a male heir, then we might try to keep the place in the Logan name.

"I'd prefer to pass it on thataway. But, our son-in-law and Sarah's fiancé are town kids with no interest in keeping it free of weeds, fences up, stock or crops to take care of. Or renting it out."

Nathe stretched to his full height, then leaned his chin on his shovel. "Two hundred and fifty thousand and you and Carolyn get to keep the homestead in your name including the surrounds—buildings, the orchard, and the garden plot."

"Oh, my, Nathean, are you sure about this, my friend?" Harvey snared the bandanna back from the bib of his overalls. "You've given it some thought?" Nathe and I were topping off our hole.

"Well, according to that same rumor mill, I've got to get my bid in before Gene puts a blade to the ground for his country club and snatches it away from us."

"Yes, it'll be a shame to scuttle the ninth fairway . . . . It's where we stand as we speak. Gene wants to build a stone bridge over the Run, right there somewhere." Harvey waved the bandanna toward his barn. "Keep the buildings as a shelter for the golfers, maintenance facilities. Be a magnificent setting, near the trees and all. Murtaugh said we could move the house. Our expense. Otherwise, they'll tear it down."

It *was* a nice sight, I decided, the Logan homestead, the redwood and taupe of it nestled under the canopy of giant firs. And I could visualize the bridge arcing across the Run, with vines creeping up its limestone and the waters tumbling over a little spillway.

"I told Murtaugh I would move it before I'd let them tear it down. I know every plank, dovetail, and cabinet hinge of that place."

"That you do, Harv. I remember you and Carolyn working well into the night on it. For years."

"Yep. We were young and hopeful then. Now we're old and hopeless." Harvey Logan winked at me and we all laughed together. Harvey's rheumy eyes, a balmy old blue, glistened in the waning sunlight.

Nathe stepped forward and extended his hand. "You and Carolyn can live out the length of your days . . . right here as far as I'm concerned." Harvey took it in both of his and unabashedly let the teardrop meander down his ruddy cheek. The bandanna again rose to service as Harvey wiped his face with uncommon vigor and blew his nose.

"Well, I see I've become a sentimental old codger. I was hoping we might strike a deal, Nathe. It belongs to you or someone around here with some history. When I knew you were back, I was going to speak of it. You're like kin you are, ha-ha." He turned to me and hooked his thumbs in the bib of his pin-striped overalls. "Claude, your cousin, famous as he was, never forgot his roots, y' know.

"Even though he made movies an' such an' was bigger than life on the screen, when he came home, he wanted everyone to treat him like he'd never left the country." Then Harvey Logan shook my hands as well. In both of his. The deal seemed sealed. The first land transaction I'd ever witnessed.

We gathered our shovels and braced the freshly planted posts while Harvey drilled new screws into the blond-colored 2 x 6s keeping Standing Ovation at home. "I don't hammer things anymore now that I've got this drill. Much easier on these goofy hands of mine. Now that you're adding my place to your holdings, Nathe, surely you're not gonna tell you're taking up farming with all its risks and the gamble and hard work, are y', you an' young Claude here?"

"Hmmm. Claude and I have discussed it, but then I recall what the farmer said when he was brought before the judge . . . . 'Your honor, I know I done wrong, but I'm just a simple farmer.' And the judge bangs his gavel down and says, 'Case dismissed. If this man's a farmer, he's not mentally competent

88

to stand trial.'" Harvey whooped as if he hadn't heard that one in years. And we parted, the bull corralled, Harvey back to the house he built, and Nathe and I to our car and tractor.

*   *   *

Nathe drove the disgraced Town and Country out of the Run and Logan's pasture, and I ventured out on the lane, in road gear, another first. I was not speeding by, the fence posts and roadside shrubbery a blur. Rather, road gear seemed confined to a pleasant plodding, the caution lights clicking, the little gray Ferguson thrumming contentedly along, the grasses and budding wildflowers barely nodding in its wake.

It was my mind racing, not the tractor. *Do I dare ask the guy? I've only known him for a week or so. But then Vic is here and Mom may be about to seal her mind about him. It's urgent.*

After we put the Ferguson away, I climbed into the Town and Country for the ride back to Shadeland and asked Nathe if there wasn't more to buying land than just a handshake in this corner of Pennsylvania. And he confirmed it: "Oh, yes, we've just begun, Logans and us, but I had to strike while the iron was hot. I've wanted to visit with Harvey and Carolyn about their place. It's one of the keys if we're going to keep things rural around here. Opportunity knocked, you see, thanks to your mom's little mishap."

We pulled up the drive and parked. Vic and Mom were on the front porch. *Was I going to broach the subject on my mind with them looking on? It appeared so.* Nathe sensed I wanted to talk and looked my way, curious.

My mother's laughter pealed down the steps, cascading our way.

"Vic makes her laugh." I said, "I mean really laugh," I said. "She hasn't been very happy for a long time."

"She's been through the mill. War asks too much of our wives and widows. Hope Vic is what she's looking for."

"Nathe, ah . . ." *That knocking—was it my knees or Opportunity?* "What if Mom had really banged up the Town and Country. Ah, would you have been, y' know . . . ."

"Furious?"

"Yessir."

"No, of course not. Cars, even old ones, can be fixed. I could buy a dozen old Town and Countries. Provided I could find 'em. If I couldn't, there's always the Ford Sportsman, 1946. Or the Lincoln Zephyr, Packard Victoria—there's a pair to draw to. Total elegance, eloquent from every angle. The '48 understated Nash Convertible—only a thousand of those built. Or the '48 Continental. And no wood to contend with to boot.

"Daisy wasn't injured. That's a relief."

"Other than being embarrassed. And scared to death."

He laughed, "Well . . . she looked pretty charming, all so helpless and in distress, backlit there in the mud puddle. I wished I were as gallant as ol' Vic. He was Sir Galahad out there."

I torqued my courage up to its highest notch: the Door of Opportunity was no longer ajar but thrown wide open. *Ask!* my mind screamed. *He's totally exposed. Before he takes cover.*

"Right, an', if Vic weren't in the picture . . . would you be interested? . . . I mean would you, ah , find my mother attractive?"

By the look he bestowed on me, I had caught him off guard. I kicked myself.

What a flub and blunder. I shuddered. Then I relaxed as he grinned and blushed as hotly as I felt.

"Well, your mother has a fetching smile. I can see why Cousin Blake was so taken with her. Would you be doing a little matchmaking, my friend?"

*   *   *

CHAPTER 15

Silver Nights, Golden Mornings

"A couple things to bear in mind, son. There are quite a few years between your mom and me. Thirteen or more."

"Vic's forty-three."

"I see. Well, uh, she's on her way. . . with him, career-wise."

"But . . . you're just a couple years older than my dad."

"Right. True, but then there's all this business about falling in, you know, love and such. Gets perplexing. And complicated. There's an old movie line I remember. A young guy about your age asks this old timer about 'what is it what makes folks want other folks?'

"And the old gentleman says, 'Boy, I'm obliged to tell y', that's the one question mankind has never developed a good answer for.'"

"But if Vic weren't around and in the way, what would be the chances then?" *I marveled at my boldness. Were my knees quivering just now? What he must think of me.*

Nathe tapped a little rhythm on the steering wheel and went through what Uncle Albert described as a "rumination." Finally, he looked at me with an expression I'd never seen before and can recall vividly now: a blending of resignation and remorse. "I dunno, Claude.

"I've had two marriages go flat. I may not be worth the risk. I know one thing and it's nothing new. Your head gets caught up in some yearning and your heart is no help. Therefore, you have to go with your gut. And the gut's answer is not always what your head or heart had in mind." He looked over at me and shrugged and I read him right I think: he was sympathetic. And I felt as he did perhaps, the tug from some brooding sense of loss.

Later that night, I pondered and stared at the moonlit ceiling above me. One's Head, then his Heart weighing and presenting, then debating, squabbling, declaring a truce between them. Then flaring back up at each other until Gut arrives on the scene and settles the matter. "Things getting all muddled up and that's no good," I said aloud to the darkness around me. Still, if we could get Vic out of the way and if Nathe would fall for my mother, then things would be nicely "redd up"—as they say in P. A.—in my corner of the world. I kicked free of the bed covers. Outside, the evening was pouring inside.

I crept to my window. Sleepless, I marveled at being wakeful, as if I were finally engaged in something adult. Now I could truthfully report: "I didn't sleep a wink, I swear. . . tossed and turned . . . couldn't quit thinking about . . . wish I could drop off like you kids."

Below, my first-ever glimpse of Shadeland bathed in silver. My room looked down on the drive, now a little river; the gauzy front lawn, the ghostly fields and fences stretching on toward the rolling hills, hills older than fossils. They looked rumpled and curmudgeonly annoyed with the thousands of trees stirring and now leafing across their ancient buckled knobs and ravines. Budding young leaves they were—maples, oaks, sycamore, beeches and birch—curling, stretching, awakening to their first-ever benediction of a full moon. They likely were basking, shimmering in the radiance, marveling at each other's raiment, quivering in anticipation. The leaves must be asking one another: "From now on, will every nightfall bring us such magic?"

The hills grumbled. They'd seen a million moonlights. Those stolid and grumpy old things. Like some folks I would eventually know, were they so jaded they might never know joy in the morning?

Me? As young as I was, I knew how important to welcome it often. I knew, as I grew older, the importance of a daily dose.

How badly I wanted to step out my window and float to the ground. I even cranked the window open, allowing the breeze from the evening air to lift me over the sill and set me down upon the lawn. There I met my father, Blake. And we laughed and left our footprints in the dewy grass glittering beneath our feet.

*   *   *

I must have found peace that night. For I awoke refreshed and found the house stirring. Shadeland would soon be a place of departure. Aunt Margy's friend Anne Doolittle, the first. Anne promised she would return "if things work out. It may take years. But, until then, I'm going to work very hard, Marg—"

"I know you will, Dear. You call me whenever things get rough."

"I'll be the best doggone mother-in-law I can be to those two, I'll tell the world—I do so want us to get along."

"Yes, and those kids need their grandmother. We know that one thing for sure."

Anne had finally decided to move to Florida where both her sons and their families lived. She had succeeded in arriving "on terms" with her daughters-in-law, both of whom Anne described as "high maintenance, trying to outdo one another.

"But I think they've mellowed. Troubles can cloud or light our way."

Then, Mister Vic and my mother would be jetting off to Las Vegas within the weekend. Vic's pilot and personal assistant had been rooming at Shadeland as well. Soon, it would just be Aunt Marguerite and me, rattling around in a house with four bedrooms down and five up.

But not for long perhaps. Word came, confirming that Bethany, Marguerite's only child, was indeed loading a rental trailer this time. Her worldly goods and seven years of marriage crated, wrapped, stacked, and wedged into a six by twelve foot box. "We divided the wedding gifts," she told her mother. And Anne told me, "it sounds final. It's good you're here, Claude." She patted my arm.

"Your Aunt Marguerite will need someone to lean on. I wish I could stay. She and I've been through the thick and thin of this Bryan and Beth saga, but my kids need me down there now, more than ever. Your aunt and I were the only girls in our families, so we're both the sisters neither of us had."

*   *   *

If it was a silver midnight a few hours ago, what lay before me was a golden morning. A cloudless sky, the light breeze blowing across the meadow, spring birdlife returning to Shadeland. "The Bird and Tree Club counted thirty different species of songbirds alone hereabouts," said Aunt Marguerite, "and that's just around the firs, up by the Springs, and the orchard. When they're nesting and then fledging, the air's so full of chirps, you can't hear much else. I see you've found the bike, Claude. Good. Tires flat?"

"I found a pump and a patch kit. It's a good old Schwinn Predator."

"Yes, that was the one Bethany wanted, kind of a boy's bike we told her. But she was a tomboy back then. How times and kids change. Part of her problem in Texas."

"Oh?"

"As I've said, the Van Strassels expect Beth to be as competitive and as driven as they are. At the kids' wedding reception . . . Mr. Van Strassel, her new father-in-law, came up to me and said, 'Well, Missus, don't expect you've ever seen a clan like ours.' I don't think he even heard my reply, just kept crowing about how Bryan had been groomed . . . pushed to excel . . . particularly at football —'had the pros looking at him, he did. Did your daughter tell you Bryan held a national FFA office?'"

All ears, I leaned across the giant butcher block table. "Did he say anything about Bethany?"

"No, Claude," she laughed, "how perceptive of you—I mean, wouldn't you think? I expected to hear what a lovely bride she made for his Bryan—and she did too—you should see their album. But not a word about my daughter. The old goat . . . wanted me to know how he raised all his boys to be better than those of his brothers. 'But, hell, it's the same with my nephews—hell, you can't imagine the touch football games we've had on this very lawn—sweat and blood—no holds barred. Same playin' hoops. Be better, get on top, be first—kind of the code my brothers and me lived by, passed it on.'

"'I took a page out of Ty Cobb's book, Missus Kay. They say Cobb always had to be first, not just on the field but getting on the team bus, lining up to shave in the morning, checking into the hotel.'"

"And I said, 'I see, Mr. Tee. Well, Bethany's been raised by Romans 11:16-18. Are you familiar with it?'" He was too busy swilling his drink to respond, so I quoted a bit: 'Be of one mind toward one another and if at all possible, live peaceably with all men.' I left out the part about being conceited."

She laughed, lost in the memory and the mixing bowl in front of her. Then she looked toward me, her electric grin all the more radiant across the sunny kitchen. "So, I smiled at him sweetly and said, 'Beth has backbone, your son will learn. It could be a colorful marriage . . . *Mister Tee.*'"

The exchange delighted me, especially the punch line. "And what did he do then?"

"Well, he kind of snorted, said he needed another toddy, asked me if I wanted one and walked off before I could say yes or no."

"Sounds pretty proud of himself and his kids an' all."

"Oh, there's no shortage of pride in the Van Strassel realm. They run the town and surrounds. You'll meet Bryan. He'll be up here within a week, trying to get Beth and the kids back. Such I do fully expect."

*   *   *

The morning begged a ride on my "new" bike, so I set out to explore my sunny world where now a few cotton ball clouds bobbed along a sky of robin egg blue. The day compelled one to get involved . . . in something. As I meandered along the lane, I couldn't help but reflect on the chat I had with Aunt Marguerite over the week's batch of bread. I felt her confidence in me growing. I wanted that.

I wanted to get a look at this Bryan too. Cousin Bethany I liked. From my dad's funeral, when she told me: "I miss my dad but he calls and I call him. I have a feeling someone will take Uncle Blake's place for you. Won't be the same but . . . maybe."

As I pedaled past the cows, some of them looked over and a klatch of calves burst free, running alongside with such headlong joy, they seemed destined for a pile up, a heap of hooves, legs, and tails all tumbled and tangled. *They'll sort it out,* I thought. *Like life.*

Relationships, I was learning, seldom follow rhyme or reason, like the predictable seasons or the phases of the moon. Take my mom. Was she falling or going to fall in love with Vic? How did Aunt Marguerite and her husband arrive at a "modern" marriage, one that seemed to work best when they were apart? Now, Bethany and Bryan Van Strassel seemed headed for the divorce court with two little kids in tow.

And what of my own hopes for Nathe Summers, former motion picture star, and Daisy Kinkade, widow of the highly decorated and fallen hero of The Gulf War? Could they create a new marriage unwedded to their old ones? They'd each had two.

Could I blame Mom if she now felt free to take up a new life, living it on some of her own terms at least, "giving it my last best shot, son. I need this or I will always wonder." Or was she as reckless as a gamboling calf in a meadow?I could not help but harbor the hope and notion: *If it doesn't work out, maybe she'll come home to P.A. and Nathe and me.*

*   *   *

CHAPTER 16

No Abfustication Permitted

Just down the road in my new state of the nation, "P. A.," spring was inching its way toward us. Farther south, the grounds of Fort Campbell, Kentucky, were coming to life with forsythia and daffodils brightening what little ground the U. S. Army had provided us at quarters.

Mom loved her little patch of bulbs there and dug them up before she left the army for Aunt Marguerite's, P.A., and the farm. "Later today, we're going to plant them, Claude, in a little special place, a little final together time, okay? The label says it's not too late." Both of us were avoiding the subject of leaving, pulling away.

"No way to sugarcoat departures," Aunt Marguerite said this morning. "My last trip was to Texas to see the kids. We were going to meet my plane that Saturday right after Wren's soccer match. So, we're at the game, trying to enjoy the morning and there goes his dad charging up and down the sidelines, yelling, 'hustle, Wren, hustle. Don't let up, boy. Y' gotta hustle now.'

"It was noon, hot, humid. The kids were tired, getting cranky, and losing their game. So, Wren—that spunky little cuss—is kicking the ball on the run when he comes to a dead stop, lets the ball roll on, and yells at Bryan—'I am hustling!' Everyone snickered. Or laughed outright. Bryan was embarrassed of course and likely crabbed at him later. I looked at Beth and she knew that I knew the marriage was raveling.

"She was not happy at home with him and such is not how you want to leave your daughter. I boarded the plane in a blue mood, flew home, and as soon as I walk in the door, she calls and we're on long distance for nearly two hours. Her, me, and even her 'Auntie Anne' for a spell. Oh my.

"At least I think you and Daisy are separating but knowing you're both happy . . . excited, something new in the offing."

"We are, Aunt Margy. Mom's off to 'see her rooster' and I'm liking this bein' a farm kid—a lot."

She laughed. "You've a good heart, Clauders. Yes, we hope this rooster is a happy new chapter for her. For all of us. Lord knows, that's all we want, wherever our corner of the world." I didn't say so, but I hoped Mom's rooster didn't send her off the barn roof with a 30-foot plunge like the one my dad escaped as a toddler. She might come down hard. I knew Aunt Marguerite felt as I did: hopeful for her but ready to share the disappointments that might come Mom's way.

*   *   *

A column of dust rose into the blue of the morning. Mr. McIntyre at work. The ball field, under his seasoned eye, had begun to "flesh itself out, Kiddo. We want just a slight crown slivering off toward the outfield. No low or soft spots, y' see. That's a vibrating roller over there. Use it a lot for driveways and the like—it'll force any rocks down deeper yet and bring up the sand. Then we'll top 'er with crusher fines and sod. Geez, Nathe is spending a wad on this." He doffed his new Pirate's cap and readjusted the bill to his preference. "But it will be a good, a great surface. Y' got a crew ready for tomorrow?"

"Yessir. Six or eight of us at least." The future Pickett Township Panthers were assigned the job of raking the infield and rolling the outfield out.

"That'll do. We got enough for a team, y' think?"

"Ten."

"Umm. That's a little tight. Only one guy to spare."

Mr. Mac's "we" inspired me to ask: "Sir, are you going to manage?"

"Aha. Coach a little maybe. Nathe's trying to get Lawrence, James' son, to manage. He played in high school and junior college. Pretty good athlete. Naw, I shouldn't take the time. I'm subbing on too many jobs this year. This Bobcat time cuts into my Cessna time." Mr. Mac laughed again, that thrifty bark I would learn as characteristic.

"Y' been up to the house?" A car crept up the Summers drive and a gray-haired, slightly built man wearing a gray suit stepped out. Mister Mac sidled up to the fence and leaned over the top rail. "Looks like that fellar's wearing a clerical collar. Nathe say anything to you this morning?"

"Nossir."

"Hadn't heard of Albert ailing," said Mac, scowling deeper than usual.

It gave me pause. I'd begun associating clerical collars with sober matters.

Then Nathe emerged from the side porch and bounded down the steps. The two men embraced and engaged in a hearty reunion it appeared. Mister Mac and I were waved up to come join them.

"Guys, this is Reverend Peter Benedict formerly of Hollywood and now doing the Lord's work as an Episcopalian."

Mister Mac scratched his ear and said he was omnivore himself which drew a hoot of appreciation from the minister. Mac then excused himself as having to "meet the accountant" but not before accepting the pastor's compliments bestowed on the Mister 'Mac'McIntyre Chevrolet Cameo, advertising "Landscaping, Excavation, and Tree Services".

"Nathe and I drank from the same hand pump out here years ago. Now, he drives old Chryslers and I drive ol' bowties . . . bowties are Chevrolets, Reverend. We caught the same fever, just different symptoms. Nice to meet y'."

"And you, sir. We Episcopalians set a pretty good table at times for you omnivores should you ever want to stop by." Mac said he'd think on it and pulled out and down the drive.

"Well . . . Claude," said Nathe, motioning us to the rockers and settee on the porch. "Can you join us or has Mac got you working on the diamond today?"

"That's tomorrow. A bunch of us are laying sod and raking stuff."

"No school today, Claude?" asked the minister.

"Nossir. Teacher's meeting."

"Ah, yes. Blessed relief. Especially in spring when a young man turns to baseball and shaking off the dead lice of winter, pardon the expression."

"My mother used to say the same thing, Pete." Uncle Albert eased his way through the door with a tray. 'You young'ns— get out from under foot and work off those winter lice . . . and some of that energy!' Here's a fresh pot and some zuccini bread Marguerite sent over." The gray-haired gents greeted each other as if belonging to the same fraternity, agreeing it had indeed been a long time.

"And they were good times, Peter. Nathe and I have said over and over, if the film world had more folks like Pete Benedict and Richard Strauss, it wouldn't be the cesspool it is today."

"Well, I wished we could have put things together back then. We would have made a good company out of it had the money been there. You, Albert, managing the funds and the books; Nathe our star; George Fenhurst writing and directing."

"Claude, Peter directed and produced a film called, um, *More Precious Every Day.*"

"Right, 1958. *More Precious* Each *Day*," Peter corrected Albert. Reverend Benedict smiled at Nathe and asked if he could tell Claude the short pants story.

"Sure, it's bound to come out. Especially once he sees the film."

"Well . . . *More Precious Each Day* tells the story of a British family dealing with the outbreak of WWII. War's been declared and Nathe's older brother and cousin are off to the fight. Nathe's character, Clive, is left stewing behind and he joins up with a group of young lads who are kind of a home guard, training with toy guns, drilling, helping out where they can, watching for Nazi spies and all that."

"I remember one of the lines, Pete."

Reverend Benedict laughed, "Really, it's been thirty- odd years ago."

"'Oh, but can't you see, Father? School can wait. Our lives are at stake and I could be a part of it behind the lines, not at the front of course. Andrew and his brother are working in the family plant down at Gloucester, building all kinds of canvas goods and the like. He said I could join them, work night and day, and it would do me good.'"

"That's remarkable. You always were so predictable, Nathe. Never witnessed you forgetting or bumbling any delivery. Can still do the English accent, I see."

"Passably. Cousin Faye schooled me on such. I copied Freddy Bartholomew, too closely, I suppose. But Cousin Faye drilled me for fair."

"Anyway, the scene shows these boys acting like soldiers and wearing these outlandishly short pants and so here's Nathe climbing over a stone wall and he rips the seat out, right in full view of the camera. So we wrote it into the scene."

"Hated those pants, everyone did."

"Yes, kind of a row over the pants. But short lived, the boys were pacified with a ride on a schooner under full sail as an outing and as a reward for wearing the dreaded pants. Part of the film, it was. Supposed to be a training exercise. Basic seamanship. The short pants served as swimsuits for one scene. Which I guess was their original intent."

"The new president of my budding fan club—Darlene—wrote how sorry she felt for me when my pants split and all the boys laughed. It was a spontaneous moment."

"Totally unrehearsed and it worked into the film quite well as we had you complain to your father about getting some new shorts. And he said, 'until you can grow into some of your brother's, I'm afraid there's nothing to be done about it, m' boy. We've all got to endure. Privations and shortages will be our lot, I fear, for some time.'"

"See, Peter, you can recite some lines yourself."

"Well, I wrote much of it, remember."

"It was a good film. Thank you, again, for letting me be in it, short pants and all. It was our first real association."

"It *was* a good film. How I bristled at the critic who said we were knocking off *How Green Was My Valley* or *Mrs. Miniver*. Not at all similar."

"It may become one of my favorites." Nathe nestled his steaming mug in his hands, and again I witnessed that wistful expression start at his brow—ever so slightly pinched—and descend downward to his lips, lightly pursed, thinking of something well beyond us and out of sight. "I grew from that film. I had to stretch for it. It served me well."

*   *   *

It developed the Reverend Benedict would be taking lunch with us but before then, we all trucked out to what I learned was "the range", a set-up Nathe had designed and built years ago for sighting rifles and shooting clay pigeons. I found it amusing to watch the minister shed his jacket, role up his sleeves, don earmuffs, and go banging away, cradling the shotgun butt next to his ecclesiastical collar and yelling "Pull!" while Nathe or I launched a clay pigeon down the way.

Then trigger pulled, he'd laugh whether hit or miss. Nathe was the best shot of us, and soon Uncle Albert puttered up on what he called his "go cart," an all-terrain vehicle like Harvey Logan's with a cased long arm across the handle bars.

"Heard all this ruckus and decided Gene and his cronies were attacking our rear flank."

"Gene?"

"A developer who's making waves hereabouts, Pete. One of the Forsythes who used to own this country and lost a good bit of it and now is trying to buy it back, by hook or crook."

"Need to get m' .30-30 up to snuff an' defend our holdings, Reverend."

"Yes," said Nathe, "and we need a man of the cloth—any persuasion will do—to settle things and prevent bloodshed. Before Pop here gets Gene in his sights."

"Oh, well. Don't remember shootouts being covered in seminary. How be I just go off and pray about the matter?"

"Nope," said Albert. "Laymen and ministers alike need to take up arms. No abfusticating, Reverend B. All for the cause." He then dismounted the "go cart" with surprising nimbleness and set about loading an unusually handsome lever action rifle for firing. "Can we count on you . . . as chaplain?"

"Pass the ammunition."

*   *   *

CHAPTER 17

Finding Our Boyhoods

"I hear from Darlene Schue every Christmas, son. She says she always writes to you. I send her a little note.

"Darlene, Claude, became the president of Nate's fan club back, oh, around the time we made Peter's film. In fact, she organized the club. Pretty plucky for a twelve- year-old girl. But she proved up to the task."

"Yes, she stays devoted," said Nathe. "I reply, write a little something on my card, tell her where I am and what's doing and ask about the year she's had."

We were sitting on the side porch, enjoying the sunny afternoon and its spring breezes, and cleaning the guns from our morning's "shoot," as Nathe labeled it. Peter had left for an evening appointment in Pittsburgh.

But not before he and Nathe had recited the number of failed marriages between them. "Both of my ex's have remarried and one's divorced.. That makes three, Pete, on my side. How many for you?"

"Doris has remarried and divorced and so that makes two for the two of us. One of my children split, so there's another to make three as well. Mary—that's my second wife, Claude—and I would still be together had she lived. We were soulmates. She's the reason I turned to the ministry."

As the Reverend Benedict drove out and around the circular drive, he waved through the open window, beeped the horn, and I couldn't help but marvel: W*ow, how many lives become entangled and disrupted when we stumble into things like marriage, family, then calling it quits.* As if Nathe were reading my mind, he said, "Splitsville and the next stop, Quitsville . . . seems Peter and I have spent time enough in both those towns."

Uncle Albert squinted through the bore of his rifle, then wiped it down. "I suppose. Pete's found his calling I think. Darlene lives in Ohio now, Nathe. She might pop on over."

"Yes, I know. I'd be pleased if she did. Would like to see her again."

"She's not married. She never married far as I know."

"Ummm . . . yes, her Christmas letter is always about trips and travel, her pets and such. No mention of spouse and family."

"Be wary, son. She might set her cap for you."

"I've slipped through enough traps." Nathe winked at me. "Still, I would try marriage again. Probably not to the president of my old fan club of thirty years ago, though. She'd find out I wasn't as wonderful as she imagined. And I wouldn't want to be a disappointment. Tabloid headline would read something about the former fan club president and wife finding out her hero and husband, ex-child star Nathean Summers, was such a fraud and nowhere near the blissful marriage she had hoped."

I smiled back at Nathe. But Uncle Albert laid his rifle across his thighs, folded his arms, and gazed across the fields stretched before us. "You . . ." he sighed, then paused to collect his thoughts, perhaps to carefully carve what he wanted to say. "You were . . . *presented* . . . as that clean-cut, quintessentially wholesome American boy. One that every father wanted his daughter to bring home.

"Your fans wanted you that way, the studio packaged you as such, the industry wanted you as such, and your mother and I supported the notion and added to the image as best we could

... because that's what we and everyone wanted you to be for us."

"Nothing wrong with that, Pop."

"I suppose not, but . . . still."

"I wouldn't have had it any other way."

"Yes, perhaps, but were those expectations fair? You didn't have a life of your own . . . at times, trying to fulfill everyone's expectations, live out their dreams, not yours. Plus, you became an outsider in Hollywood, and we all helped cut your career short because we wanted you to be that perfect son-in-law, not what the studio wanted." Albert sighed again and looked down at the rifle in his lap. "I've never said this . . . but I wonder if things between your mother and me had been smoother, you might have had a better marriage to model after and wouldn't have made a couple of mistakes."

"Dad . . . don't let that weigh on y'. Mom was not easy to live with, I know, especially when you and I were out there in the business and she was holding down the farm here. Mom, Claude, did not care much for the motion picture business. Not at all, in fact. The honeymoon was over before it started for Mother."

"Yes, true," said Uncle Albert. "I felt the same, later on, truth be known. Had your sister wanted to try her hand at it, I would have said absolutely not. Even back then, the business had its share of creeps and lechers, unprincipled men, lacking honor and respect. We were lucky we got on board with guys like Peter and Richard Strauss. Think of sweet, naïve' Audrey falling into the clutches of the likes of Roland Stranahan, Heinz Laher, that jerk that was producing some of the early TV westerns—"

"Bancroft."

"Bancroft, what a joke, producing westerns. He didn't know which end of a cow got up first. He was the first guy I ever punched. How people like him get ahead in the industry— it amazes me. Had the personality of a caged animal."

"Audrey?" I asked. "That's your . . . daughter."

"Yes, Nate's younger sister, Claude. She's the public librarian up in Belleville, near Lake Chautauqua, north of here. She used to go with us on location some."

"The camera would have loved her. Remember Spence Kamfort, wanting to screen test her? He said it would be fantastic box office, her and me, a brother and sister duo in the same film. Perfect for Disney, according to Kamfort."

"Oh, yes, and he might have been right. But, good night, trying to keep two kids in the business from falling into wrackanation and ruin. I would have gone berserko."

"Yeah, Sis wouldn't take the scrutiny. She was too . . . thin-skinned to deal with the pressures on the set, the screaming, the criticisms."

"Too sweet and genteel. Some of the most beautiful girls on those sets had the foulest mouths."

"The way you raised her, Pop."

"Yes, and she's found hers, speaking of callings. Books and quiet obscurity."

Nathe scooted his chair toward mine. "Once, Claude . . . this guy Bancroft pulled me aside and said, 'Look, cowboy, your career is washed up—you might as well face the fact your looks don't measure up anymore. Better you get behind the camera if you want to stay in pictures. You're too, too . . . cornpone-country, so-so, average American kid off the farm. No one wants to go to the movies to watch their brother on the screen.'

"'You need a brooding persona like James Dean. Y' need to look like Rock Hudson, get y' a pout like Sal Mineo, look haunted like Perkins. You just don't have any charisma anymore, kid, sorry. The farm kid look is over.'"

"And I said, politely, 'Well, Mr. Bancroft, we'll see. There's room in this town for plain-looking folks I've noticed. Besides I don't want to kill myself in a car wreck or hide a secret life to be successful, now do I?'"

"And he said, 'You cheeky bastard', and that's when Pop 'decked' him right on the set. Several people applauded, everyone hooted and hollered."

"What did he do then?" I asked, savoring the image in my mind of this guy rubbing his jaw and announcing Nathe would never work in films again. "Did he say you're finished in Hollywood?"

"No, he was the one on his way out and everyone knew it. Including Bancroft. The studio had given him an ultimatum that if he threw any more tantrums, he'd be canned. There he sat, blood all down the front and that shut him up for the rest of the shoot. Last we heard he was dealing cards somewhere in Nevada. Good riddance, everyone's opinion. He wasn't suited to the process, though he was convinced he was. You can push that nasty bombast so far and pretty soon there'll be someone to call your bluff. Pop called his," Nathe laughed. "I was so proud of you that day, Dad!"

"Well, I was as surprised as he was. I simply saw red, like the proverbial bull."

"Bancroft pulled the tirade thing once too often, insulted too many people and cost the studio a lot of money with some big name stars walking off the set, cast and crew members quitting. Once you become too expensive or extravagant, the studio execs lop off your head. Unless you've proven to be cash cow and talented. And he was neither one."

"Welp." Uncle Albert rose and sheathed the rifle. "Getting on toward dinner time. Why don't we put these guns away, son, and you show Claude some of the archives upstairs? I'll call Marguerite and tell her you're supping with us, Claude, all right? Nothing fancy, I'll warn you. Road kill garnished with a few leftovers."

He started to leave but paused at the open screen door, heedless of any flies or millers and moths that might fly in.

"I hope, Claude, you won't find it uncomfortable when we talk frankly an' such about the olden days. Or about today's times for that matter. Marguerite says you've proven an uncommonly good listener. She and I and Nathe, your Gram Bea, we all consider it important you get to know your family, small as it's become. Blake would have passed this on, had he been given the chance."

"Yessir," I answered. "I know he wanted to. Eventually."

"Yes, and good for him. He knew its importance." He studied the door, noting an area needing patched. "Well, we tend to live in the past hereabouts and that's not always healthy. We've got a future to think of, yours, Daisy's, ours, the properties on which we dwell it appears and so things, topics . . . conversations get a little weighty and such around here and over at your Gram's. Wish we could just focus on baseball and what's for dinner tonight but you know, we all know, there are issues and matters that must be aired. Some about the times past and what lies ahead, the good times and the not so good."

I nodded my understanding and Nathe said, "There's a college degree of experience between the two farms—Blake said such not so many years ago. One of the wisest statements he ever made. And he made a few, especially after he'd sampled life and war."

Uncle Albert merely smiled and excused himself, saying he had stuff on the stove. Nathe stood and leaned against the porch pillar, a common practice I was to learn. He looked off toward the barn, a movie pose if I ever saw one.

"A part—a big part—of your boyhood might take place around here. I hope I can find where I left mine behind."

*   *   *

CHAPTER 18

The Filmography of Nathean Hale Summers

Nathe described the Summers house as 1880s vintage, about sixty years younger than Shadeland.

"It's more farmhouse whereas Shadeland is more manse, certainly grander than this place. Here, we've five bedrooms up. Down that little hall, you'll find the maid's room and it retains much of the Shaker flavor of the original place. One bathroom back in those days and eventually decrepit until we renovated everything a few years ago. Now we've got three baths up and two and a half down. I'm like your Aunt Margy, like to have plenty of plumbing for everyone.

"Families were big back then but the Summerses were modest. Two, three kids per generation. You'll meet my sis, Audrey, sometime soon. She and her husband check on Pop every couple months. Like he needs such as he is very independent and careful about everything. But, as I say, not many 'youngin's' around. Audrey and Frank never had kids. And my daughter . . . Temple . . . is estranged, thanks to Sherylinn, one of my ex's.

"So, Claude, if you stick around here for a spell, you may end up the grandkid Pop never had."

"I see. Fine by me."

"He is totally energized by this Little League idea, I can tell you."

"So . . . you never see Temple?"

"Once every few years, if I make the effort. Sherylinn is so driven and driving Temp so hard that there's little room for me. I expect it all to come crashing down, and my nightmare scenario finds her coming home, here, to dry out or lick her wounds. She's never seen this farm."

"She's in the movies?"

"On television some, bit parts in soap, commercial work. I advised against it, but her mother became a starstruck agent and that was one reason we split back when Temple started doing some ad work. Should have read the handwriting on the wall.

"Temple's talented, no doubt about it. Sher throws it up to me—'Well she gets her stagecraft from you, and you had your chance. Why deny Temp hers?' goes the argument and around and around we go. I know the business, I say. The business has changed, says Sherylinn. And we get nowhere. Now, Temple's in the business; heartbreak, rejection, and all that glitters and goes with it. For better or worse."

"That could become Mom's story," I said and Nathe looked at me, pursing his lip again and nodding.

"Yes, m' friend, it could. We all hope not . . . ." He pulled a leather-bound coffee table book from a glassed case. "Well, here's a place to start. You said you wanted to see mementoes and such. Here's a good overview. Dad put a lot of these albums together. Mother started to keep stuff but became disenchanted with the film business and my being in it. I understand her better now, now I'm a parent." I began leafing through the album and soon became absorbed.

"Take your time, son. About two dozen bigger than that one, a book for every film at least plus stuff in between. I've some bills to pay here. We can visit about anything you see or want to know."

I returned to the beginning and here I found what I was looking for. The book I held in my hands seemed a capsule of Nathe's life in film, in Hollywood, on locations here and there.

There were a few publicity stills, some informal shots around the set it appeared, and a few captions all bundled under the title:

A List, Some Descriptions, & A Few Quotes from Nathe's films

1. *Wagon Train to Sunrise*, released in 1954, filmed when Nathe was eight. Nathe plays Lars, one of the younger children in a troubled wagon train of Scandinavian immigrants heading west. Highly acclaimed performance by a newcomer. His final scene "the most tearjerking under prairie skies we've endured since *Shane*," wrote one critic, known for his typically acerbic reviews. Grudgingly acknowledges Nathe as a "refreshing departure from the usual parade of dismal child stars we're asked to love and cherish. Perhaps there's hope."

2. *Hoot 'N' Holler*, 1954; Nathe, eight years of age. A very loosely plotted farce showcasing a number of well-known radio and country music personalities of the era. Nathe had three lines in this "dismal waste of film" as lamented by family cousin Faye Summers Tattersall: "Anyone seen my toad?"; "I can't find my goose."; and "Now, why'd that ol' coon get in there anyways?" Generally dismissed by the press and critics, one who recommended "its simple fare suitable for those curious to learn what these country music-makers look like." One country-western artist objected to the title.

3. *The Remington Rifles*, 1955, Nathe, nine years of age. Nathe's character is instrumental in thwarting a band of gun runners supplying renegade tribes with single shot Remington rifles on the Bozeman trail. Nathe is kidnapped but escapes and shoots one of the ringleaders with a Remington. Filmed in Kanab, Utah. Big hit with audiences across the nation but no award nominations. Nathe was given a prop rifle as a souvenir.

4. *The Timberline*, 1956, Nathe is now ten years of age. Nathe and his father are caught up in a crossfire/manhunt in the mountains of Montana and Idaho. On location near the Lochsha River. A tale of survival. First of five films directed and produced by Richard Strauss. Known for its haunting choral musical backdrop and overture sung by Tennessee Ernie Ford. Typical of a Strauss production, the cast and crew spent several months on location.

5. *The Wolves of Wind River*, 1957; Nathe is eleven. Plucky lad that he is, Nathe's character, Vasily, helps a band of Russian immigrants of a religious order, deal with perils of crossing the Wind River Range of Wyoming. Filmed near the Green River on location. River crossings, avalanches, wolf pack, marauding outlaws. A Strauss film, again celebrated for its scenery and thus advertised. Nathe's scenes included swimming in cold river water, effecting a rescue of one of the girls of the party. Drew the attention of those who enforce child labor laws and stunt doubles within the motion picture industry.

6. *Where the Sun Now Stands*, 1958; Nathe turned twelve on location. Depicts the flight of the Nez Perce across the wilds of Idaho and down through the Bitterroot Valley of Montana, to the Big Hole, Yellowstone, and north to the Bear Paw Mountains. Hailed for its authenticity, scenery, musical score. Nathe nominated for Academy Award for his performance as Daniel Adams, the indentured runaway who takes up the cause of the Nez Perce. Filmed in the Green River country of Wyoming largely with some Yellowstone footage that had to be carefully secured. Pioneered aerial shots from a Piper Cub which was quite startling to the industry. Nathe's final lines as the dying Daniel: "It's best this way . . . always had a feelin' . . .

wouldn't be stayin' long this side of the world. My luck's been a short string." Nominated for Best Picture by the Academy of Motion Picture Arts and Sciences. Aerial work included the Nez Perce tribe traveling down the valley. Nathe's narration is "another factor in setting this film well apart from the usual western fare," notes one critic.

7. *More Precious Each Day*, 1958. Nathe at age twelve. Shot in the pastoral San Juan Islands of Washington State and panned as melancholy, this well-liked film portrayed English country life before WWII. Nathe has a supporting role, largely lamenting the departure of his older brother and cousin, wishing he could enlist and be "a part of it, Father. I could do something behind the lines, perhaps." Nathe had to adopt an accent appropriate to the region and was so schooled by his cousin, stage actress Faye Summers Tattersall. Several weeks of location filming, including Nathe training for the home guard with toy guns. Nathe's fan club is formed, its female president especially enthused about this film and "Nathe's good manners around his elders and at the table." Film was accused of being a knock-off of *Mrs. Miniver.* Not a Strauss film but one by Peter Benedict, who became a close friend of the Summerses and who left the film industry for the Episcopal ministry. *We're Here*, the schooner filmed in *Captains Courageous*, appears in several shipboard scenes.

Benedict also wrote *Wingspan* a year later but the project was shut down just as principal photography began, a very disappointing development for him, Nathe, and Albert. Was proposed for a Saturday television series but Sky King and its popular reruns commanded the skies at the time. Nathe took flying lessons in preparation for the role.

8. *One Hundred Horses*, 1959. Nathe is thirteen years old. Nathe, his father, and brother are Quakers who steal a large band of horses bound for New Orleans and the war with

Spain in Cuba, 1898. Kanab, Utah, location. Praised for its insightful interplay between Nathe and father. Nominated for Best Screenplay that year. Some minor awards. One of Nathe's lines: "Pa, I'm not one to buck thee, but I believe, we're dealing on the wrong side of right here. Can you tell me we're gonna be proved . . . to have done the right thing? Should thee be sent to prison, whatever shall I do?" A Strauss production but directed by John Hazeltine, whose niece, Sherylinn, Nathe met on location and married twelve years later.

9. *Children of the Oregon Trail*, a 90-minute long television series of twenty-six episodes per year, ran for two years, 1959-61. Nathe is 13-14 years of age. Filmed in California but with numerous episodes and trail scenes done in Kanab area, Jacobs Lake, and on the North rim of the Grand Canyon and the Kaibab Forest. Nathe's fan club visits him on the set and they play baseball with the cast. Wins several industry awards plus parental and scholastic awards. Peter Benedict writes a few episodes, collaborates on others but is not involved in the direction or production end. Reflecting upon this series at age nineteen, Nathe said he held it in highest regard.

"Although we may have caught a glimpse of its importance during production, it's over the years that I've become very pleased with the depictions of the history and hardships of the Westward movement of the country, especially the *Trail's* treatment of the Native Americans and minorities. If I had done nothing more in the film industry, I would have been pleased to end my career with *Oregon Trail.* Such a good experience it became for the cast and crew, and I'm especially grateful and humbled when it achieved such wide appreciation and acclaim."

10. *Stage to Red Hill*, 1961; Nathe at fifteen. A family trying to cope with running a stagecoach line through Indian and badland country, hiding any number of gangs. Another filmed in Kanab, Utah area. "Aptly named, Red Hill. Enough blood shed hereabouts to stain every hook and hollar." Lauded for its inventive musical score and gritty depictions by an eccentric, demanding, and mercurial Irish director Roland Shanahan. Shanahan was mean to almost everyone on the set. Died after a long convalescence from a boating accident and his will left Nathe with a prized, expensively ornate A. H. Fox shotgun with a note apologizing for being "such a foul-mouthed blighter. Please accept the fowling piece, befitting a young gentleman such as yourself, as a form of apology. And in hopes it might bring you pleasure so you'll entertain a favourable memory now and then of a misguided soul who, above all, meant well. You seem the natural gentleman I always envied, Nathe. Stay that way. Damn few of your kind left today, that come by it from the ground up and not tacked on. Well, I see I've killed myself, going too hard, too heedless. Let me be a lesson to y', now. I could have been a good one, even one of the great ones."

11. *Gentleman Jim and Lady Jane*, hour-long television series, weekly, thirty-nine episodes per year and ran for three years. Nathe appeared in about two-thirds of them. 1962-65. Nathe is 16-19 during its running. Filmed in California largely and depicts turn-of-the-century Denver. Often light-hearted and frivolous thanks to the chemistry of the actors portraying Jim and Jane, it nonetheless becomes quite popular in its heyday until rating competition forces its eventual cancellation. Reunion special in 1980 was a highlight for Nathe and his last appearance before the cameras. He wonders why he ever left this industry as this filming was so enjoyable, then notes how many cast members clog the phone lines between scenes, calling their agents, trying desperately to line up work.

12. *Finding Redemption*, 1964, Nathe at eighteen. This made-for-television movie involves a widow and her son trying to help reform a boozing outlaw, who takes on a new life as a farmer and sheep breeder on "New Leaf Farm". A Willa Cather-like account, adapted by Peter Benedict from a Boyd Kendall novel. Essentially Peter's last feature film. Well received and widely recommended. Later, Nathe and Peter collaborated on some television productions. These often included Peter writing Nathe into decent roles for various western serials both in prime time and on Saturday morning television occasionally, titles of some episodes included: "Cross the Cruel Land"; "Bronze Sun, Silver Star"; "Daylight Pass"; "Samuel and Blue Roan". Alan Bancroft, unfortunately, directed a couple of these, always an unpleasant experience.

13. *Cascade!* 1965. Nathe is nineteen. Nathe teams up once again with Richard Strauss and produces a magnificent, spirited tale of the early lumbering industry in the Northwest. Steamboats, steam powered locomotives, breathtaking scenery portraying the Cascades and Puget Sound. Nominated for musical score, art direction, best picture. Lavish sets and singled out for its alpine scope and adventure in the forests. Wins an Oscar for Cinematography. Filmed in Cinemascope and Stereophonic Sound, its "look" is spectacular. One of the most expensive motion pictures of that year and the times. Very successful at the box office where Nathe is heralded as a heart throb. Filmed in the Cascades, Canada, and Alaska. Nominated for Best Director, Strauss died after its premiere and such presented a big loss for Nathe.

14. *Maui Melodies,* 1965. Nathe at nineteen. A light, teen romance set in Hawaii that was never released, to Nathe's relief. Directed by Alan Bancroft, a vitriolic, irascible, thoroughly unpleasant tyrant. Bancroft came from a film industry family and thought he was untouchable. Eventually, his temper and arrogance preceded him and he fell from grace quickly, shunned through the Hollywood grapevine and tagged as "troubled." In this pathetic film, Nate's a bit player, the scolding, disapproving big brother to a vivacious little scamp played by Meloday Rivers, a face and personality this particular studio was banking on for younger audiences easily wooed by froth and beach scenes. Meloday appeared in few films aimed at younger audiences but faded into drugs and booze. Found dead in her apartment of an overdose, 1970. Studio executives tried to fabricate a romance between the two. But Nathe squelched it, to the PR department's annoyance, by dismissing it as someone's "front office fantasy." From that point on, a low mark in his career, Nathe was tagged as "becoming difficult" plus typecast as "not quite right for today's audience. Westerns are not drawing the audience to theaters—thanks to the television oaters. The genre's become tiresome and the public wants more police dramas, thrillers, and contemporary settings," so says one industry observer. In a letter to Albert, Nathe vents: "They want me to chase skirts and crash cars now. Last two scripts have been miserable."

15. *The Candle's Wick*, 1966; Nathe is twenty. Nathe plays Caleb, a promising baseball player who must choose between supporting his father's Mission Farm and a career in sports after WWII. Highly praised for several of the performances, including Nathe's but no academy nominations other than Best Director and Best Art Direction. Nathe displays his stunt, catching a fly ball behind his back for the screen. His pitching excels and he is scouted by the majors. Groundbreaking treatment of black characters hailed. Instead of stereotypic and comedic roles, they are revealed as sensitive and intelligent supports for the dilemma playing out between Caleb and his father. Set in the Lexington, Kentucky, area and praised by Sydney Poitier, the actor fresh from his triumphs in meaningful films for black actors, including *Lilies of the Field, The Bedford Incident,* and *A Patch of Blue.* Nate's last feature film as it turned out, and it washed away the taste of the previous film. The score is punctuated by a solo harmonica throughout, under Nate's soft-spoken narration.

Poignant last scene shows a bus full of baseball hopefuls departing for the tryouts and possible Triple A league berths, leaving Nathe on the tractor and behind. He and the farm collie, Daisy, drive across the field toward home.

*   *   *

CHAPTER 19

The Little Winchester

"So, the dog was named 'Daisy' in *The Candle's Wick?*" I asked Nathe.

"Yes," he laughed, "after your mother.

"No, Daisy belonged to Howard Coates, stunt man and animal trainer. You can see him in some of our films, walking on, crowd scenes. He'd have a line or two in a film, stuff like . . . 'Stage is a-comin'' or 'Them horses took a notion to scatter down the draw'. . . . Or, 'We'd best get by with what we got and get t' gettin' or we'll get what's comin' to us.' There's a line for y'.

"His brother, Harold, went by the name 'Boots'—Boots Coates—and he took a liking to me for some reason and taught me everything I knew and much of everything *he* knew about horsemanship and driving teams, harnesses, shooting and gun handling, the works. He was a cowboy's cowboy but never arrogant about it. Just a quiet master of his craft. We all respected him greatly. A good role model for us boys.

"The other kids on the set would take off after a scene was shot, but I'd hang around until he took me under his wing. I think he liked the companionship. He was a shy guy, quiet, well liked but without many friends. Just hung around with his brother, mainly. He had a few bit parts now and then, here and there.

"But Boots was so soft-spoken he couldn't deliver a line to a director's satisfaction. He looked the part, more 'western' than his brother and as 'western' as western gets, but he just didn't do that well in front of the camera. Too self-effacing, I think, kind of a Richard Farnsworth persona but, unlike ol' Richard, poor Boots couldn't pass the eye test."

"Eye test?"

"The camera magnifies the message your eyes give off. If the actor's eyes aren't convincing, they won't convey the emotion or carry the scene and it will fall flat. Richard Strauss told me once: 'You can talk all you want, talk all you like, yak-yak-yak, but when the camera zeroes in on you, the story gets told through your character's eyes, then his mouth.' He was old school, Strauss, began directing film in the silent era. Said one well-chosen facial expression or hand gesture was worth a dozen words."

"So, he helped you a lot."

"Richard Strauss made me, Claude."

By this hour and on this particular day, Nathe's room in the Summer's home took on an amber glow that bordered on magic.

"We call this room the 'Golden Chapel', as you can see why. My mother picked out the paint, 'Daffodil Delight' it was called back then. I thought it kind of sissified but this became my room over the years and when I repainted it last year, I chose 'Daffodil Valley'. Even though it faces west and north, it's bright in the morning for some reason. And in the evening, in the summer, it's like entering a clearing in the forest with the sunset streaming through the trees."

*   *   *

We went down the winding stairs for the evening meal, and Uncle Albert told us to grab it and growl. He added, "candlelight would be nice for a change, since we have a white tablecloth and a guest."

Nathean explained his mother, Peg, always insisted on a white tablecloth for dinner, if at all possible. "Our home life was not to her liking during much of my teen years when I was busy out west."

"Yes, then her health became an issue in the '70s. Those were turbulent times. Thank goodness for Audrey helping to steer the waters. Nathe, when he could come home for a spell. Marguerite too was a ministering angel. What did you two get into upstairs?"

"One of the albums and the Coates brothers."

"I became kinda jealous of the Coates brothers. Nathe was spending so much free time hanging around the stables. But then, my hours on the set especially were bizarre. Often working until midnight, keeping the bills organized, things paid. Nathe would be bedded down, sawing away, and up before daybreak.

"We didn't see each other all that much. For several weeks it seemed."

"The Coates brothers were a pair to draw to, Claude. Boots had two horses, wonderful mounts, he named 'Fungus' and 'Mucous'.

"Mother was appalled."

"Did you show Claude the .22?"

*   *   *

After dinner, Nathe and I again climbed the stairs to the Golden Chapel and to view "the .22." "The.22" was an exquisitely crafted piece I learned was a Winchester 1890 pump action, .22 Long Rifle caliber.

"The shooting galleries used this and later versions at thousands of county fairs the country over. Only they were in .22 Short caliber for greater safety. Didn't need much more as the range was about 10-12 feet.

"Wow." Nathe showed me how to open it, check its loaded status, fit it to my shoulder, find the sights.

"Mr. Chapmann, Chapmann Hardware in town, must have tired of us fondling it. Finally we had enough bucks to buy the thing and he handed it over. He had the newspaper send a reporter over and get a shot. I was back in the area between pictures and . . . here it is."

The clipping was a bit yellowed but protected by a plastic sleeve. It showed two blondish teens in matching plaid wool jackets with a bespectacled gentlemen, smiling as he passed the rifle we were now admiring across the counter. The caption read:

In town . . . Hollywood film star Nathean Summers and his cousin Blake Kinkade stopped by Chapmann Hardware for a Saturday morning's shopping. Nathe is fresh from Stage to Red Hill, *a Paramount Pictures motion picture filmed in Utah and soon to be released. Said Summers: "It's good to be back in Chapmann. Thanks to everyone in the area who's been writing to me about* Children of the Oregon Trail. *Yes, wish we could keep it going. But, it looks like we're heading back to Hollywood soon for a new series. It's been nice to see so many old friends on the streets."*

Nathe smiled down at the image of the "twins." "It *was* a nice day. Lots of folks. Some even parked their cars and got out to say hello or get an autograph. Take a photo if they had a camera handy. Blake was gracious, not envious of the attention I was getting. I asked him if it annoyed him and he said not to worry, that he liked to tag along 'cause the girls would date him later. I was too unreachable."

"Neat."

He looked at me, then back to the print. "It's hard to describe, being admired. Does something to you, inside. Can be harmful or helpful, I decided. Like too much of a good thing, ice cream or the like. Boots Coates told me that's why he named his wonder horse, "Fungus".

"Oh?"

"Everyone admired the heck out of Fungus. He could take a fall, jump a coulee without a shred of hesitation, plunge into a river, let you do anything on his back or under his belly. Folks, even a couple well-known stars, wanted to buy him, 'state your price, Boots'."

"So . . . he named him Fungus because?"

"Boots said with an ugly name, it helps the horse keep his head on straight. Not be swayed by all that fame and acclaim. Something to remember, he told me and I never forgot it." He pointed to the rifle in my hands. "This was your dad's .22."

I tried to utter something, then choked. *My dad's very own rifle. When he was a boy.*

"I-I never knew there was one."

"Yes, I 'spect there's a lot for you to discover here, Claude. I'll help you all I can. I want to."

"T-Thanks." I beheld it in my hands. Something my dad had carried, caressed, used.

"Blake and I partnered on that rifle. He didn't have enough to get it before it was sold out of Chapmann's so I filled in the balance. Cost us $150 back when you could get a garden variety .22 for $29.50. We thought it was a special order model, modest engraving but well executed, very nice furniture— that's gun talk for the wood. You don't find that kind of walnut on the day-to-day rack. It is custom all the way. Crescent butt plate of brass, highly polished bluing, folding sights."

"It's beautiful. Kind of a work of art."

"Glad you think so. Accurate too. There's a. . . note . . . goes with it." He handed me a small envelope engraved with the initials BDK. Inside, on paper of matching vellum, his handwriting read:

125

Ol' frien':

If I should go off somewhere and never return, would you see that son Claude learns to shoot our little rifle safely? I would be much obliged.

Your grateful cousin,
Blake.

I set the rifle down on the bed for I could feel the tears welling. And I didn't try to hide such. I turned and embraced my father's cousin and clung to him as the closest boyhood friend of my departed dad when he was young and full of life.

"I never got to say good bye like I should have," I bawled. "He got lost somewhere on the other side of the world and I couldn't find him. I dream 'bout it all the time and I can't find him. I thought once I could hear him calling me and now I can't hear him anymore." I sobbed it loose, all of it, like I had never done before with Mom or anyone. I needed to share my sorrow man-to-man and grieve over things my mother never knew. For to me now, a son's loss seemed different than that of a wife's. We missed him for different reasons.

I saw him today for the first time as he was then. Not much older than I. Captured in an aging newspaper clipping and unaware what lay ahead for him in the years to come and thousands of miles away from Summers Run.

I felt so very full of loss for he looked so very full of life.

If the author of our futures has written, "dying too soon," can such not be changed? I mourned not only for my father, then, but all in the prime of life who would follow him.

We sat down on the bed—still in each other's arms—next to the beautiful little rifle Dad treasured. Nathe offered me a tissue. "Claude . . . I'm a-thinkin'. Now that you're here, there's a good chance you'll hear him again. No promises but that's the way it can happen, I'm told.

"You come back to a place he loved and he'll meet you there somewhere, somehow."

* * *

CHAPTER 20

The Bearcat

Tonight, the hours spent at Summers Run Farm became my baptism into the world shared by my dad. That he'd been in the "Golden Chapel" made it a hallowed place.

And I would venture in only by invitation, I pledged, with a sense of wonder. If he never spoke to me from his spiritual place, perhaps he wanted me to look for him among the clippings, family albums, the oral histories Nathe could certainly supply.

Yes, Aunt Marguerite stood alone as a primal source of lore about her brother on a day-to-day basis, but Nathe knew Blake Kinkade as a kindred soul, guy-to-guy.

I have the *Tribune* clipping now and keep it in a guarded place where I visit it from time to time. Its emotional power stirs me just as it did on that night seventeen years ago when I first looked upon it. Two teenage boys captured on the cusp of manhood in the hardware store. The photograph tells me they were spiritual twins quite apart from the similarity in dress, haircut, facial features. They have no need to relate their conversation to me. For I can create it nearly verbatim. So vivid is the exchange between them it's as if I were there and we were a trio.

That night, over dinner, Uncle Albert had proposed "we three form a gentlemen's club. Perhaps we include Banks McIntyre and Peter Benedict as ex-officio members. We've already had one recreational event at the range this afternoon. An organization dedicated to preservation, honoring the memories of those who've entrusted us with the world of Shadeland and Summers Run. Amongst other things. Such as baseball and . . . Blake's Wood."

"Hear, hear," said Nate and we clinked the family crystal together. "Pop is the official historian of Shadeland, Claude, and this place too."

"Well, Shadeland is more illustrious than Summers Run, son, as we know. Big-wigs have dined there on trout caught in the Run, deer and pheasants harvested in the meadows and forests of the olden days. Some notable judges, local potentates, state senators, personages from the theater have lodged over yonder."

"True," said Nathe. "It's all documented. Albert 'no-stone-left-unturned' Summers is the consummate historian. Brings all that exactitude from accounting to the pages of history. You'll be in his archives soon, Claude. Date of your arrival and so on."

"Great," I said. "Hope I'm up to snuff." For me, the importance of finding my dad among the shadowy corners or sunlit corridors of Shadeland and Summers Run had become the focus of my life right now. Along with baseball, of course. A Gentleman's Club might help unearth some of his unknowns and mysteries. Truth be known, I relished becoming "up to snuff," a frequent family expression shared by the Summerses and Kinkades. I also pledged to fulfill the expectations of them both. I'd noticed recently as well, that The Enchanted Forest was being referred to as Blake's Wood here and there in conversation.

When I mentioned such over dinner, Nathe agreed. "Yes, there's been talk of officially christening it as The Blake D. Kinkade Memorial Forest or simply Blake's Wood. We need your input. The families are getting some documents drawn up, Claude, for preservation an' the like."

*   *   *

I pedaled home, back to my room in Shadeland, in a daze. The moon seemed full again, filling my world and lighting the lane ahead with . . . hope. Something about being in the presence of Nathe, Uncle Albert too, gave a boy like me a sense of presence. That I mattered, that they were committed to my destiny, that as I followed their pathway, I would find the ripples to be less jarring than it had been for them.

A car approached. I dismounted and pushed my way into the shrubbery of the roadside. Didn't want to be seen and I nursed a pang of resentment at its intrusion. *This is my part of the earth tonight, don't y' know? I have it reserved. Really no need for moonlight or the harsh glare of your headlights, certainly. I've been to a place so special the afterglow is shining still and guiding my way.*

The car passed by but not before it shone on two deer crossing the lane, their dusky buckskins blending with the gravel of Summers Run Road. I put my bike back on that gravel and took up my trip home again, the tires grinding against the grain of the road pleasantly, my thoughts a rhythm of renewal and resolve. When I bounced over the washboards surrounding a curve, I felt him near.

As I rode near the tree-shrouded area where the whitetails had passed, they leaped from the brush beside me, within a shadow's length, and bounded back from where they came. I skidded to a stop. Something rustled near the road. I saw movement ahead of me, and I awaited a black panther's scream. Summers Run Road stood dappled in the moon's light but bright enough I could glimpse the four-legged critter skittering away. It barked.

I resumed my pedaling. The dog floated up the road like a phantom. In fact, it seemed a good night for ghostly apparitions. *No need to be alarmed,* I assured myself. Panthers are black, not vaporous white. The dog ran solo, not in a pack. Mr. P.

M. Murphy might be about on some nighttime foray. But if I meet him, he would seem kindly, I felt convinced. He'd be about, just innocently foraging for some exotic mushroom or botanical wonder that appears only under cover of darkness. *Why would he startle the local Farm-Kid-In-Residence, representing Shadeland and Summers Run Farm, his benevolent neighbors?* Yes, come P. M. or panther, it wouldn't matter, I decided. There's a guardian spirit here in the form of a warrior, one who looks out and over the wanderings of a mere boy.

*   *   *

Saturday, my crew arrived by bike or hopping out of the family car. As promised, James and Lawrence Alphonse pulled in with two truckloads of gray crusher fines from their pit. Jules and August rode with them. Shortly thereafter, a huge semi from Holland's Turf and Trees drove up with our new outfield rolled and stacked in neat, uniform bundles.

Nathe strolled over to meet the eight future Pickett Township Panthers. They stood as if in the presence of something hitherto never seen in their young lives; a boy knows the signs of boyish awe. Gaze moving up and down the slender frame; glances exchanged with each other; undisguised scrutiny, unvoiced questions (Did he look like you thought he would?). One boy volunteered his family had "every movie of yours we can find." His buddy elbowed him in the ribs.

Nathe laughed and signed ball caps of those requesting such. "Appears I'm still kinda popular around here, good to know. Well, we got us a ball park, men, once we get it off the truck. Here's a signup sheet and if you know your sizes or not, guys, please give us a good guess." We worked away, comparing our necks, legs, waists, trying to reach a consensus with anyone who really had a gauge on what size shirt or jeans he wore. A uniform that fit well was almighty important.

Mister Mac came bouncing along with his Bobcat and positioned himself behind the Alphonse trucks while they slowly raised their beds and let the crusher fines sloosh their way into his bucket. "This way's slower," I heard Mac tell them, "but we won't dig up our subsurface so much." The trucks left leaving the infield in heaps. Mac jumped off his machine and approached us, doffed his cap, scratched his ear, and took the clipboard from Nathe, rolling his toothpick and speaking with authority.

"All right, gentlemen. Good to see so many of you out this morning. Everyone brought a birth certificate. Good. Who is Benjamin Anders?" One of our taller Panthers raised his hand.

"Got a position, Ben?"

"Ah, third . . . please." Mac smiled. He approved of the "please."

Mac ticked off the infield, pointing with his yellow pencil. "Jules at short and Gus at second." The twins shuffled about enough to notice.

"Man," said Jules. "First time that's happened lately."

Mac looked up and smiled. "First time what?"

"That someone got us right the first time. Most folks can't tell who's who."

"Well, I can tell a lot. Who's interested in first base?"

Another tallish boy I knew only as Aaron raised his hand. "Sir, I'd like to try. I'm Aaron Oarcaster."

Mac cast a squinty appraisal eye upon him. "You're a lefty. Gotcha a first baseman's glove too I see."

"It was my father's."

Mac nodded. "I knew your father. A fine man, son." More scribbling on the clipboard. "Now, catcher. How many catchers we got? Names?"

"Carmine Catalino."

"Aha!" Mac barked. "One of the Catalinos. Hoped some of your clan would show up. Good. Need at least one more, two would be better."

"I'd like to try."

"That's the spirit." Mac pointed his pencil at a solidly built, ruddy-faced kid I hadn't really met yet and learned his name was Kevin Wingate. "Any other catchers?"

"Am I too small?" asked a boy I knew as Gamoski. Mac cocked his head. "Well, you look kinda tough. I take toughness over size. Okay, we got the makings of a three-man catcher unit. Catchers control a lot of the game, fellas, and that's why they make good managers later on. They know a lot of stuff about how this game is played. What's your name, bud?"

"Ryan Gamoski."

Mac filled in his clipboard with "Ryan . . . 'Bearcat' . . . Gamoski." I didn't look around but I could hear everyone smiling. "Catchers gotta be smart too, figure out what's coming next, what the others side's up to.

"Now . . . outfield. Mr. Summers and I agree . . . in Little League . . . especially, the outfield can make the difference between winning and losing a game. Y'got a fast outfield with strong arms, on a field like this, and you often choke off a run, throw a runner out on the base path, or keep a game from getting away from y'. Right field, who wants it?" I raised my hand.

"All right. Claude Kinkade. Left?" Mac leveled his pencil at Luther Ludlow. "Guess you got it, frien'. Could you play center?"

"Yes," he said. "Anywhere."

"Where's Trent Smythe? Got his birth certificate here."

"He had a funeral or somethin' out of town."

"Any one know his sizes, position?"

"He's about my size, Mister Mac," I spoke up, "and would like the outfield or anywhere in the infield too."

"Ah, utility guy. My kind of man."

"Okay." Mister Mac tucked the clipboard under his arm. "My name is Banks McIntyre. Most of your folks know me as Mister Mac. That's the name of my business over there and that's the name I'll go by here. Most of you boys know my Nancy from school. I'll be the assistant coach at least for now. Mr. Summers will act as the trainer for drills and practices. We're hoping to get Lawrence Alphonse to manage. He's played ball in college, knows a lot about winning as his team went clear to the semi-finals in P. A., couple years ago. Well, would y' look at that."

We all turned to see the crane hoisting the first bank of light poles, ready to be anchored to the concrete poured last week.

"Man, we're going to playin' under the lights. How cool is that?"

Mac's furrowed brow relieved the customary scowl. "Mighty cool, all right. We might need those lights to get the town teams out here."

"Yessir. Nothing country about us Panthers, that is for certain," said Jules Alphonse, "When they come to play us, they're going to see we're here on first-class field." This time I heard Mister Mac smile over a memory from years ago.

"Yup, we're here . . . and we're back."

*   *   *

CHAPTER 21

Nicknames

Instead of bats on our first day of baseball, we were wielding landscape rakes and hoes. I'd been assigned to chop out a place for the pitching rubber. "Let's run another tape on it, Albert. Got to get this down to the half inch or we'll get scolded," said Mac. Banks McIntyre served the project as "straw boss."

Everyone had a job. Uncle Albert running the tapes, planting the survey stick; My new teacher, Mrs. "Mac" McIntyre, helping Aunt Marguerite with lunch; Grandma Beatrice and Mom spraying orange and yellow paint where directed. Nathe was driving equipment including Harry the Ferguson, pulling rollers and drags, then a water tank to soak down the infield and warning track where the crusher fines had been spread as smoothly as a coat of paint. We gathered for the noon meal.

"Good ol' crusher fines, James," said Mac to Mr. Alphonse. "Sure glad you make this stuff. Perfect for what we need."

"That is for certain. Boys, if you'uns look at those fines closely, you'll see they have little teeth that cling to each other. Makes th' bond all that stronger. Unified."

"Not a bad symbol for a life or a team," Uncle Albert said. "The Pickett Township Crusher Fines. Bit of a challenge though to find a mascot. Perhaps James' trucks with a load in the bed."

"Wasn't there a team over east that called themselves the Black Ash Widows?"

"Yes, Mac, for a spell anyway. They played once or twice right here, on our old field. Then there were the Copperheads from up by Corry. Poisonous snakes and spiders seem a bit discomforting. Might be best we stick with the Panthers."

"We'd better, Dad. The printer's already run the logos and is ready to print the shirts as soon as he has the sizes. Until then . . ." Nathe reached into his cardboard box. "Here are the caps."

"Whoa," said several Panthers in unison. "Cool colors too. Just like I wanted."

The remainder of the noon break was taken up with my teammates fitting their hats and shaping the bills to their liking; discussing the merits of retaining them in the original flat and broad configuration; peaked in the middle like the Japanese wore theirs; squared off on the corners for maximum sun blockage; or curved overall to honor the concept of baseball's basic code of roundness.

"How should we do this, Mister Nathe?" Jules asked. "We can't decide for sure."

"That's up to you, boys. You work it out amongst yourselves. Mister Mac and I'll copy your lead. Or . . . no one says you all have to all look alike. That cap's part of your personality. Maybe you want yours to have its own special style."

*   *   *

"I've hooked a manifold to that water tank, Claude. You take two of your guys and spray that water out in a mist. Soon's she dries a bit, we'll start laying down sod here, then do the outfield. Try to keep it even and we'll see if we have any low spots. Supposed to rain tonight and that's perfect to settle everything, give that grass a drink."

Mac became a man on a mission. It seemed little wonder he was a success at what he did, landscaping and earth work. He watched us start. I looked to him for affirmation and he nodded, gave us a thumbs up. Then with the Harry, here came the sod. Nathe and I loading, me driving to the envy of my teammates I hoped, and the Panthers rolling out the beautiful grass like velvet ribbons around the infield.

"Pack 'em tight to each other, boys. We want this to look like a pool table out here, no gaps or folds. We'll roll it later. Once you're done with that, I'm going to turn you over to Mr. Nathe. He needs y' to throw some baseballs around."

While Albert, James, and Mac tweaked the infield, including cutting the scallops around the bases, Nathe had us assemble on the Summers lawn where he rolled out the prettiest carton of baseballs we'd ever seen. It resembled a Milky Way of white leather and red stitching.

"Hmmm. I take in the aroma," said Jules, holding two, one to each nostril. "And I bless the horse that gave us these."

Nathe laughed so heartily it took us all by surprise. The man was human. "Yes, thank the horses. Okay, men, pick up a couple balls apiece and let's see who can hit those gongs. They'll ring right smartly if you hit 'em square."

First thing this morning, using the Ferguson, Nathe and I pulled the target gongs, which were mounted on skids, from the rifle range to the expansive yard of Summers Run Farm. Now, it appeared they would be doing double duty clanging for accurately thrown baseballs instead of bullets. "That first one is about forty-five feet away, two feet in diameter. Let's see who can hit it, then we'll move to the 60-footer."

Soon Nathe's gongs were ringing and my teammates glowing, especially if both balls hit their target. "Okay, good. That's about from the pitcher's rubber to home plate. Now let's try the distance from, say first to second." Possibly fewer gongs, I decided, more misses. I felt pleased with a solid hit on my first, a "tick" on my second.

"Okay, everyone stay put. I'll gather up what's in front of the gong, then everyone take your mark right on the paint line here and at my whistle, meet me at the second gong. We're gonna see who has the wheels in this bunch."

We lined up, then tore toward Nathe and the second target, in a 20-yard dash.

"Great. Looks like Claude, then maybe Gus, Ryan, Aaron. Normally, we'd warm up and stretch before doing all this, but Mister Mac got your kinks out over there this morning. Okay, little demonstration.

"Who's our third baseman? Ben. Find y' an orange square over there a-ways, Ben, and who's on first, Aaron? Take that mark. And, right field, Claude. You'll find a mark over there. I'm going to show you what happened to me once back when I was playing Little League years ago."

Nathe had Ben and me throw to Aaron from our marks. Then to count our steps to first and report. "Nearly the same distance," Jules spoke for the group.

"Right, in Little League, remember the outfield is just that much closer to the infield. Don't do like I did once. I hit a nice sharp grounder between first and second and—thinking, 'hey, another hit'—but, to my surprise, I got thrown out at first by the right fielder! Talk about embarrassing."

"You mean, you didn't run fast enough, Mister Nathe?"

"Exactly, Jules, I just thought, 'well, I got it made' and instead of churning for first, I lolli-gagged my way down there and this kid in right came up with the ball and made a shot to first. Caught me dreaming."

"My dad calls that 'counting your poultry before they're plucked,'" Jules told us.

"And a darn good thing to keep in mind. If all goes according to plan, you guys playing the outfield are going to be like an auxiliary infield, backing up every base and even making infield plays now and then. The purpose of this little skit is to show you, one, the importance of getting to first in a hurry and second, how you outfielders can be mighty important to your infielders."

"Sir, are you going to show us how you catch fly balls behind your back?"

Nathe laughed and shook his head.

"Like you did in that one movie?"

"Yeah, well, remember I got cussed by the manager for pulling that little stunt in a game. The movies can make things look pretty neat . . . and easy. I guess, Lute, we'll save that one for later. Well, let's get some more drills in before Mister Mac calls us back to the field. He'll be needing us to roll out that outfield pretty soon." Nathe had us work on bunting tennis balls for much of the rest of our first ever session.

"Bunts win games, guys. Quite often, they're the source of mistakes. No one's just sure who's supposed to pick it up and where to throw or they get excited and throw wild. And that's where a team handling bunts well can rattle a team that doesn't. Everyone likes to drive one out and deep, but it's the bunt that moves runners around the bases quite often. Or scores a run."

The first practice of the Pickett Township Panthers over, I returned to our field with my teammates feeling pretty buoyed by the experience. I could hear the murmuring, "Man, I think we gots us a good coach," and "that's fun" or "I like hearin' those gongs go 'twang'—bet no other team is doing stuff like that," and I couldn't help but feel a modest swell of pride that it was my cousin at the helm.

Two of the boys had acquired nicknames before things were over. Nathe labeled our likely and regular third basemen, Ben, as Benjamin "Air Rifle" Anders as he could indeed deliver a shot across the 85 feet from his base to first. And it was agreed Aaron Oarcaster should be tagged as "Scoop" for he could snare bunted tennis balls or those thrown at his feet with determination and familiarity. Something inherited from his departed father perhaps? I didn't know his story but my interest rose, piqued. In time, perhaps.

*   *   *

By the hour we arrived back at Shadeland, Mom and I barely found time to set out her bulbs before the thunder rolled over and the rains passed through. A quick little storm but more threatening just beyond what we could see of our horizon. A metaphor, I decided many years later, as I reflected back on those few moments we shared before her Las Vegas departure. Yes, there were clouds, we agreed.

"But, hon, I've sailed through some awful blows. That time when you were about seven, and we hadn't heard from your dad in weeks and no one could tell us a thing, so hush-hush an' all. Nothing to do but plod on and hope and pray and pull ourselves together if worse came to worse. Usually turned out to be some top secret CIA thing, special assignment. How I hated to learn of such. Thank goodness for your grandmother Ronnie keeping our spirits perked up. And Marguerite too. She phoned often, bless her."

To ward off the chill, Mom and I bundled ourselves in a wool blanket under Aunt Margy's gazebo where there were other bulbs, perennials, vines and flower pots in abundance. Our little planting would enjoy good company, it appeared. "Aunt Margy's idea to put that mesh around them to ward off voles. Or moles? I forget which but anyway, I hope they do well here. If they do, this will be your daddy's little special place."

"There are a lot of special places here for him, Moms."

"Yes, I know but this is one we put together, you and me."

"Right, I'm sure he'd like it here." From the glazed, troubled look crossing her face just now, I knew ashes were on her mind. She felt as did her mother and dad that things were not really settled until there were remains. My grandfather wanted Arlington for his final resting place and wished he could "pull some strings and get Blake some kind of recognition there or somewhere where we could go and pay him honor." Mom wanted his ashes scattered at Shadeland, should remains ever be found. No military cemetery, Dad, she would tell Granddad C. J. "I've had enough."

Nor would my mother entertain the idea her husband and my father might return by some miracle. Should any motion picture or television drama present such a theme, she couldn't click it off quickly enough. "No Hollywood back-from-the-dead stuff."

Blake Kinkade remained a source of conflict for her. She loved him dearly. Of such I was assured repeatedly. However, his career was, "the other woman in our lives." That I reminded her of him compellingly evident: "You have the same cowlicks and that little thing you do with your eyebrows—my Lord, how you are your father's child. I catch Aunt Marguerite watching you walk or your mannerisms when you speak.

"The other day, she said to me, 'Daisy, it gives me such pause. I just go numb sometimes—it's like he's come back to us.' And once she started to cry. 'Mom says so as well—we're a couple of old fools, Granny Bea and I. Perhaps Claude shouldn't hear us go on, but it's so comforting sometimes to know the hole in our hearts is slowly being filled by his son.'"

"Then, Moms, you shouldn't tell me if Aunt Margy didn't want you to."

"I know, but I think you're aware of the effect you're bringing to this house."

Mom opened the door. I felt presented with an opportunity to poise Shadeland against Las Vegas.

"Yes'm, I've noticed. Folks look at me like they're seeing someone else. Like they're remembering something he said or did. Dad was mighty important around here."

"The heir to Shadeland. Such became his dream once he retired. To bring us back here, build a little cottage, return to the life he knew as a boy."

"So, now we're here. Let's stay."

"Well, son, you can come back here once you're 18 or so. Go to school. Buy a little place, one of these farms, maybe.

Me, I have other plans. Hopes and dreams. The things you can't get out of your head."

"Maybe Vic would buy some land or a place around here."

"Oh, I doubt that."

She looked up at the clouds churning above us and smiled. "They look like a basketful of gray and spotted puppies tumbling over each other—Claude, would you like a dog here? Margy told me she wondered if you shouldn't like a dog. Every boy needs a dog sometime in his life."

"It would be okay here but what about in Las Vegas?"

She didn't answer, distracted. Rather, she brought up that moment at the airport in Pittsburgh. "We haven't discussed it much.

"I know I sounded so silly when Nathe met us at the baggage carousel—you were embarrassed with me, I could tell. But, I swear, seeing Nathe walking toward us was like Blake coming across the tarmac after being somewhere horrid. Suddenly here's the family's celebrity—for a minute there, I just couldn't catch my breath."

CHAPTER 22

The Homestead Room

The Saturday evening before Mom's departure, Aunt Marguerite hosted a supper in what she called her "Homestead Room," a den just off "the little kitchen." Shadeland had two: one kitchen for the family and a large commercial layout built during the remodeling of a few years ago. Dr. Seaborn, Aunt Margy's husband, so designed it in the event Shadeland ever became a bed and breakfast or even a white tablecloth restaurant: fulfilling his vision more than Marguerite's, I learned. Likewise, there were two dining rooms.

Shadeland's formal dining area bore an ivory tone overall accented by blue Wedgewood china on display, highly polished cherry wood high boys, a long, richly carved and warmly glowing mirrored side buffet, and a dining table capable of service for twelve. All were antiques handed down through both the Forsythes and Kinkade branches. Its curtains were Bedford style hung on simple rods in a print featuring themes of a Currier & Ives harvest.

In contrast, The Homestead Room seemed more masculine with an equestrian and leather motif. It presented prints from the field and stream and featured stone gathered off the meadows of Shadeland with wrought iron hinges and fixtures, supported by forest green, tartan plaids, and an oval hooked rug to establish a warm hearth and rustic homespun character. It served as the "TV" room.

The ambiance complemented my mother's dress and appearance that night. She seemed flushed from the fireplace's cheery glow and as I recall, radiant. During the course of our meal, I divided my gaze between her and Nathe trying to decipher what each might be thinking. From what Mom said earlier in the rain and at the gazebo, she might find the attentions of Nathean Hale Summers of interest. After all, didn't she admit Nathe reminded her of my father Blake?

Over dinner, Uncle Albert and Grandmother Beatrice traded stories and anecdotes on each other. Mom and Vic Delveccio seemed quietly amused as did his pilot, a young fellow named Trane and Mister Vic's personal assistant, a young woman I knew only as Sophie. Nathe and I kept our peace largely while Aunt Marguerite moderated. While she might have been holding court, she did so in her usual calm and methodical manner, supplying a date or name for Grandma Bea.

Uncle Albert provided the occasional rosy affirmation, his cheeks glistening in buttery satisfaction, toasting and congenial as ever. No curmudgeon, this Uncle Albert of ours. To picture him as Scrooge—a role he once played in a production at the local Grange one Christmas—seemed grandly out of character. It was said even P. M. Murphy attended the play in a rare public outing, the first many could recall by him in years.

"You're quiet tonight, Claude. Mister Mac worked you boys for fair today."

"Yes, ma'am, but children should be seen and not heard," I answered Aunt Marguerite which drew a laugh from all.

"Claude, I grew up with that old saw. Pretty stifling to my mind, then or now," said Uncle Albert. "Of course, today, children can become too chirpy. Look at some of what you see on television—my, they are precocious. Like caricatures of kids, not real kids. Seems like when Nathe was in the business, the kids were more natural in their actions and delivery."

"True, Pop. Way over-animated. Like they're programmed to say a line, not listen to the people in the scene. Of course, these are sitcoms where everything seems over the top. Strauss taught me to actually listen to what the character was asking or telling me, not just wait for a cue or be thinking of my line. Carry on a real conversation, he told me. Just as if you are at home or in school."

"Speaking of school, how do you like it by now, Claude? And Mrs. Mac?"

"Fine, really do. We're getting a deaf kid this week. So she's had us working on signing, Mom." I looked down the table at her. "We need Grandma Ronnie up here."

"Well, Claude . . . wonderful. You'll be a big help, son." Mom clasped her little porcelain hands together under her chin, a mannerism that I thought made her especially appealing. "My mother, Ronnie, had a very good lifetime friend who was born deaf and so Ronnie became so good at signing, she taught classes here and there, wherever they were stationed. Claude and Mother would practice, especially when those two wanted to keep a secret from Dad and me."

"He reads lips some, I guess. He's deaf but he's not mute."

"Does he play baseball, Claude?" Nathe asked. "We're short a man. Two would be a welcome cushion."

"You might end up signing a girl, cousin. What do you think of that?"

"If she plays as well as you did, then that's a thought," said Nathe over his coffee.

"I go on record as opposing girls playing boys' Little League," said Uncle Albert. "Girls should have their own team. Old school, old fashioned, I know, but this age, this league is a boy's last bastion of boyhood before girls and growing up and the pressures from school, military, careers and the like. Girls will come soon enough—let the boy enjoy one last joy of boyhood with his chums—they need that and without the opposite gender mixing in.

"For when his boyhood is over, it's over—never to return. He doesn't need to share it with the girls and that's my last word on the matter. What a grump I am these days," he laughed, raised his cup, then set it down immediately.

"Besides, this genderation business—it manipulates kids, pushes them when what they need is their time and space away to explore on their own. Last fall, I read about some father down in Pittsburgh suing the school system so his daughter could play high school football—now let's be sensible. Who wants her to play? The girl or the old man, looking to relive his past glory?

"Phooey on this peerness and this adult pressure to succeed, compete, meet all these expectations. This is a veteran of the film industry talking, mind you. Case in point, those ten-year-old actors you see on TV talk shows trying to act as if they're age twenty. Let 'em be kids one more year or two, I say."

"Amen, Uncle. Case in point, the Ballingers," said Aunt Marguerite. "The Ballingers, I should explain, were college folks who tried to live out here. Their girls were raised by all the latest methods and theories, schooled back east, sent to hoity-toity camps where they were expected to come home with trophies and recommendations and the like. European trips heavy on learning and academics. They ended up, one lawless hippy escapade after another, busted for this and that. They were living their parents' dreams, not theirs. Look at these ice skaters and tennis phenoms, pushed off to camps and if they don't make the grade, then what's next? Drugs, anorexia, suicide?"

"Yes, the poor fool Ballingers. The butt of neighborhood jokes. Of course, I should talk. We tried to get Nathe back home here as often as possible. But he was doomed to a Hollywood boyhood—deprived of natural boy things and too much adult stuff and business for our liking. Second-rate at best I—"

"Now, Dad, you quit beating yourself up on this—I had a great childhood. Unusual yes, but you and Mom and the rest tried to keep me grounded. I knew that an' was grateful for our times together, away from the set. Remember, in Utah, how we used to take off and go tramping the Kaibab for the day? Or up Kodachrome Canyon? Remember renting that house boat on Lake Meade where Mom fell in?"

"Yes and those days were precious and rare. But take Little League. Son, I don't think you ever had two games in a row. Baseball and your boyhood seemed to be in such tatters at times. No wonder kid actors go bad. Your career came first and off you had to go on location or to a late shoot at the studio. Miss practice, miss the game. Peg would get so irked—'can't they let that boy have a day or two with his team?'"

"Well, I emerged unscathed. I'm making it up now," Nathe laughed. "See? Here I am coaching a team and knowing darn little about it. Yes, I just missed growing up here, on the farm— wasn't to be for the most part—fly in and fly back and that's just the way it turned out." He set his cup back in its saucer and leaned on the table. "Speaking of growing up too fast, I read Maria Arounek, the darling of the Five Star company and those folks . . . found she'd taken an overdose last week."

"Oh?"

"They pumped her out. Almost another Meloday Rivers. Might have suffered brain damage."

"How sad."

"I remember her father from the *Trail* series and I think he was in the Nez Perce film. A Hollywood family, born and bred, third generation. So, it isn't as if they didn't know the dangers."

"Sir, when I knew we were flying in here, I read a little bio sketch where it listed *Wingspan* among your films. Is that . . . available? Would love to see it."

"It was scrapped, Trane. You pilots would have loved it—lots of nice aerial footage too that ended up in some other picture. Or in the vault. But the day principal photography was scheduled, we got the word—'Fold it up. You're all coming home.' Great disappointment. We were stunned."

Uncle Albert shook his head and frowned. "I don't think Pete Benedict ever quite recovered, Nathe, do you? Nor did we. We had so much emotional capital invested. It was an excellent screenplay, just *excellent.* Pete told me later that fateful day, 'I hate to throw in the towel, Albert, but this is it. I'm through working for these fools and dummies.'"

Nathe sat back in his chair and studied the beamed ceiling overhead. "I recall uttering nearly the same statement years later. Hollywood loves to shoot itself in the foot. Oh well, if I were still fighting the battle out there, I wouldn't be here and living at home with my dad!"

Everyone laughed and raised their glasses, following Nathe's lead. "Say, folks, tell y' what. Relocating these last few months have been some of my happiest and—last month— finally moving back home, back to my old room makes life the best it's ever been for me."

Vic Delveccio then raised his glass. "Well, here's to home fires and goin' back to your roots. Nothing wrong with that."

"Thanks, Vic. Odd, is it not, you're plunging ahead with your new hotel—all those wheels turning—and here I am, going backward. On my way to becoming as reclusive as P. M. Murphy up the lane. What a contrast."

"Now, Nathean, I'm going to give you a scolding," said my Aunt Marguerite.

"Oh-oh. She was always boss," Nathe told the table. "Fire away."

"You're not becoming a hermit just yet. Folks won't let you. You're coaching the Panthers and look at this community development thing that's brewing. Everyone wants you to take charge, provide the leadership. There's a migraine in the making, cousin. I don't think you'll have much time for brooding in your garret, writing your memoirs. Or even whittling away your hours on the porch. You came back home and now you're in the thick of it, I'm afraid."

"Wow, what a grim sentence you pronounced, your honor. Home, Sweet Home."

"Hey," said Trane. "I'd go back to live with my folks in a minute . . . if I could make a living there and fly planes of some kind."

"And where's home, Trane?" asked Aunt Marguerite.

"Nova Scotia."

"Trane wants to fly the bush in Alaska," said Vic.

"Beavers, Otters?" Nathe asked.

"Right. Jets and automation are fine. But, for hands on, the true classics are the deHavillands for sure."

"Yes, we used them in *Wingspan*. Pipers and Cessnas too all on floats. Got to ride in a Beaver and even handle the yoke, like you did the other day, Claude. . . . *Wingspan* . . . just . . . something that was not meant to be. I might pitch it again somewhere to a young, hungry producer, likely a female filmmaker, but it's probably too old fashioned. Not enough violence and special effects."

"Try it, son."

"Until the money runs out, Pop? Could be a rat hole or worse, a badger hole. No, I'd rather write a column of some kind. Call it The Homestead Place—that should appeal to ladies and gents alike. Could I set up shop in here, Marg? Over in the corner there by the window? Gaze outside and tell folks how they should live their lives in the country?"

Marguerite bestowed that magnetic smile and once again, I saw the childhood days of her and Cousin Nathe, reflected in their affection for each other.

*   *   *

The prospect of a girl Panther might loom. Which could be all right. Too, I nurtured the hope our new classmate, the deaf kid, would prove to be a baseball player. In my mind's eye, I worked out a collection of signals for us outfielders to exchange. We could become a formidable unit, a deaf player making us even more tuned in to the game.

*   *   *

CHAPTER 23

The Candle's Wick

Mom and I held hands during most of the movie. After all, she said of it, our last night together for who knows how long? Boys indulge their mothers.

I hoped it would prove only weeks before she would be back in P. A. and entertained the notion she'd fly in for my first Panther game. But, from appearances that evening, it seemed Mom and Vic Delveccio were soon to launch onto a new and distant orbit together. Months might pass before we would see each other again, such the far-flung whirlwind both she and Vic had in mind. A galaxy away from my little world now on a Pennsylvania farm.

After dinner at Aunt Marguerite's that Saturday, we had all gathered ourselves in front of her television to watch one of Nathe's films. He had recorded *The Candle's Wick* on videotape. Such a treat and innovation, home video, and to see a member of one's family on the screen, well, it made a night to remember.

Daisy, the border collie, appeared early in the film to Mom's delight. "Oh, I am honored. How adorable—look at those ears." Daisy did capture one's heart, tilting her head, questioning, sticking one ear straight up while the other remained folded, conveying her pleasure or concerns in oval-shaped tones.

The film revealed a world to me so rife with issues, decisions, the impact of choices, the risks of disappointing those around you, the denial of one's dreams, the unrealistic expectations we place on each other. It kept my mind buzzing for days. Nathe's role was major.

He played the son of a minister who had by sheer will power and force of personality developed a farm and colony devoted to helping folks and families recover their worth and dignity at Mission of Hope Home and Farm. As the farm expanded, more funds were needed, and the Reverend Millard Penstock was compelled to take his story "to the hinterlands as well as the great metropolitan centers of this great land. To the humble and the mighty, to the privileged and those who know affliction and who will respond as one when we present our story of lives changed and burdens lifted."

Atypical of Hollywood's usual treatment of protestant ministers as slightly deranged, secretly decadent, shystering those innocent widows glued to the weekly broadcasts of "The Truth" in its various guises—the gospel of, the herald of, the messenger of, the hour of, this film plowed new ground. The truth as presented by Reverend Penstock was indeed . . . true. The Mission of Hope Home and Farm pointed with justifiable pride to its strict accounting, modest salaries, verifiable results. No scandals or expose's.

Its promotional radio spots featured farm personnel, especially "the apple of my eye," Reverend Penstock's son, Caleb, played by Nathe. Caleb, however, is torn between enrolling in seminary or agricultural school and playing semi-pro baseball. He becomes the conflicted heir apparent to all his minister father had built while yearning to prove his mettle on the diamonds of Lexington, Nashville, Charlottesville, Morgantown as an outfielder or pitcher on the mound.

During the weeks and summer following that evening at Shadeland, I found myself returning often to the sentiments *The Candle's Wick* stirred within me. Concerns about priorities, decisions, options lay ahead for me and my mother for certain and others of Summers Run. The film said weigh, balance, and listen: your gut instincts are speaking.

At times, boys open easily to the softest knock.

And seeing my cousin play such a penetrating role certainly tapped my normal reserve. Truly, as I had read and been told, Nathean Summers had become that capable of an actor, so convincing and enveloping, surrounding the script with a sense of palpable gravity and universal understanding.

His character Caleb waves, haltingly, at the bus load of baseball player hopefuls riding down the dusty road toward their various destinies. The dust swirls around the bus as it disappears into the waning sun and obscurity. One can only guess where those boys ended up and how. But most telling for me was his hand, now centered in the screen. The message from gesture.

Its wave both expressed its good wishes and the regret it wasn't making the journey. Nathe draws it back to his chin, then lowers it to his lap where he studies it wondering if it will ever grip another baseball and hurl it toward the plate in competition. Daisy, the farm collie, appears in the scene and stands up on the footrest of the Ferguson, cocking her head first to the left, then right, asking, "May I come up? A ride would be nice."

"Hello, Daisy-girl," chokes Nathe, his final lines, essentially the last he'll utter in films for more than a decade. "Yes, you're important to me too." Nathe lifts her to him and buries his face briefly in the fur of her neck and then, resolve restored, he says, "Let's go home together." *The Candle's Wick* seemed one of those milestone pictures in one's life. It made me think. It does yet.

I sat on the leather hassock. I remained captured by Nathe looking over his shoulder for one more glance of the future awaiting his friends and teammates and that's the image haunting me even to this day. For as I studied my cousin of years ago, his youth and persona preserved thanks to celluloid and electronic wizardry, I could see my own reflection next to him on the screen. I awaited my future, I knew. What had its author written for me? In six years, would I mirror Nathe's image on the screen?

I wanted none of the parting comments from beyond The Homestead Room to intrude on my moment. No goodbyes or urgings, no wishes for a good night. no thanks for a marvelous meal. Nathe came back from the foyer and leaned against the door jam, blessedly silent as he could see I was engaged.

For I realized, while I sat enraptured by the final scene of *The Candle's Wick* where my cousin bid farewell to his dream, I was looking at myself in not that many years to come.

*   *   *

"Many thanks again, my niece, for such a dinner," Albert hugged Marguerite, then found the handrail down the steps.

"You're welcome, Uncle. Better than your usual fare of road kill I hope."

"Oh, infinitely. Miserable burnt offerings of late. Especially that last critter I scraped up by the airport. Still not sure what specie or breed. Might have been that annoying little ankle biter that chases your car over by Tiffens. Hope so."

"You're incorrigible. See you tomorrow then."

We all made our way toward bed. It had been a long day, full of physical labor and output for sure, but bristling also with the emotions laden into pending departures. I thanked Aunt Margy again for the lunch and gave my mom a hug.

"Thanks for helping today."

"I'm glad I didn't miss it, son. Such a nice thing Nathe's doing for you and the others. It'll be important to you down the road." We didn't broach her coming back to see a game or two but rather exchanged our *better-to-not-discuss-it-right-now-maybe-later* look.

*   *   *

We drove in two cars, the head-turning Town and Country and Aunt Marguerite's plain jane Oldsmobile painted in Evening Jade. We met the awaiting Citation where Trane had the engines warming the interior, the steps unfolded, the tanks topped, and the cookies baked. We all marveled at the creamy interior, butterscotch leather, the latte'-colored pecky pecan and the cranberry accents and trimmings. Then we disembarked and said our goodbyes. I was last in line.

"Fasten your seatbelt, even if you're just going around the corner to the store," I scolded her. "Did you have it on when you broke through the fence? I forgot to check." My mother took heat from all of us—me, Granddad C.J. and Grandma Ronnie for being negligent about this matter.

Mom nodded, her eyes closed, her tears starting to puddle the mascara.

I said, "All right then." We embraced and she added she'd been through so many of these with Blake and "now it's me taking off leaving you behind."

"Hey, I'm here. Just a phone call away, Moms."

She dabbed at her face, started to pull the compact from her purse and thought better of it. "Do you know what I'm most afraid of? You'll become so much the man of the family, you won't be my little guy when I get back."

"Nah, I won't change. Don't you neither, okay? We'll pick up right where we left off. Nobody changes. That's the rule, all right?"

She nodded again and I told her jets burn a lot of fuel. I walked her to the plane and we pecked each other on the cheek while Aunt Margy, Grandma Bea, Uncle Albert, Mister Vic, Nathe, Sophie and Trane looked on or away. Then I shook hands with Vic and Trane who said he'd take me up sometime. And I stupidly mentioned I'd recently flown a Cessna.

"Good for you, Claude. That's where everyone starts." I liked him for that. He, the last to enter, the door latched, and the white and silver swan glided out of sight behind a row of hangars. We waited.

Crows began cawing to each other in the morning's stillness. Then, a dozen pigeons barreling away from the runway became our first indication flight had begun. Bursting from behind the hangars, the Citation came rocketing down the asphalt, wet from the early morning rain. And as its nose left the earth, its engines hunkered down, the heat from their exhaust sending two plumes of steam arcing behind the plane, giant geysers like platinum bows launching the arrow carrying my mother skyward. Someone said . . . marvelous.

Murmurings were heard. Cornerstone morning. What a sendoff. What an adventure for her, bless her. She deserves a turn. Daisy dear, the poor girl. God bless her, yes indeed. And though I suspect it came to mind for us all watching her take flight, no one uttered anything about going to see or find her rooster.

It was Easter Sunday, Easter being late this spring, and we Kinkades and Summerses trooped off to church.

*   *   *

CHAPTER 24

The Neighborhood

The sermon focused on the wonders of rebirth and renewal. I confess I drifted away, my mind's eye watching the Citation climb sharply through the puffy remnants of the morning rain and then turn west toward the desert far away.

I could imagine my mother weeping and watching the quilt of a Pennsylvania countryside slip by below. I hoped Vic would pat her hand.

The final hymn sung and the benediction rendered, we drifted toward the aisle amidst many well-wishers who flocked around Grandmother Bea, who was in her element. She bid me to her side: "May I present my grandson . . . May I present Claude, Blake's son." I dutifully shook the hands of many, oldsters mainly, little thin frail hands knobby with arthritis, bigger paws thickened from hoisting sacks of potatoes and grain, country hands devoted to homespun arts and working their seasoned way around a winter's wood, their garden plot, or a grassy meadow ready to be shorn. Soon I was enjoying meeting these people, and I also confess I basked being in the center of their attention. I liked them. A lot.

"Hon, this is Blake's boy . . . oh, of course, how nice to see you . . . meet you . . . have you here . . . have you home . . . I heard you're Blake's . . . yes, so good . . . so nice . . . well, welcome home, son. . . welcome."

One balding gentleman gripped my shoulder firmly and told me he was Blake's Sunday School teacher. "I'm a machinist by trade. Many of us are 'round here, old tool and die guys, railroaders. Blake was one of those you never forget. My wife, she's gone now, always hoped our daughter and him would pair up but you can't force those things. Is your mother here today?"

Explaining our family's situation and Mom's absence put me on the spot and I managed to dance through it with: "Mom left today for Nevada on some . . . business things she had to tend to. I'm sure she'll be by and meet you all later." I didn't care to mention dreams, night clubs, or her possible marriage to a casino owner.

Or I'd add. "Dad used to talk about folks up here a lot." Or, "he really missed this place."

One lady rubbed the sleeve of my sport coat and said through her tears, "And we miss him. He was a neighborhood fixture. Our boys and him got along so well. Everyone liked Blake and Nathean too, though we didn't see much of him. But do you know? Nathe remembered me even though we haven't seen each other in years. Of course, Albert and us have known each other since high school. Albert raised good stock. Apples don't fall far from the tree."

Between Grandmother Beatrice and the rest, I became roundly introduced and it consumed such time my stomach started to growl. Today's light breakfast went down hours ago. Nathe had reserved a table at The Chapmann Inn for its fabled Sunday brunch. "We'll fill up there," he said.

On our way down the walk and to the cars, a family approached and Nathe recognized the husband as "Rob . . . Rob Wilson—"

"Willotsen. That's pretty good after all these years, Nathe. This is my wife Bettye and our girls Mandy, Felicia, and Bridgette."

"Wow, what a flower garden. Beautiful dresses and black patent leather shoes all around."

"Yes," Bettye laughed, "Easter's a big deal. Have to get everyone gussied up." Nathe "presented" me and we were joined by two boys, one older than I plus a fourth grader I'd seen at school.

"Heard the big news that you're starting a Little League team out at the place," said Rob. "Hope it goes well. We need one in the area. Jason's ready to sign up but he's too young yet."

"Too bad, Jason. We need another boy or two. Guess this guy's too old by now," Nathe said, looking toward Evan who said he was 14.

Hands on her hips and surveying Nathe critically, Mandy asked: "Are you the one who got shot when the Indians stampeded?"

Nathe considered the question and allowed: "Well, likely. I've been shot a number of times. Bullet holes all over, even an arrow or two. The worst was getting snake bit, and oh yes, and getting torn up by those wolves and jumpin' in that cold river. It's a wonder I'm here to tell the tale."

"My cousin tells about her and a girlfriend going to see *Where the Sun Stands Now* eight times," Bettye told him. Nathe laughed and pulled out his money clip. "See that she gets some ticket money back, would y'? Such loyalty needs a reward."

"No, no, it was their big thing that year. They used to act it out in the backyard. They never missed a Nathean Summers show. Have you seen all of his films, Claude? Maybe he'll get you into the movies, ever think about that?"

"No, ma'am. I don't think Nathe would let me."

"No, indeed. We need him in right field this year. Jason, come practice a little with us. And get older, soon."

*   *   *

Brunch at The Inn hosted a few families making a day of it. Church, family, Easter egg hunts, boys clad in ties and sport coats. I felt fine in mine, a light blue blazer with a tie my dad picked out and showed me how to knot. A British Regimental on a field of blue with red and white stripes pointing down to one's heart. I have it to this day.

The Summers-Kinkade party drew a few furtive glances and folks nodded as we took our table in a quiet alcove. As we worked our way through the buffet, two little girls in their Easter frills and black patent leather pointed at us and giggled. Before we left, Nathe signed autographs for all the wait staff and a couple visiting family from Erie. We were noticed.

Right or wrong, I felt some pride in such. Here—just fresh from church where we are exhorted to shun self and arrogance—I was shameless. I then remembered Fungus, the modest and unassuming movie stunt horse: *what he must think of me.*

*   *   *

We drove home to Shadeland. *Home to Shadeland.* The phrase sounded less hollow than a few weeks ago when we first arrived on an unsettled day in March with our hopes teetering. Uncle Albert decided to stay for tea and "walk home, son. Don't bother about me. I need the stroll. Besides I'm enjoying these ladies in their finery."

"Yes," said Aunt Marguerite, "does us all good to have a lazy day and stay dressed up for a change. Instead of getting back in harness and our working togs." Aunt Marguerite favored smocks, usually dusted with flour.

"You both look stunning, my dears."

Grandmother did look like an advertisement for some upscale senior center and luxury spa. She wore a violet paisley print bloused from shoulder to shoulder, a string of pearls and a broad straw hat that framed and flattered her face's shape and complexion. She might have passed for a well-preserved

Greer Garson or Myrna Loy. Aunt Marguerite nearly matched her colorwise with a purple/violet turtle neck, matching pearl necklace and earrings, a coordinated heavily pleated skirt and a well-tailored jacket of faux doeskin. One would look twice and be charmed. Still a country girl, her, freckles undisguised, but one with a clear sense of style for certain.

"Well, it's been a grand Easter." Albert summed it up. "Good to see so many old friends and such. Nathe, why don't you and Claude take a turn around the neighborhood. You have man stuff to talk about, I know. Put the top down, roll the windows up, but put the top down, you two. Nothing like an open car on a sunny day in spring."

"Okay with you, Claude? No homework, book report?" asked Nathe.

"Nossir. All caught up."

"Good. Let's take in the local attractions then."

He slid behind the wheel after we did as we were told, snapping the top into its boot and rolling the windows up. Then we drove off. I detected the family's effort toward easing my transition into life without Mom. "She might be over the Great Plains somewhere by now," I told Nathe. "Hope it's clear so she can see a long, long ways." I wanted to ask if he found her charming and attractive last night, but how would one go about such?

*   *   *

We glided along but slowly enough to be passed by those out enjoying a drive in the country. Folks smiled and waved and a couple tooted their horns in recognition? Approval? Open road camaraderie? I couldn't tell which but it buoyed me on a day that might have been sunny outside but gloomy for me personally. I was beginning to feel a kinship with my surroundings and my extended family whether Summers or Kinkade. Nathe began a narrative of the houses and farms we passed.

"The Malford Hayden-Cawleys, WASPish, New England aristocrats who made sure you knew they were descended from Plymouth Rock stock. First hyphenated surname I'd ever encountered. Blake tried to sell them a cord of good old apple wood once, but they turned up their thin little patrician noses, said the wood might be 'wormy and let bugs in the house.' Did you ever smell an old apple wood fire? Nothing quite like it for aroma. Like a new baseball, you never forget. Place is so broken up now, sold for lots and houses, you can barely see the original farmstead. Bank took it over once. All that old money from Plymouth Rock didn't keep them afloat. Ballingers lived around here in one of these places. There's a house that could tell a story. . . .

"Adell Quince, widow woman for as long as I knew her. Used to collect my memorabilia. Did you know I was on a dixie cup ice cream lid for a couple years? School tablets, book covers. Never had a lunch box, though. You had to be really big time to get a lunch box, someone on the level of Roy, Gene, or Hopalong. Rode in some parades with cowboy stars—that was fun—Wild Bill Elliot, Gabby Hayes. Rode alongside of Roy and Trigger once. I've got his autograph somewhere. Nice fellar, Roy Rogers . . . .

"The Cornell Lundquists, college dean and administrator. Became a recluse after his wife died. He and dad were good friends but poor old Corny, as Dad called him, never recovered from losing Madge. She and Corny were soulmates. I think Dad envied him in that respect. He and Dad belonged to the gun club, shot trap together. Big old house that's been added on. It's a private orphanage now called 'Fountain House Home', run by a minister and his wife. Your mom and Marguerite took a load of stuff over to them the other day. Your aunt canvasses the neighborhood for can goods and clothing. Lots of needs as there are lots of kids. Lots of cars and vans around usually. . . .

"Sherm and Gertude Woolsey, raised Merino sheep. Always wonder if their surname was part of that decision. Gertie was a spinner and weaver, Woolsey Woolens. We have some of her pillows and throws around the place, so does Marguerite. Did grand work with nature's bounty. 'Simple gifts, simple pleasures'—says one of the throws we have at home. Nice to have someone's handiwork about. Both gone now. Their kids sold it to some people from Pittsburgh for a summer place. You see them poking about some when the weather's nice. . . .

"The Breckinridge Farm, grand old place—look at their view. Kids live there now, work in town. Mister Breckinridge was a model train enthusiast. What a treat for us kids to see, three or four trains running at a time. I can hear those little whistles yet. Whole basement was laid out in HO gauge. The kids didn't sell the farm's frontage. Good for them. Would have been a travesty. . . .

"Vernelle Merganthorpe, school teacher for years. Lived with her sister and mother when I knew her. Rented their farm out. They used to spend summers up in Lake Chautauqua. Blake used to keep an eye on their place some. After baseball's over this year, we'll go up to Chautauqua for a few days. You'll hear music there like nowhere else on earth. It's a colony devoted to learning and the arts. Just like the Merganthorpes. Aaron Oarcaster and his mother live there now. It's not farmed. Oarcaster was a builder, died a couple years ago, fell off a scaffold. . . . Used to be a Forsythe place before the Merganthorpes. . . .

"The Castleton sisters, Madeline and Eunice, another set of spinsters. Old, old farm. They kept a roadside stand for years.

Always remarked the stand became their lifeline since they were living in 'reduced circumstances after Poppa died.' We'd buy stuff even though we didn't need it much. Had marvelous raspberries though, couldn't keep up with the bumper crops some years. Sweet corn, truckloads of pumpkins. All gone now. Great old place to visit and pick berries. They were dear hearts, good-hearted souls. 'Good eggs' as we say of folks around here. . . . Both gone now. Dad bought this place a while back, rents it to a Forsythe descendant, ironically. . . .

"Used to belong to Charles Tarleton Pendergraff. Place burned down once. Supposedly connected some way to the Forsythes. Raised Christmas trees for years and started the 'cut your own' thing. Now what's left of the plantation has grown into huge thickets. Lots of whitetail winter under 'em. Blake took a big buck out of that thicket. He wouldn't have made it through the winter. Got tangled in someone's fence, cut open and suffered an infection. An old mossyback, marvelous head. Mounted in the Montana room at Shadeland. Smythe's live there now, another Panther of ours. . . .

"Abel Murfitt and his brother Ward, bachelors. Allegedly moonshiners but never proven. Used to build beautiful lampstands, coffee tables. Dad has a nice set of end tables from the Murfitt's workshop. Still there, working away at their wood now and then. . . .

"The Vaughn Hollaways, dairy. Was on the cover of the *Pennsylvania Farmer* years ago for its carousel, modern, state-of-the-art milking parlor. Think they gave it up with the big dairy buyout. Dad kept their books some on the side. Gentlefolk, very devout. . . .Once part of Shadeland and owned by the Forsythes way back when. . . .that fancy barn is idle now. . . . The big dairies over by the interstate, Clawton Farms, ship all the milk out of this country now. I remember when every place had a stand by the road and a few cans there for pickup. I remember riding the milk cart and helping my friends wrestle the cans out so they could be picked up. Tommy Joslin's family milked—we spilled part of a can once. . . .

"The Taylor Tiffen place. First to try being a bed and breakfast around here. Guess they're still going. Used to have a cider press there and folks would bring their apples from miles around to have the Tiffens press their Northern Spies, Winesaps, Macs. We used to truck ours over there. They were beekeepers too. Had wonderful clover and buckwheat honey in the comb. I'd go over there some and end up signing autographs for all the girls. Had several who wanted to date me, thought I was quite the prize. I think Blake liked one of the Tiffen twins, but he got annoyed since all she wanted to talk about was my latest film or TV episode. . . . The Tiffen place was once part of Shadeland as well. . . .

"This little corner is called Griffin Hollow. James Alphonse and his family live back up that lane a ways. His gravel pit is just over the hill there, on the old Griffin farm. To my mind, kind of a homey, cozy little place tucked in the trees. The Bradshaw girls live there next door with their aging father. Run their sheep here and elsewhere, wherever their neighbors want some weed control. New family, the Kenilworths, live here and do blacksmithing for folks hereabouts, call their business 'The Forge'. New family, haha, been here ten-twelve years at least. They make all kinds of signs, brackets, hinges and such. They do nice work, husband and wife team. You can see some of their handiwork around the place, over at Margy's too. . . .

"Well, here's Carmine Catalino and the family orchard, vineyards. They do well but it doesn't come easily. Always dealing with frost and the weather. Good, natural husbandry plus they match the latest against the tried and true of trees.

Hard workers. Blake and I both helped there some, bringing in the harvest an' such. Great times and wonderful meals, of course. . . ."

As we approached Shadeland and Summers Run, we passed by Harvey Logan's farm where Standing Ovation stood near the road, not far from where Mom breached the fence and planted the Town and Country in the mud. As we slowed down almost as if to pay homage, His Royal Obsidian Omnipotence looked our way disdainfully, befitting a monarch. Nathe said of him: "There's a guy who doesn't need any reminder of who he is and where he came from. Kind of like a fellar I used to know."

*   *   *

CHAPTER 25

Meeting Tim

"Well, Clauders . . . have a reasonably amusing and moderately interesting day." Marguerite left me out at the school bus stop where I scanned those kids waiting and felt confident I had identified my target.

"I think I will, Aunt Margy, by the looks of things. See you tonight."

The Olds and Aunt Marguerite drove off on their way to town and I proceeded toward my quarry, standing off a bit from the crowd. I felt sure it was he.

I greeted my new friends from the neighborhood and passed through them toward the slightly built boy wearing a dark jacket, trimmed in yellow, and jeans, black hair, ruddy complexion, white cross-trainers. The jacket was mine, an old one I had outgrown, and it appeared the shoes might be mine as well. Clearly, he was from "Fountain House Home."

He saw me approaching him deliberately and his look of unease with the group narrowed, focused as we were on each other. He drew back in concern? mild alarm? as if I were a huge dog bounding across the lawn as he stepped from the car? Was I friend or foe?

I signed "Hello."

He reciprocated, timidly, bewildered, and then I signed, "C-l-a-u-d-e" and took his hand, shaking it. He nodded, relaxed and signed, "Tim." I spelled out "K-i-n-k-a-d-e" and

167

he spelled back what I thought was "Hardaway" and then got it right: "Hathaway."

"What's going on, you guys?" asked one of the older kids.

"We're signing," I told him. "He's deaf."

"Oh, yeah? Can he talk?"

"I don't know. For now, he does this." The guy and a companion laughed, sharing some off-color remark between them, I decided. At that moment, the bus arrived and I pledged to avoid their scrutiny if possible, escorting Tim away from the back. He seemed relieved, his black eyes growing more trusting and the scowl relaxing as we sat beside each other. I felt confident of my signing largely though I told him I was a bit rusty. He waved it off, signing he'd been learning lip-reading and could manage if folks spoke slowly enough. As we bobbed along the back roads and made other stops, I had to smile. My grandmother Ronnie Jarrett would be pleased.

*   *   *

After Saturday's practice, Nathe and I loaded the Town and Country with groceries, some camping gear and drove to what the family knew as "the lake." Through the padlocked gate we went and up a two-track lane until we arrived to where there was a picnic shelter, a little cabin with a veranda all around, a storage building, a boat dock, and a hand pump and portable toilet.

"There's a cop that comes up here about every weekend. Brings his family. Everyone knows it and so no one messes around with things. No one gets on the bad side of Constable Carney. He'll hunt down anyone up to no good."

"He lets you come up and stay here then."

"Yup, he does." Nathe smiled over at me. "I own it." We pulled up on the concrete pad under the picnic shelter. "Mr. Carney mows the lawn, the weeds, takes care of the upkeep, and he can use it year around if he likes, no charge. In turn, my investment is protected, fiercely, and one less worry for me. It's called 'a working arrangement', Claude. They come in handy at times.

"The flora and fauna hereabouts are pretty diverse, it being a lakeside. Usta be an old homestead here—that's why you see those apple trees. Most of the orchard's gone but for a few old soldiers. Lots of elderberries in the summer for your jams and pies, goldenrod for your allergies. Lots of birdlife too: Herons, kingfishers, killdeer, shorebirds like sandpipers. I once spotted an American Bittern in that big clump of Reed Canarygrass over there. Nestled himself in there—would even sway a bit when the breezes would blow. They point those long ol' beaks straight up and you'd swear it was a part of the vegetation, they blend in so well. You wonder if such fools the foxes, don't y'?"

Nathe and I settled ourselves into setting up our fire and a supper cooked over the fireplace he'd designed himself.

"Not my own design totally. Borrowed some ideas from a Swedish stove maker, and a Navajo I'd met in Kanab, and a blacksmith who worked on the *Trail* series for us. It draws well, the main cooking surface is under cover, and most of the smoke goes up and away from us."

"Wow, everyone had a hand in it, looks like."

"Yup," Nathe laughed, "plus I had an Amish stone mason build it for me. I call it my put-together-by-a-committee stove. Dad thinks I should patent it. He's always cooking up some enterprise."

"So the money won't run out."

"Yes, he's the incurable money manager. Like I told you, Pop owns a few of those places we drove past last weekend, including the Fountain House Home."

"Really? Our new kid Tim lives there. Says he'll be at practice Monday if you want to see . . . y' know, if he's up to snuff. He's the deaf one. But he's really fast, fast as I am. We raced."

"Fine, speed is always welcome. We can work around the deafness. Baseball is a game of signals anyway."

"Yessir." I had to smile. Nathe, I had noticed thus far in our relationship, always seemed to take a sensible approach to things.

"What?"

"Ah, well, you always seem to have the right answer."

"Sometimes I wing it, frien'. Take this Little League thing. We're at sea. Need old Red Floyd here to advise."

"Uh, the manager in *The Candle's Wick?*"

"Right, the Kenneth Tobey character. There's a guy who always had the answer. Life's answers are easy in the movies." Nathe wedged another log under the grate. "We'll need the heat more than the coals if we spend the night out here. The cabin is plumb cold this time of year, not insulated in there. Yet. Did you take to the film all right? I noticed you seemed to be caught up with something from it. After it was over."

"Yessir, some parts are really sticking with me. Well, it all did but the ending where, you know, Caleb decides not to try out but go back to the farm. . . . That would seem so hard. Sad I thought."

"Right. Had he chosen to play ball, the film would not have succeeded, I've decided. There was an ending which had it that way—Caleb goes off with the team, spends several years in the minors and comes back home bitter because he never made it to 'the big show.' He ends up hating the farm, mad at everyone and himself. I argued against that one. Normally I didn't speak up but the director didn't like the 'downer' ending either. I'm not sure I would have portrayed it well. Simply because I felt the first ending was stronger and reached out more to the audience. Lots of folks had been there—a lot of my fan mail said so.

"Then . . . the screenwriter also wrote it to where Caleb tries out, plays a bit, finds out he doesn't like it, has a terrible time of it, and gladly comes home and settles into running the farm and mission, putting baseball behind him, relieved it's over and glad he had the chance to try it for a spell. We all thought it seemed the weakest ending."

"I liked the ending." I shuffled my boots about on the concrete pad. "Mom and I both . . . got teary. A little, just a little. Mom, moreso."

Nathe smiled. "Me too. That's Dad's favorite film of mine. It says a lot to both of us. Caleb made a decision that wouldn't tell him if he might have been good enough for the majors. That was his dilemma, the unknown. Did he give up too soon? Was he happier staying and building his father's dream for the farm and him? Did he do the right thing by himself and all the others depending on him? Would he always feel envious of those who tried, especially if some of them did make it? Would he kick himself for not trying at least? Lots going on."

"Boy howdy. Makes y' think. A lot. About giving up your dream an' such."

"Exactly, son. That's the way it became for me out there. I had foolish hopes of becoming this big time leading man, a household word. Big pictures, big budgets, on television talk shows, lots of money, half a million per picture. That fell through with a bang. Then," Nathe poked another log into position, "Then, I turned to sports, became an announcer for a baseball team in Sacramento—you heard me mention such. There are some clippings of me at the microphone and some tapes back home. And so I thought, 'Well, hey, this isn't bad. It's not films, not year around, but the fans seem to like me and I like the job.'

"Turned out, the club owner had a nephew who needed that same job and he was in and I was out. So much for those four years, down the drain. No one needed an announcer elsewhere, clearly not in the majors, at the time. I peddled myself hard, sending tapes around, interviewing but it was always, 'maybe next year, Nathe. Sure miss seeing those westerns you used to be in. Could we get an autograph?' Talk about humbling.

"In the meantime, I'd been working on some television pilots and screenplays during the off season. Peter Benedict and I had a property—not *Wingspan*—that was catching attention and we were hopeful. Peter had remarried and was dabbling with getting into the ministry but willing to give films one last shot. Peter is a very good writer—that's why he's a heckuva minister, I think. He understands the human condition. Anyway, we were required to partner with a subsidiary of the main studio for production and distribution and all that—things out there get very complicated and mysterious. Incestuous even. And that bunch ended up stealing, or trying to steal our end of the project, the rights and such, yanking the rug out from under us.

"Well, they thought they had us squeezed out, but it developed I knew a guy who knew a guy who was a very shrewd copyrights lawyer, and he found they hadn't done their homework. Long story short, we sued them and collected around five million dollars after the attorney took his and Peter got his due. The project was scrapped and so was my film career, m' frien'."

"Oh? So no one liked you anymore."

"You can say 'Boy howdy' again. If you are really big and really important, you can sue anyone in that town and they love y' all the more. But, if you're small and you're lucky enough to win as I did, then the word goes out he's poison, he's an ambulance chaser, he's a lawsuit ready to happen. No one wants you or your project hangin' around. I took the money and left." Nathe sighed heavily and I pondered all this.

Life again. Sorting it out and what to do with it once you have it sorted.

"So then, I got into magazines, publishing, books and the like. Meanwhile, my second marriage was failing and I said, 'all right, so much for the family and the marriage if this is the way she wants it,' and poured myself into this firm tirelessly, working night and day, developed an ad agency on the side and was building some reputation and putting out some nice products. We grew and I moved up the ladder, Editor-in-Chief, Vice President of Special Projects, member of the Board of Directors.

"So along comes this bunch of MBAs, hired from a couple big universities down south—called themselves The New Confederacy. Several were fraternity brothers and they were swinging a wide loop and they became everyone's darlings and finessed their way up the ladder too and wanted to change my approach to the magazines in particular. Essentially gutted the concepts I'd developed in favor of a traditional business model based heavily on advertising rather than subscription revenue . . . which was my strategy. My magazines were largely lifestyle: The Country Gentleman, Country Hearth & Home for the ladies, The Farmer & Rancher's Digest, and The Small Homesteader's Companion, Classic Cars, Trucks & Tractors—five of 'em and we had a lot of subscribers who took all five every month. Very loyal readership.

"We packaged our editorial so it could be transferred, if appropriate, among the different mastheads and it worked quite smoothly. No ads, all loyal subscribers. We made tons of money, numbers growing every year. Excellent columnists with sound, sensible advice. Packaged some of their work into books.

"No conflict of interest, no prostituting ourselves to big advertisers, no competition with other magazine look-a-likes. It worked. Beautifully. You can see copies at the house; I'll show you some time. But the MBA boys thought my approach was old-fashioned for their sophisticated taste and too honed on a genuine love for 'dear hearts and gentle people'. Too cornpone, they said, too country kid once again. Remember? Just like when Alan Bancroft said my looks and screen persona were too average and so-what for the big screen.

"To get to the point, the Southerners looked at the dollars the mainstream farm and home and garden magazines were pulling in and started drooling. They wanted some of that and dropped the subscription only idea and started filling the pages with ads. Folks cancelled by the droves, by the thousands! One magazine lost ten thousand subscribers in a year, nearly half its base. And that's how a magazine sells itself, by the numbers of readers it can deliver who will see your ads in its pages. Ad revenue fell. Drastically.

"The MBAs hung together to defend their turf, justify their actions. We had some battles royal and they conspired to get me removed from the board and off the masthead—fired essentially. Meanwhile, the Board of Directors reads the profit and loss statement, meets in an emergency session. Meanwhile, my quiet little ad agency where I'm a silent partner pulls all our clients out of their pages and starts placing their ads elsewhere. Meanwhile, ad revenue plunges even faster. This time, I pulled the rug out from under them.

"The Board starts lopping off the heads of the MBAs. They are panicked and jumping ship, crying foul, threatening lawsuits, bringing lawsuits, dusting off their resumes, desperate for work. I'm getting nasty calls, guys screaming into the phone, crying, calling me a bastard. Now, they're the ones who are poison, not just in town but across the entire magazine industry. It's a scandal, just the thing those industry watchers like to feed on. Hiring an Ivy League or big school MBA became the kiss of death—reversed the trend. All five of those guys left the industry in disgrace.

"It was hardball, Claude. And yes, sweet revenge. And nothing I'm proud of. The publishing house went belly-up and what was left sold to a holding company. All my work for naught as it turned out. The magazines I pioneered and put out to the public became history. That's the sad part. Lots of good writers and artists lost their jobs and had to move elsewhere.

"In the summer and autumn of '91, about the time of your dad's memorial, I found myself in Japan pushing urgently on a deal and to get it to the market earlier, I financed it with my own money. The last book published under the Country Home & Harvest imprint. A book about minorities who farmed and ranched and formed communities all across our country. It's in the local library. Marguerite has a copy too. It's up for some awards this year, somewhere, by some industry folks. Nice book if I say so myself. But it was over.

"When it went to press last fall, I packed everything up— nearly 20 years' worth—and came home to P.A. Bitter. Jaded. Fed up. Done to death with the corporate world—they can have it with all its deals and wheels, greed, big shots, intrigues, lawsuits, greed, bullying, posturing, gossip, innuendo. I swear, if I had a son, I don't know how I would advise him today. Just like the folks in *Candle's Wick* who said: 'Hmmm, Caleb, 'pears the road ahead for you is kinder foggy, don't it?'

"There . . . Claude, you have the story of where I've been and how I got here. It ain't pretty. Two bum marriages, aborted my film career, sued my way out of Hollywood, couldn't jumpstart my broadcasting career, and for all the work I put into publishing, I have nothing to show for it but a few nice coffee table books. They probably catch more dust than they're read. 'Oh, pitiful days,' as Marguerite would say." He stirred the fire.

"But, at least, I'm back home, back to family and where I started. Back to where I might find what I left behind. Back where I might find what I lost when I went out into the world as a mere boy, younger than you. Singing for my supper of approval, adoration . . . proving my ability to carry the picture, deliver the goods each issue.

"I think . . . turns out, Blake has likely proved the smarter of us two. He loved being an instructor, loved it. Loved figuring out how to make complicated things or missions simple, make simple things better, safer, loved his guys and loved to see them come home, intact, from the places where he sent them. He was rewarded, honored." Nathe coughed and jabbed at the fire in front of him, an angry gesture.

175

"The army loved him. I wonder what that was like—to be so . . . secure, so highly regarded over the years, held up for all to copy, revered. I was loved by my fans and later had a lot of nice compliments from those who read our stuff and what we published. But, such as that is fleeting, for the most part. Folks forget quickly. There was nothing long term except indifference. Blake was unique and the army knew it. It held on to him as long as it could."

Somehow, from somewhere I knew I had to do this: I moved my little camp chair closer to his and touched the back of his hand that held the smoking poker. "I think," I started, "I like to think that maybe my dad disappeared saving some guy's life or somethin'." I forced myself to look his way and found him glowering toward the flames reflected on his sober face.

"I think maybe that's how he found his rooster. Over there, being a hero. Maybe . . . Nathe . . . you will still find yours. Around here, somewhere."

He looked at me and his expression softened. He took my hand in his and said: "Bless you, m' boy. Bless you."

*　　*　　*

CHAPTER 26

Las Vegas on the Line

A pattern seemed to be emerging. Both Nathe and I were adjusting to our new lives, our surroundings. Perhaps our visions were taking shape and with such, expectations—both our own and those from them around us. I pondered too: what did he expect from me and I from him?

I decided he'd read my curiosity. There was no hiding such. I wanted to know everything, wanted to read every bit I could get my hands on about both Nathe and my dad, Blake David Kinkade. View all the family photos, the videos of Nathe's films. I was in the words of Marguerite, "insatiable, and I am so pleased, Clauders. You need every scrap you can find around here. There's nothing hidden—no scandals or horse thieves—that I'm aware of anyway."

While I sought remnants of my father, I remained in awe of Nathe still. How he began a business career, essentially at age eight, by emoting in front of a jaundiced film crew who often applauded his depiction in a difficult scene. How he became a respected supporting actor, even sought after, and rose to such heights he brushed that rarified level of becoming a household word in thousands of American homes. Was he a legend?

Well, all things considered, probably not. But for the folks in Chapmann, Pennsylvania, Pymatuning County, Pickett Township, yes, he had attained such a stature he could do no wrong. He was one of theirs and though Nathe would scoff at the idea, some folks would insist, after all these years, "he put us, this little ol' place on the map, yessir." Nathe and my mom would likely agree: applause is almost chemical in its allure. It makes one want more.

And I sensed Nathe wanted me to know all about his life and times. Hence, the narrative and the descriptions concerning the neighborhood, his career moves, his personal life. Nathe, I decided, needed to "unload." He asked me if I was keeping a journal as my mother suggested. "Perhaps, if it's not too much trouble, you could jot down a few notes for me as well. I feel the need to get my thoughts and perspective down. Seems like the best stuff comes to mind when you're miles from a keyboard and there's not a pen or pencil to be found."

I said, fire away, adding: "I want to know everything—even your brand of toothpaste." And so began the earliest career move of my own, the official biographer of *Nathean Hale Summers, born May 15, 1946, Chapmann, Pennsylvania; child actor, appearing in more than 15 feature films and television serials; active, 1954-1965.*

In compiling my cousin's commentaries, we agreed: "Might be a means of learning a lot about your dad as well, Claude. He's a fixture in my life. Grateful for that. A privilege to have known him."

We arose the next morning to a rosy dawn. I told Nathe I'd slept well under the picnic shelter other than wrestling with a short nightmare. "I dreamt the Chrysler was 'bout to eat me."

He laughed. "Yes, I can understand such. Bedded down as we were, right in front of that toothy maw. Pretty grisly, getting ground to bits in all that metal and chrome. Sorry about that, shoulda backed it in here, instead of front first."

Nathe stood at his committee-built cookstove, grilling the morning's catch of smallmouth bass from the lake. When I peered over his work, he said, "they tend to be firm this time of year if a little lean. Add a few bacon bits, a little lemon juice, and olive oil, salt and pepper, and there y' are. 'Breakfast fit

for a couple misfits,' as Pop would say. Claude . . . how are y'
feeling about things, son, by this time? Your mom doing all
right out there? Vic treating her right?"

Speaking of roses, I didn't want to paint a picture as
glowing as this violet-hued morning full of promise and high
hopes. But, it seemed inescapable to report otherwise. I secretly
hoped Vic wouldn't look as glossy now and that her memories
of Nathe strolling our way in Baggage Claim would prevail.
That he, cutting a dashing figure, would be haunting her.

However, my mother crowed she was "floating on cloud
nine" and busy "meeting people, rehearsing with this little
combo at the club. Been a couple parties—I met the mayor
of Las Vegas, hon—and just settling in. Vic gave me a nice
'homewarming' gift certificate at one of the shops in town.
Got me several new outfits, accessories. I needed to spruce up,
Claude. Most of what I didn't leave behind in Kentucky was
starting to look dowdy and worn.

"Oh, and guess what? We're going out Saturday to a
benefit and there are supposed to be a bunch of celebrities
there. It's black tie and I'm getting a fitting tomorrow for my
gown. Wow, what do you think of that? I hope they don't ask
me to sing—not quite ready for that crowd. How are things
at school? And Aunt Margy, Grandma Bea? There's so much
going on here, Claude—you'll love it. And this city is great,
not so big you feel overwhelmed. Hope your grades are going
to hold up, dear."

"They will. School's going well. Mrs. McIntyre is having
me sign quite a bit to make sure Tim—that's the deaf kid—
understands the assignments and things. He seems really smart
and takes to stuff easily. Everyone likes him—"

"Well, I am so proud of you. You tell Grandma Ronnie.
She promised she would call you this week just as soon as they
get settled in Arizona. She says the desert is beautiful. You
know, I haven't seen anything country since I got here—it's

been such a whirlwind. Flowers around the condo are pretty and everything is in bloom—you should see—it's fabulous."

"Mom, you know, that Tim, he was wearing that blue jacket that you took to the home? My shoes, too. So he's an orphan—I don't know the full story. Don't think he wants to talk about it yet. But, yeah, I'm helping out quite a bit and showing kids how to sign basic stuff and to speak slowly so he can read their lips—"

"Great. Maybe I can send some things for the home from here. They have a couple fabulous secondhand stores downtown. I took some of my old things in and even picked up a couple nice cocktail dresses I'm going to have someone work over—every girl needs that little black dress for evening wear around here—there's something doing every night. It's nice you're being a friend, Claude. Help him all y' can."

"I do. When I told him some of the girls think he's cute, he said that was a change. He told me: 'Mostly they avoid me or think I am a freak.' I think there are some at the home that tease him some and make fun of the way he has to talk. He has trouble with his speech. Everything's kinda breathy and hollow-sounding and folks might think he's retarded, but I'm supposed to work with the speech therapist some next week and we'll see if we can help—"

"Well, like I said, we're all so proud of you. You all seem so far away, but like I said, the flight was fabulous and so fast—we just seemed to zip along. It won't take us long to fly home if Vic and I decide to get married at Aunt Margy's."

"Okay. Uh, Annie's down in Florida and doing all right, I guess. Bethany and the kids will make the house pretty lively, I expect."

"I 'spect. Help out where you can, son. You have a lot to give. The mayor's girlfriend was telling me about some charity she heads up for girls and I thought I could get involved. They have a benefit later this year and I might sing for it. Gosh, it's been so fabulous to get my vocal chords back in the game—

this combo is really good and once I get on my feet, there are a couple big bands in town who like to have guest artists come in. Working on 'I'll Be Seeing You' and 'Somewhere Over the Rainbow', maybe 'Harbor Lights'—I dunno at this point. One day at a time. The vets and their wives like the older numbers."

"Uh, the team's shaping up. The field looks really good. All the lights are up and they put up some bleachers the other day. Our first game is next week if it doesn't rain, been raining a lot so we've been practicing in the barn and—"

"No rain here. Folks say it's getting dry out in the desert, but they must get their water from somewhere, all these pools and fountains. Everything's watered by these little drippy things and misters. It's so nice to wake up to the sun and then see the sunsets."

"Uh, anyway, Nathe set up these two huge batting cages in the barn—really nifty—and a couple of pitching mounds. I'm going to pitch and Tim, too, as he's a lefty. We use hand signals a lot and he's tuned in to that."

"Well, be careful, I don't like pitching much. Seems like you're too close to the batter and some of those big kids . . . well, just be careful. I think you should wear helmets out in the field too, not just at home plate."

"That would be such a pain, Mom—"

"I wish you still played T-ball, myself. You're growing up, guy. Nothing I can do to stop it."

"Any chance you might get back to see a game? Later on, when we're better?"

"We'll see. It's getting busy around here for me, son. It's a zoo. Vic has so many people under him, meetings, phone calls, plus setting things up for me. If not me, I know your grandparents are coming through when it starts getting too hot in Arizona. Granddad has a place rented on the Finger Lakes somewhere near Watkins Glen where they have that big race and said he'd take you to the races there, rent a boat, fish some. That's not too far from where you are."

"Right, the Little League world series is south of there. I looked on a map—"

"Anyway, I need to git. There's a luncheon today honoring some of Vic's cronies and I am supposed to 'put in an appearance' and that'll be fun."

"Okay. Don't work too hard, will y'? I do a lot of chores around here for Aunt Margy and I know she—"

"But work is what I need, son. I'm starting to thrive on it. After all these years, imagine. Vic says I'm a duck to water. And he's right. I've never felt so alive, so energized."

"That's good, Moms, I'm glad for y'. Oh, and I hit one over the fence the other day. It was just in practice but it sure felt easy. I didn't try to power it out and Mister Mac—"

"That's nice, dear. I hit one myself the other night at the club. I did this pretty hot version of 'Everything's coming up roses' and the emcee said, 'that was a home run, little lady'— the crowd lit up, wow! Claude, I'm in my element. And Vic is so well connected with so many of the right people here and their wives seem nice and including me. I think they respect the Delveccios so much. They're fixtures in the community— supporting the arts and charities an' all. Aren't you happy for your Moms?"

"Yes, that's gr—"

"Well, hon, I really have to get in gear. Vic is very punctual and we agree on that. Just like clockwork. He runs a tight ship, you can tell. Bye now. I'll tell Grandma to be sure and call soon. Bye—love you."

I hung up the phone and left the house, deflated.

*   *   *

The fish were so sizzling hot, spitting and cracking, I thought they might take a notion to burst off the grill for one last leap toward freedom. Nathe plopped them beside a generous mound of spuds and onions and I dug in. It was "fabulous" I told him just like Mom found Las Vegas and her new life.

"Sounds like things are off to a good start out there, anyway. You're not comfortable with it though, Claude . . . something's nagging you about it."

I studied my steaming breakfast and let its vapors climb my way. "I wish she wasn't so giddy about everything. I just think she's cruising for a fall and, darn it, I wish she would take a tumble and come back to earth. Is that wrong of me? Seems like it is and I feel . . . ."

"Guilty?"

"Yessir. Like I want her to fail and to not forget about Dad. And me, of course, but especially Dad. Not fail, just be sensible. About show biz, getting married, getting carried away. Sometimes, my mother doesn't make the best decisions."

Nathe nodded and did that lip pursing thing I was beginning to expect. "Give it some time, son. . . .

"Your mom's off on a rooster hunt and things tend to fall in place once the hunt . . . or the honeymoon's over. Things are usually not as rosy as first thought . . . and what looked grim and unthinkable may not be as bad as predicted. There are silver linings. Like when *Wingspan* was in development and then it failed and we couldn't find backers.

"Well, Pete and I forged a real strong bond then. We became kindred spirits. I tried to help him with his marriages and the death of his wife and he tried to help me with mine. *Wingspan* crashed but Pete and I became strong pillars for each other. I've only two lifelong friends, him and Banks McIntyre really. And there was Blake, of course, in the early going."

"No lady friends? Over the years?"

"Oh, yes. In fact I've been engaged once, nearly twice, since my last divorce. But the one had a career crisis, took to drinking, and one day, I found her with another guy. My latest was a nice girl who deserved better from life. But she came with loads of baggage.

"Her kids were in one mess after another, her ex was a bad-tempered Russian, and her folks were following her around, needing support, someplace to live. Met her at the magazine and she had high hopes I could bail her out, like some life boat. I liked her. But I didn't truly, deeply love her, not like Blake loved Daisy. I felt sorry for her and wanted to rescue her and she wanted rescued. And that's not a great place to start a life together."

"Do you think Mom wants to be rescued by Vic?"

"At this point, I wonder if Vic isn't tired of sorting through the gold diggers and the party girls looking for a red carpet ride. He might . . . *might* see something in your mom he's been looking for and hasn't found until she came along. Claude, there's a 'you date California but you marry Minnesota' thing. Vic might want a sweet, genuine girl from humble circumstances that won't demand much or become high maintenance. Your mother might want rescuing right now, and she's willing to let him run her show and career and their marriage. She wants to start over and Vic's giving her a chance. I could be plumb wrong but that's the way I read it from my viewpoint."

"Do you see her as kind of . . . I dunno, helpless or something? I don't rightly have the words for it."

"Gullible? Vulnerable? Easy prey? Like a quail with Vic being the fox?"

"Yeah—yes sir. I don't want her to get tossed aside when some new woman comes along. Or for her to find out he's no good and she gets herself stuck and can't . . . love him." I felt my throat getting hot, talking about attraction and love. "Or Vic decides she's using him to help her singing and her career. That would be bad. I hope, if they decide to marry, it's for the right reasons, whatever they might be."

"Blake . . . that sentimental dad of yours . . . was so in love with his 'Li'l Daisy', Claude, I could hear the lump in his voice on the phone. Said he couldn't wait until he could get her and you and him settled down and living the quiet life he yearned for. If he hadn't loved his job so strongly and been so darned good at it, it would have been easier for him to quit the army and start over at home, at Shadeland or buy one of the farms nearby. He was that way growing up, devoted, intensely loyal, a true 'man of the clan.'

"He was a Scot to the core, to the hilt of his sword. The army demanded such and he paid their price. And the army rewarded him. In its own way—ribbons and medals, citations, awards—not the way your mom wanted, out of harm's way, not the way that might have been best for you. But such was its way.

"Now, life with Vic will be so totally different, your mom may be in love with the change as much as she might love Vic. The older we get, the more life affects our decisions. It may be true love, more or less, but there are other things entering in by the time we're in our forties or fifties. Money, family, kids, fear, health, complications of all kinds. I could have been married again, a couple of times for sure, but there's always baggage to deal with, hers and mine plus any kids who have a say. Plus, a lot of folks marry two or three times because they don't want to grow old alone. No one wants to repeat their past mistakes. However, we tend to gloss over the doubts."

While Nathe's answer didn't really address my question, his thoughts and memories, and his experience might help me sort things through. So many questions, so much I didn't know about life, men and women, attraction, love, marriage, the works. I felt overwhelmed. And I think Nathe detected such but didn't, or couldn't, offer me the perfect solution right now. At this point. Later perhaps?

I let it settle in, like the breakfast filling my belly. Perhaps I should quit hoping. Not even begin trying to matchmake Nathe and Mom. Just as the machinist said at church Easter Sunday: "You can't force those things," meaning matters of the heart. Whether country boys or city girls—I was beginning to realize, one cannot simply make two people want each other, despite how nicely it might work out for me.

It seemed best to let things take their course, leave the romantic part of life and this puzzle of relationships to those who are directly involved, not those on the sidelines where I stood. And where were Mom and I at this point?

No, I didn't truly want her to fail. Yet, I didn't want her becoming Vic's wife, if . . . if she turned so starry-eyed she dismissed or forgot I now belonged to the Clan Kinkade. Or ignored how my loyalty was spreading its cloak over the Summerses as well.

*   *   *

CHAPTER 27

Load and Flow

"Before Pete left that day," said Nathe, "when we were coming in from the range after our shoot, he told me he'd met someone. She's a widow. Like him."

"So, there's a chance he'll marry again?"

"Maybe. I'd bet on it. He's more careful about things now that he's a minister and such. It's a glass house they live in. The Episcopalians tend to be more tolerant than some denominations on some matters. He and his lady friend are sorting it out."

"Seems like he deserves to be happy, losing his wife an' all. But then, that's Mom's deal too. I want her to be happy even if I have to give her up some day and she changes her name from Kinkade to somethin' else."

I looked at Nathe, hoping he might add something in return, like "but not this soon perhaps" or "not to this particular guy" or "maybe Daisy'll decide to wait, perhaps meet someone else." He was frowning slightly and looking off over the water.

I surveyed the lake as well, its light changing as we spoke. "A while back, Mom asked me if she marries Vic, would I give her away rather than my Granddad C. J. Do you think that's strange? I said I would."

"Well, such would honor your dad, Claude. And you. C'mon down to the lake." Once there, Nathe stripped some line from his fly rod, then cast it with such grace and precision, even I was impressed, though I certainly knew little about throwing a fly line with finesse. How one starts the presentation behind one's shoulder, then jets it, letting it arc over the water, then settle its lure on the surface as gently as thistle down lights on a spider's web. I was watching something close to perfection. Something like an unhittable curve ball. Or, an effortless swing and contact driving the ball to the stands.

"There's been a plot brewing behind your back," he said, watching his fly intently and folding the line into his palm, ready to set the hook should there be a strike. "Marguerite's the leader. Your Grandmother Beatrice. Even Albert Summers is definitely involved. Namely, now that the Kinkades have you in their clutches, they're not going to let you go. You belong here in some way, where your dad was born and raised. I'm a-thinkin' . . . Daisy knows this and will honor such. She knows you come from good stock."

He handed me the bamboo. With a light ripple now on the water, the rod felt like a long and living stem of Reed Canarygrass in my hand. The line, a string plucked from a harp vibrating, singing in harmony with the rod. Nathe slipped his hands over mine, like living gloves they were. "And she knows you will forever be Blake's son as long as the sun sets and rises.

"Just pull the line out and let it fall in wide ovals at your feet. Then point the tip of the rod flat, even with the water . . . hold the line taut—right about here—for just a second, bring the rod back and let the rod load and lift that line *Back* and *Up* and *Over*. Let it lift the line up high and fine, to where the clock says 'two', then bring it forward smoothly without a pause to where the clock says 'ten'. Wrist stiff, elbow close to your side.

"Then draw it back and let it load behind you and then flow ahead . . . let the rod take command of the line . . . load and flow . . . feed a little more line . . . two and ten . . . *Load* and

Flow . . . Load and *F-f-l-l-o-o-w-w* . . . and let it light where you want it to go.

"And you've cast your first fly . . . just as your dad and I did over Summers Run back when we first learned together. . . . Anyone glances your way, Claude, and they know as Daisy knows, that this boy was seeded and rooted by Blake Kinkade."

*   *   *

Before the morning was over, Nathe and I had treated the Town and Country to a wash, wax, and oiling of its wooden surfaces. "Fella who makes this wood replenisher. . . is a small town, one-man shop. He might, *might* make a small fortune with his formula, selling to custom car guys, furniture restorers, woodworkers if he went mass production. If some company didn't steal it from him and drive him out. Bet he's had a dozen offers to sell his secret. People who drive woodies like this one swear by his wood treatment.

"But he prefers to run things himself, advertising by word of mouth, mostly. Craftsmen . . . a dying breed—some think. But I 'spect they're coming back. Or will down the road when we all get tired of mass-produced junk. . . .

"Remember, Claude, it doesn't cost any more to go first class—you just don't go as often." Nathe and I were on opposite sides of the Chrysler, oiling away, the wood absorbing the magic elixir, and me, soaking up the narrative my second cousin and baseball coach was imparting.

"The publishing industry . . . used to crow about 'thinking out of the box', but that's mostly lip service. They want everyone in the box when it comes to the bottom line—don't try anything too . . . unconventional. When my business model succeeded, it blew everyone and their theories away. They didn't think it would work. But I sensed there were thousands of readers who were hungry for just such magazines as ours.

Readers were suspicious after our magazines . . . folded. They wanted us back and didn't want to trust an imitator.

"I could have started them up again, but I was burned out. Fed up. I wanted to go home and be a country gentlemen, like I wrote about in my books. I was done with the corporate world, publishing or film. I wanted to be a loner, recognized for doing something special. Heck, that's the way I lived my life. It usually brought me pleasure.

"Take the guy who built that bamboo fly rod over there. Learned his trade as an apprentice, then began crafting maybe three or four dozen rods a year. . . . When he puts his name on it . . . he wants it to perform well, wants it to be cherished by those who have enjoyed his workmanship and plan to pass it down to their heirs. A bamboo rod, natural as the earth, is still the acme. Fiberglass, carbon try but just don't bring that special pleasure. . . . Rarity is half the appeal. . . . Some craftsman enjoyed building that gun or rod before you got a-hold of it. There's history there, lore . . . love of one's trade and the beauty of crafting something unique, building something few others can match, craftsmanship of the highest order, on the surface or hidden.

"But . . . one can get along with a $50 fishing rod or a $200 shotgun, son. Believe me, you can—don't get the wrong idea. When it comes down to it, it's nice to have and use fine things, the best money can buy, but they're still just trappings, Claude, tools. Something to fish or shoot with, transportation to and fro. Like someone said, 'The best things in life aren't things.'

"Take the Brits. Those that can afford it, buy very pricey double guns for big game, shotguns an' the like for field or competition. Highly engraved pieces of art, but they use 'em. They don't keep them home as safe queens. That's the power of balance in your life, seems to me. Use such, enjoy such, but don't treasure it so much you keep it out of sight or for display only, like the holiday china. Then you end up being owned instead of owning. Be ready to lose it all and be happy.

"Just like this car, Claude. Some of my old classic friends are appalled I'm out here driving it around through the dust and in traffic, parking it on the street . . . hauling groceries and running errands, crashing through fences, slopping around in cow pastures—'Nathe, you're an idiot. A T & C should be hauled to shows and kept under wraps—it's a trailer queen, not a daily driver.' One guy insisted I sell it to him where it would 'live out its days in a proper climate-controlled museum,' Oh *ta-ta,* I had to laugh, 'Heck,' I told him, 'what fun is that? Besides, it's been so modernized, it's no longer authentic.'"

We'd awaited the soaking period the formula prescribed and then began the buffing process along the grain of the maple and mahogany using the special heated paste wax and lamb's wool as Nathe had shown me. The wood seemed to relish it, as if drinking in the aroma from a new baseball. Or savoring a good scratch such as Standing Ovation might enjoy against the trunk of his favorite, accommodating hickory tree. It became a pleasure, watching the wood take its sheen, feeling the silken smoothness left behind by my efforts.

Prior to this morning, I'd never considered furniture much, other than the occasional dusting of my room or if Mom asked me to help her "get this house 'redd up' as your dad says" for guests or Blake's long-awaited homecoming. Odd, one might think, why these few simple, physical moments remain so dear to my heart.

Perhaps for the pleasure derived from watching the results of my elbow grease take shape. Or, most likely, the association of two guys working together, sharing observations of life and how it might be lived.

So vivid were the minutes of that Sunday morning, I am tempted to relate them all, for I remember every exchange we made, every response—his and mine—every pause and reflection. I felt full. Overflowing. Bursting. On the verge of turning points. Arriving at pivotal moments. Experiencing epiphanies. Life to its fullest. The lot.

191

All this energy being unearthed during a lazy sort of day. Even the sun was choosing to snooze a bit behind the haze of a buttermilk sky. The lake became so quiet, it shown like the surface of the car we were polishing. Nathe was extolling, contrasting, waxing philosophically. And I gathered he needed to talk.

About craftsmen and craftsmanship . . . idlers and doers . . . effort and perfection . . . self-assurance as opposed to ego . . . the conduct of compliance . . . teamwork. . . folks he had known, places he'd been. . . . Were the misfits really the ones to be envied? . . . Would the Parsimonious Murphys of every community end up our heroes, locally or across the globe? . . . Would the artist in bamboo finish his life fulfilled?

Would the kitchen table chemist who served those eccentric enough to drive wooden cars, would he complete his turn around the galaxy, satisfied with obscurity, knowing his brand of genius was honored in a very small universe?. . . Would he be remembered? Fondly, like Roberto Clemente? Or with ambivalence, like Ty Cobb? Would one of us Panthers play our way to glory, someday. . . .

We discussed the pleasures from doing common things well. . . . And the benefit of attempting difficult things, like fly fishing or hitting a fast ball, and succeeding just enough to where zest fueled both the challenge and the desire to meet that challenge. . . .

The longitude of achieving significant things, the latitude of modesty and companionship and good will toward all—The Clemente-Cobb of things. *Life*.

*   *   *

By the time we were finished with the Chrysler, rain had become a possibility. I'd taken my turn with the fly rod, practicing my cast, Nathe quietly commenting and encouraging. Any fish in the quadrant of my attention seemed to have left the scene.

192

"Guess all my thrashing and slashing has scared them off," I laughed, a bit humbled by the mysteries of fishing and fly rodding in particular.

"Well . . ." Nathe said gently, "they've likely become bored with us. We were a novelty this morning, something new to talk about down there."

We took up the shotgun and "clay pigeoning," as Uncle Albert called it. Nathe uncased a gun I hadn't seen, though I'd read the note accompanying the Shanahan gift. Here it was in its perfect marriage of wood and metal, a bequest from a motion picture director whose genius failed to nurture his humanity. Even in the lukewarm light of the fading afternoon, the magnificence of the shotgun built by A. H. Fox was stunning.

The mild blue and bronze of the case hardening was overlain with lacey engraving, minutely executed. Its "furniture," fashioned of crotch walnut, displayed shadows and highlights so splayed across the butt the effect became a rainbow fashioned in woodgrain. It shimmered in what light the sun bestowed upon it.

"I always yearned for a Fox when I was your age, Claude. It was a magnificent gift, the kind of gesture you might expect from a wild man, fundamentally a generous man when the mood struck him. Like he said in the note, Roland Shanahan could have been one of the great ones had it not been for his personality. And its flaws. Ranahan Shanahan—some of his detractors tagged him such.

"Poor ol' Shanny," said Nathe, admiring the checkering and the golden quail suspended above the hunter and his dog. "I don't think he ever shot this. He called it a gentlemen's 'piece', what he so wanted to be." He looked at me and shook his head. "Accepted as a gentleman. He was a tyrant and he knew it. I think he brooded about his unlikeability after the shooting was done for the day. Drank heavily at times. Thought people were talking behind his back. Which they likely were. I heard such, a little here and there.

"Being of a suspicious nature, he'd single people out—big name stars, didn't matter—and spend the day picking on them, belittling their interpretation, mocking their delivery, or chastising them for their walk, mannerisms in the scene. The actors called it, 'being in the well' and most of them bore up under it as just part of the job. I thought it was awful and prayed I wouldn't get picked. Tried very hard to not get picked. But it was embarrassing to everyone on the set. Very mean-spirited and needless. Early each morning, the cast would bet on, 'okay, who's going to be in the well today?'" I never entered a bet. The movie business was less than fun, those days."

"Were you ever 'in the well', Nathe?"

"Only once did he pull that on me. I had to catch this wild horse—and it was a real wring tail—no movie horse but straight off the mesa, thrashing about in the corral. Well, the horse wrangler had gotten in a tight the day before and was laid up with a dislocated shoulder, and the stunt guy my size was having no luck with this critter.

"In the scene, I was supposed to wade in and catch this horse and snub him to a post. Shanahan's having a fit, railing at the stunt guy, shouting at the hazer, swearing at the lighting and camera crew. Now ol' Boots Coates had shown me how to throw a loop and snare the horse by the front hooves. By now, Shanahan's screaming, the horse is screaming and nothing's getting done. Said horse is bucking and crashing around the corral, threatening to jump out and becoming a real danger to himself and anyone around.

"So, I step to my mark, throw my loop, and *bingo*, catch him just as I'd been taught and down he goes, *ker-plop*. I run to the snubbing post and take a dally and tighten everything down just as one is supposed to. The whole cast and crew are stunned to silence. Fortunately, the director of photography and his camera guys were rolling and caught it all, beginning to end, enough footage to make the scene.

"But Shanahan wanted more fireworks and dust and such, hooves in the air and so on, so he starts railing on me. I let the horse up and whupped him on the butt with the rope and he starts flying around the corral. I draw my loop, throw it again and down goes said horse. By now, Shanahan is screaming at me—'No, no, you bloody fool kid. Do it like you did in that one *blankety blank* film when you were a such a sweet—*little sweet boy*—not a *blankety blank* snot-nosed adolescent know-it-all. You're supposed to be afraid of him—now do it like you're afraid of that horse.'

"I turn loose of the horse, he gets to his feet and by this time he's winded and I just throw my loop over his head and draw us up to where we can both blow up our noses and I lead him out of the scene. By now, all the big shots and stars are on the set, watching, and it's so quiet, all you hear is the horse heaving and snuffing and the cameras whirring. I pass by Shanahan and tell him, 'That's the problem. I'm not afraid of the horse . . . and he's not afraid of me.'

"Here I am, leading this horse off the set, out of camera range, and that just wasn't done. Behind me, I hear Rolf Admunson—an assistant producer who was an old drinking buddy, ol' World War Two buddy of Shanahan's—tell him, 'Roland, that's the damndest thing I have ever saw. If you don't use that footage, you're a *blankety blank* fool'—only guy around that could talk to Shanahan thataway.

"Then I hear Shanahan . . . 'Cut . . . print it.' And that was the last trouble I ever had from Roland Shanahan from there on out."

"Whoa-aa," I said. "Cool."

"Hmmm. One of the best scenes in the picture, even if I do say so myself." Nathe smiled ever so slightly and loaded the elegant Fox. "It's a 28 gauge. Crafted in the city of Philadelphia, P. A. of good old Pennsy steel, better and stronger than its competition some say. One of the strongest guns on the market back then. Still is, for that matter, guaranteed to not shoot loose. . . . Speaking of craftsman, I had a fella trim just the slimmest wedge off here, where the wrist meets the action.

"He changed the comb and pitch just enough plus he shaved a bit so it shifted the cast of the stock and it fit me perfectly. Dad said it would take a true stockmaker's eye and touch. Turned out, Roland and I were about the same size as I grew older and so, what was fitted to his build, eventually worked for me. With a little finesse here and there. Roland would be pleased.

"But I'm such a fraud, Claude. I wouldn't shoot a bird if it flew up the barrel." Nathe hoisted the gun to his shoulder and sighted down its rib. "But I do like busting clays for certain.

"I was 15 at the time, when I had my run-in with Old Ranahan Shanahan and truth be known, quaking in my boots. A toast to you, gunmaker Ansley H. Fox . . . and Boots Coates, stuntman, horseman of the earth. For being a lasting part of my life. And, to Roland Shanahan, it must be said.

"It's not always your friends, Claude, who prove to be your best teachers."

*   *   *

CHAPTER 28

The Snot-nosed Adolescent

We shot the little Fox twenty-eight until a shower drove us under the shelter. Once there, we gathered our gear, wiped it down, loaded the back seat and trunk, and put the top up.

"What a weekend. It was great." I wanted to voice my appreciation, of course, but also wanted to give expression to something else. As if some sentiment remained, lingering in the sweet air of the lake after the rain. Like the surface of the water, I wanted to say, somehow, I had changed during the day and night we'd spent on its shores. I managed, "I feel different."

"So do I, son. Funny, how that goes. I needed a change of scene for a few hours, needed to get my thoughts together."

"Oh? Hope I didn't keep you from writing stuff down. Guess you mean the big meeting about the land an' such."

"Yes, that too. Oh, stuff on my mind, brewing. Folks. Futures. I'm still on the sunny side of fifty, barely. Now that I'm back where I began, I need to determine more than just what I want to do with my life from now on. Have to decide what *good* I can do in life from here . . . until the end. Meaningful good."

He started the car and we drove out toward the dock while the passing shower pattered its rhythm on the Chrysler's canvas as we looked across the lake. "Look how the light and color shifts, even within the hour. Wonder if the bass like rain, if they're frightened by it or find it soothing. Guess it's part of their life and pattern. Every living thing has patterns. We humans call them habits. Or hobbies. Or hang-ups."

*   *   *

We took a different route homeward. This one, equally back country passing through little corners and crossroads every few miles with names like Shadduck, Drake's Mill, Henry's Hamlet. Henry's Hamlet advertised itself as a bed and breakfast in Olde English script, the hamlet being a cabinet shop and a fine old white house surrounded by ivy and maple. Then came the Borough of Beddington, Slate Creek Stables ("Horses Boarded, Riding and Dressage Lessons"), Fayette Farms, Thornville, Lee Center, Tanners Corner.

"This is kind of the Summers' side of the township, Claude, where my people originated. None left now. Dad owns a little bit here and there, a pretty good woodlot and a Christmas tree plantation. We'll take the road up to Krehbel's Knot. It's paved now. Otherwise, we'd dirty up our shiny car.

"If it clears off, we'll get a nice view. Used to be a lover's lane but there got to be a lot of drinking and vandalism. The township spruced the place up with picnic tables and shelters and such and put out the notice it would be patrolled by Officer Carney. Tidied up that mess in a hurry."

"I'd like to meet this Officer Carney. He must be something to reckon with."

Nathe laughed, "A pugnacious Irishman, for a certainty. You might meet him sometime. He umps baseball here and there in the summer. Knows the game and how to conduct it.

"This area used to be known as Krehbil's Knob, instead of Knot, because of all the rock outcroppings. But over the years, it became corrupted, maybe because the road doubles back on itself four different times or so. Here's the first switchback as we speak." The road became a sinuous thing. Nathe said from the air, it looked like two bowties on top of each other.

198

"Great place for birding. Raptors ride the currents up here. P. M. Murphy used to keep a blind up here—Parsimonious is a renown bird photographer, don't y' know. He's been published in *National Geographic, Audubon.* We used a few of his shots during my magazine stint out West. For me, a touch of home. For him, a little income and acceptance. I think he's still doing such . . . along with his other enterprises."

We pulled into the Overlook and the view was decent if not spectacular. "Sunsets are the best. Good place to mull things over, talk things out with your spouse, girlfriend, your teenager. Marguerite's been up here with Harold, I know. Last week she said she took a detour home one afternoon and spent an hour, resting, letting things settle around her. Guess you heard she's thinking of opening Shadeland as a retreat for ministers."

"Oh? I heard her and Annie talking about a bed and breakfast, but Aunt Margy said she'd have to warm up to the idea of folks traipsing in and out, coming in late, strangers with kids in her house, around those antiques and all."

"Right. She thinks having older guests for a week or two, folks looking to recuperate would be more to her liking." Nathe told me the idea surfaced during Reverend Peter Benedict's afternoon visit and that both he and Nathe were helping with the planning stages. "Looks like it might come to pass. She needs the extra income. And . . . she feels she's been given much and has much to give back."

"Helping ministers might be cool. Guess they need to get away now and then."

"Oh, yes, and recharge. Shed the load for a few days. Even Christ himself needed time away from the crowds and the pressures they brought. Marguerite would be a healing balm. Bethany would be there to help now that Annie's gone."

We drove down off the Knot and passed through a community of Amish farms. Black enclosed buggies on the road, buggies clustered around a farmstead for the Sabbath. Nathe told me he should risk a photograph for the black, white, and green of it. "But I try to respect their privacy. The rule's been that photographs are a no-no, but then, like all rules, it gets itself bent now and then. What's permitted, tolerated, or forbidden depends on the local leadership. Gene Forsythe would love to get a-hold of some of these farms for his horsey clientele. Fat chance of that."

We passed the Village of Gaffiner and around a corner—to my surprise—Summers Corner.

"Just a service station now. Neat enough though. Nice fellow and his family living there, by the name of Burkwalter. Does light repair. Used to be a couple farmsteads here but one burned and the other got moved off. Cousin Faye is the only Summers left who was born over this way. Her family home is Amish now. Dad was born in the house where he lives today. Here are the Holzer family holdings."

We drew abreast of a well-kept if busy-looking farmstead. It lacked the pristine tidiness of the Amish layouts but appeared to be industrious with lots going on: orchards on both sides of the farmstead, greenhouses, large barn at the epicenter, lots of machinery under cover, tractors moving about. Nearest the road, a large stand fashioned to resemble a covered bridge. Signs told us eggs were available 8 a. m. to 7 p. m. weekdays and Saturday. Jams and Jellies. Asparagus & Rhubarb coming. Chard soon. Sorry, no new milk customers until further notice.

"That man makes a living 24 hours of the day. Family operation, everyone pitches in. You'll meet the Holzers. Marguerite partners with them as they can't buy any more ground around here and they've built such a business, they need part of her garden to fill in. They're Mennonites—not as strict as their Amish neighbors."

"Did Aunt Marguerite set that up?"

"Yes, she approached them. Margy wanted a good garden, large enough for canning and such, but she and Annie couldn't manage the workload. Brother Holzer provides the seeds and most of the labor for two-thirds of the crop—and I mean exactly 66 and two-thirds percentage. He's a 'to the penny' man. So's his son and daughter. Isn't that refreshing?

"You'll like working with the Holzers. Always happy, like the Amish. At least on the surface. You'd think they would be a sober bunch. Well, they are about some things, but away from the doctrine and the expectations, they laugh a lot. Amish play baseball and the Mennonites go to the local school and events as they're more worldly."

"Not a bad life maybe."

"No. A bit like stepping back in time. The Amish use horses mostly. And most Mennonites drive cars, though plain ones. Some branches say they must be black, others permit gray or dark blue as long as they're not too flashy, nothing red or pretentious. Some say no chrome wheel covers, no radios."

"Wow. What they must think of this convertible then."

"Oh, indeed. This car would be forbidden, but . . . they like to ride in it, I've found. It's all a matter of balance again. What you treasure and what you put to good use. These folks . . . fish with a willow pole and worms and likely catch more fish than us hoity-toity fly guys. All a matter of taste and your comfort level. There's no accounting for taste. They lean toward the simple side of life. Simple gifts, simple pleasures, pleasure in day-to-day things. And believe me, nothing wrong with that, you'll find some day.

"Blake and I always wanted to date some of the girls but back then, in those days, just seeing 'English' or 'Yankee' boys was generally frowned on. Calling on a young Mennonite lady was not encouraged. Once they found I'd been in the movies, they were quite amused but as one girl told me, 'Oh, you dare not let on. Movies are a vile sin, we think, akin to smoking and drink.' It would take a lot of praying, likely an Act of God Himself to make me even halfway acceptable. But, word was the older Mennonite kids would sneak in the drive-in theater after dark. Blake and I saw a few we knew there."

"Including the girl who said movies were so bad?"

"No," he laughed. "That would have been a hoot. But no one confronted them. Some of our crowd wanted to but Blake nixed it. 'What's the point of embarrassing 'em?' he said. 'Watching Nathe up there is embarrassing enough,' he would laugh. We were watching *Cascade!*, and I was dressed like a foppish dandy with snooty manners until I learned I had to become a timber jack and get my hands dirty. I *was* an embarrassment, for the first twenty minutes or so. You wanted to jump up there and paste me one. But I shaped up once I found I had to work for my supper."

"Hmmm. Wish I'd been around to eavesdrop on you and my dad. Uh, well. . . ."

We crept upon a black buggy trotting along with cherubic faces looking back at us and framed by a little square window. All one could see were a cluster of rosy cheeks, bowl-cut haircuts, and black hats. I waved as we overtook and passed them slowly. Not sure they waved back. The driver was a stern-looking fellow with a beard that jutted from his chin like the prow of a rowboat. He reminded me of Abe Lincoln without the fashionable beaver skin top hat, certainly. Nathe asked me if I had something on my mind.

"Well, yes. That, uh, Shanahan . . . he called you a snot-nosed adolescent know-it-all. Guess he thought you were showing off, maybe?"

"And, I was," Nathe admitted. "I knew these horses were unbroken all right, but they had been around humans. Not very good humans. Rough stockmen—if you want to grace them with that term—who were supposedly "breaking" these horses to ride, once the herd scenes in the film were shot. Hate that term, 'breaking'. Anyway, I watched Old Boots handle rough stock and tried to do as he did that morning. Luckily I pulled it off. I thought I could and if I did, I wanted to see what Shanahan had to say or what he'd do.

"If I'd been fired, I think there would have been a mutiny on the set. Folks were getting edgy, peeved, and some downright short-tempered. It became a troubled film, *Stage to Red Hill.* "The Navajos were grumbling about the pay. The weather turned stormy. The caterer seemed barely up to snuff. I saw my chance and took it. I told myself I was not going to be put in the 'well' unless I really screwed up. Played my trump card 'cause I knew we were too far into the shoot for them to hire another kid on short notice.

"Not that there weren't equally snot-nosed adolescents ready to jump in the role, but it would have been costly with a lot of scenes to re-shoot. We were behind schedule as it was. . . . I weighed the risk and took the chance. Sometimes, one shoots the moon, like when playing pinochle. Go for the big pot. One thing in my favor, I was well-liked by the crew and cast. Shanahan knew such plus he might, *might* have sniffed a rebellion brewing, I think. He was shrewd and knew he would have the studio heads to answer to if cast and crew walked off the set—for even a day."

"Wow. Wisht I'da been there. I guess you called his bluff, then?"

"Yes, that's about the size of it. The guy's nastiness just made you want to stand up to him, let him know you weren't going to be his doormat."

"Did the crew and your other actors feel you were pretty gutsy, I mean, to stand up to him an'such?"

"Well, Virgil Tollinger—character actor—did come up to me and say, 'I wished I'd been you right then.' Of course, had Shanahan blown up and fired me on the spot, well, Virg might have changed his tune, who knows? All in all, it became a memorable moment. Those etch themselves pretty deeply. But I wasn't about to be bullied."

"Will you promise me something?" I asked him. "And do me a favor?"

"Anything I'm able, son."

"If you see any signs I'm becoming a snot-nosed adolescent know-it-all, would you let me know?"

*   *   *

CHAPTER 29

The Cornerstone Homecoming

Or a bully, I added. Nathe assured me there was no danger of me becoming a bully. "Such would run directly across the genetics of Blake Kinkade. He caught anyone bullying and he'd be on the prod in an instant."

Homeward bound, we left Summers Corner and seemed to cross a divide. We'd definitely left the Amish section of the neighborhood. Nathe called what lay before us "the eyesore of the township. You should see this mess from the air, Claude."

The "mess" included dead cars and derelict parts of mysterious machinery scattered behind a tumble down fence of broken boards and a bird's nest of net fencing, strung together with strands of barbed wire so loose and straggly, they resembled a road map. Canadian Thistle grew robust and rampant as did golden rod, morning glory vine, and miniature forests of towering ragweed. Household appliances were banked against a shed whose roof sagged so in the middle it looked like a giant canoe.

"Look . . ." said Nathe, "I remember that porch pulling away from the house when I was back here a few years ago. There it sits today, gapping away, just like when it started."

The porch appeared to be in use yet. For arranged there were pieces of overstuffed furniture, tattered with puffs of stuffing as if tawny cats and dogs were resting on the arms or backs. Apparently—one could only guess—folks found the couch or recliners handy when they paused after supper to watch the sunset or enjoy their surroundings in the evening light.

As we crawled by, a pasture bristling with thistles came into view. The effect was that of a cemetery for there were more appliances scattered about, a graveyard declaring these were the family monuments of Maytag, Hotpoint, Amana, and Tappan, who welcomed their rest, only to find themselves in this low estate. Better to be crushed and reborn as a sparkling new dryer or kitchen range, I thought, than to lie here rusting and violated by the rats one could see scampering about between their metal and plastic condominiums.

"This is the Linch clan—The Linch Mob—Dad calls 'em. They claim they 'recycle' and 'salvage' useful things. Last fall, before I moved home permanently, I met one of the Linches in town, admiring this car. Said he'd been looking for a woodie as a 'project car.'"

"Did he offer to buy yours?" I laughed.

"No, no indeed. Linches look for road kill, abandoned stuff they can drag in here to fix up but then let sit for eight or ten years or longer. I wanted to ask the guy, 'How long do you plan on living?' considering all the project cars they have sitting around. Oh, sure, they're 'going to get at it, right away.' Good intentions, Claude. 'The road to hell is paved with good intentions', someone said. Oughta put a sign up in front of all these places and their project cars—'Good Intentions Motors, Restoration Specialists . . . Eventually. Our motto: We'll get to it one of these days.'

"There are a bunch of kinda rare tractors and trucks in the back but they're getting so far gone, it's likely they'll just keep sinking into the earth. Celtracs, Diamond Ts, Reo trucks, Studebakers, Hart-Parrs, Massey Harris, couple of old Bluebird buses, a Spartan fire truck. I went through them last fall, at the invitation of the Linches."

"Were you looking for something?"

"No, just wanted to be sociable an' such. Try to get on a first-name basis with the Mob. They might become a thorn in everyone's side, given what some want to do with the community, including me who want stricter zoning to clean up eyesores like this.

"Folks that are looking for restorables can find better, more promising stuff elsewhere. And . . . it's certain the Linches will never produce anything worth selling. And they'll just keep adding 'projects' and never finishing a one. Hoping someone will come along and pay them too much for their wrecks. Pathetically the case."

"There's a kid named Jeff Linch in my class."

"Could he be a Panther?"

"I asked and he said no. Said he hadn't played any baseball and would feel stupid. Kind of a quiet sort."

"Hmmmm. A loner. That's who y' worry about, the kids coming out of here. The next generation. You wonder if they'll fall back into the family's way or break clean and make something of themselves. The sins of the fathers—they hang millstones around the necks of their offspring, to apply Biblical truths to the matter.

"Now . . . up here's another lesson. This is a Linch family too. Little more progressive but look at the house. They started to re-side it four years ago when I was back, I recall. Look— same as when I left. Siding's half on. Those windows were salvaged, bootlegged into place and they're not framed in yet. Good place for mice to crawl in and the winds of winter to whistle through."

"Wonder if Jeff Linch lives there. If so, I feel sorry for him."

After "Linchville", Shadeland looked like some English estate or royal gardens with its tree-lined drive, rhododendrons winding their way under the ledgestone wall and mossy springs, the azaleas and begonias following the fence row to the house.

I marveled. *How privileged I am to live here. Why would I ever want to leave?*

Then, I pictured Jeff Linch standing in the weedless driveway, surveying the two stories of stone, the white trimmed facia, the dormers, the shutters, the wrought iron hinges, the colonial-paned widows, the fluted columns, the copper cupolas, the dripping firs, the Boston ivy of it all. Jeff looked my way, his expression so dark and accusing, I shuddered. I don't think Nathe noticed.

*   *   *

Parked in front of the home, backlit by a sliver of sunlight, stood a confident Suburban with its rental trailer hooked behind. I couldn't help but regard it as a rescue vessel, delivering its occupants safely to shore.

Two of said occupants came bursting down the brick steps and stood at attention as we pulled in behind the trailer. They shuffled about, the boy correcting his fidgety younger sister of three years or so. Nathe stepped from the T & C and leaned over the hood, clasping his hands together and looking very much like a graying Greg Peck, another movie pose if I ever saw one.

"Well, home safe and sound. I'm your cousin Nathe and this is another cousin of yours, Claude." Nathe stepped around the front of the car and was met by a somber Wren who dutifully shook his hand, likely as instructed earlier. Wren then approached me as I got out and we did the same. "I'm Wren," he told us gravely.

"And you're six and a half," said Nathe.

Wren looked up at him with an expression of surprise trailed by curiosity. Nathe smiled, folded his arms and pondered it: "I think . . . seems I read such in a book somewhere." The boy stepped back and searched me next, as if asking: And what might you have read or heard about me? I could see his wheels turning and as an afterthought, he waved at his sister behind him. "Uh, this is Samara. She's three."

"This is my grandmother's house," Samara chirped.

"Yes, yes it is, Samara."

"I have two grandmothers. One's old and one's *really* old."

"Yes, indeed. One could say so. Well, good." Nathe knelt in front of the little girl and said: "That makes coming home even more special, to have two grandmothers to greet you." Samara hesitated and then threw her arms around him and gave him what I later decided was an unguarded hug, nothing coaxed about it. To my surprise—and I can see it yet—Nathe held her. . . for the equally unguarded moment sweeping over him.

*   *   *

All in a matter of a minute it seemed, Bethany came tripping down the walk, Uncle Albert putted up beside us on his "go cart," and Gram Bea rounded the corner with the evening's bouquet in the crook of her arm. It seemed a "Cornerstone Homecoming."

Bethany said her greeting committee "got way out of in front of me. They're wired, so glad to be out of the car. Uncle cousin Nathean—is it okay if you're my favorite uncle or cousin or both, sort of, and Uncle Albert, you're my favorite great uncle?" They blended into a threesome on the step.

"Are we related?" asked Wren, weighing his approval of what he was hearing and watching.

"Well, yes, Wren," said Uncle Albert, "but way out on an old limb of the family tree. And by marriage, as the old folks used to say. The old folks used to say, 'well, so-and-so is kind of spiritual uncle or aunt.'"

"Oh, okay. I've heard of those. Mom told us about you guys up here."

"And Claude." Bethany hopped down the steps toward me. "You handsome baseball guy—I'm so anxious for your first game. Heard you're a pitcher." We hugged and I said, "Hi, Beth. Welcome home." She started to weep. "Oh, Claude, you can't imagine how good it is." We walked toward the house arm in arm. "I've been bawling so when the kids were dozing. Once I turned on the wipers," she laughed, "thinking it would help me see the road better—I was so goofy."

The Suburban was guided around to the back and we began trooping in and out of the house with the boxes, kid furniture, and the belongings of a young family. They'd come home, yes. What awaited would unfold in the days ahead. But for now, there was homemade pizza and ice cream in The Homestead Room.

*   *   *

Not until we were well assembled, did any one notice. Nathe said it first—"Pop! Where are the sideburns, guy?" Uncle Albert brushed his cheeks with the back of his hands and grinned. "Finally, I'm getting the attention I deserve around here, all this excitement. Well, since I got these new glasses, I decided a new look was in order."

"Sir, you are an imposter. What have you done with Albert Summers? Shed the sideburns?—they've been your trademark for decades."

"Well, yes, but I decided the other day, I'd tired of looking like Martin Van Buren—he was once president of the United States, Wren—and when I put on these frail pitiful little things, I looked like Ben Franklin. So then, thinks says I, *Albert, you old duckling, it's time for a makeover* and off went the mutton chops. Wish we'd go back to the horn-rimmed frames we used to wear. Now, those were substantial."

"Martin Van Buren was the, umm, the eighth president of the United States," said Wren, who was working around his ice cream. "I think that's right."

"Yes, or thereabouts," said Nathe. We all glanced at each other, knowing looks and cocking of eyebrows all around. It might take us all to keep up with this Wren, the new element in the Kinkade household.

Later, as we were settling the Van Strassels here and there in their rooms, Wren asked me if Nathe was my dad. When I said no, that he was a cousin, he said, "Oh, okay. I thought he was your dad because he calls you 'son'." He heaved the box down on his new bed. "My dad calls me 'boy'. I think 'son' is nicer."

*   *   *

CHAPTER 30

The Panthers' Prayer

Though everyone declared the May evening perfect for baseball, the game began under a cloud. No umpires.

The schedule called for a six o'clock start and as the Panthers were hosting, the missing umpires presented an embarrassment and talk of re-scheduling. Wren hoisted the flag for the pledge of allegiance. Uncle Albert announced the rosters of both the visitors, Chapmann Bread & Bakery, and the Panthers. Our team had taken the field for warm-up and still no one to officiate. The managers huddled and agreed Lawrence Alphonse would don the chest protector and mask and call the balls and strikes.

Fortunately, Nathe,—*mister-have-a-backup-for-the-backup*—had foreseen the possibility such a crisis might arise and invested in extra equipment for the ump. And, from the visitors, a girl who played college softball stepped forward.

"Folks," Uncle Albert announced, "we are graced tonight with the presence of Mary Anne Bucci, who a number of you know as a first-rate softball pitcher and player. Played for the Chapmann Dodgers and most recently for Penn State and she's agreed to umpire the field. I think we're going to have a ball game here in just a few minutes. Thanks to these two young folks for helping us out tonight and to you out there for your patience. Getting underway shortly as soon as Umpire Alphonse cries, 'Play ball!'"

Benjamin "Air Rifle" Andrews took the mound. When I and a couple other Panthers tried to quell his butterflies, he said he would be relieved when it was my or Aaron's turn to pitch. "Be ready out there. I'd rather let them hit it than walk anybody." Ben threw hard but his fastballs could take a notion to sail high and wide.

We Panthers immediately uncorked our nerves and inexperience. In contrast, Chapmann B&B's lineup contained several returning and seasoned players plus they had already played a round of practice games. When the Panthers came to bat in the first inning, we were behind by two runs, thanks to a couple infield errors, a hit batsman, and a double. I caught a fly ball for the last out.

At the plate, we faced "Bob Holland's kid," said Mister Mac. "Speed and control. He's being groomed, don't y' know. He's not out there for fun."

I picked up that tidbit by eavesdropping, sitting next to Nathe and trying my hand at keeping score. Nathe wanted us all to learn the hieroglyphics of the scorecard. At first, we were practicing by just keeping track when the Panthers were at the plate. I liked it.

Lucas Holland didn't fan the lot of us but came close. I whiffed and so did the twins. Ben Andrews finally gave us hope in the fourth, but his liner to the opposite field drifted foul and next pitch, he struck out on a call strike. When we took the field for the top of the fifth, we were behind 7-0. I stood on the mound, foot on the rubber I had helped plant myself when we built our field just a few weeks earlier. I'd been there before at practice but never in a game and I felt . . . exposed.

I was pitching to Carmine Catalino, the most athletic of our three catchers because . . . I was throwing my version of a knuckleball.

Mister Mac, Nathe, and I discussed the wisdom of this. And based on what they saw and what I felt, the three of us decided to try it in the season's early going. Plus we had the input of an outsider, a retired player, pitching coach, and scout for the Cincinnati Reds, Bert Westermann, who said: "Well, he's got good control and his hand's larger than any I've ever seen on a kid his age. I can't say it will work but hey, this league's where y' learn things. Try it. The worse that can happen is it won't work."

There I was, trying to emulate Tom Candiotti, my granddad's favorite pitcher and one of the fabled knuckleballers of recent times. Granddad C. J. told me to "experiment and see. If you're any good with it, you might come up with a career or at least, a scholarship." In addition, Nathe dug up some interviews and training films featuring Hoyt Wilhelm, Phil Niekro as well as Tom Candiotti and I devoured them. The knuckleball became my passion.

As when Ben Andrew's fastball went awry, a knuckleball could give our catchers fits. Fortunately, I seemed to be able to keep mine in the strike zone; I'd been working on this. A lot. The gongs we used for pitching targets were helpful. But the nature of this special pitch—drifting absent-mindedly and not quite sure which route to follow toward the plate—required quick reaction and some sense of the instantly unpredictable. Carmine (we were blessed) was able to read the ball's flight and put the mitt close to where he guessed it might end up. Kevin Wingate and Ryan "Bearcat" Gamoski were not so agile or prophetic.

I warmed up and heard a Chapmann B&B player announce from the dugout: "Ah, he's slow. Kid's got nothing."

As it turned out, I threw seven pitches and got the side retired on two pop-ups and an easy grounder to Jules at short. The B&B manager pulled Holland and we faced a new pitcher. By now, we were over the opening game jitters and our bats woke up.

As I think back on it, I don't think our three-run inning was due entirely to no longer facing the ace of the Chapmann league. We simply got the hang of it. The kid replacing Holland,

"Bud" Morrill, was no slouch and had decent stuff. But we were finally inspired and feeling our oats, enjoying the ring of the bats and encouraged when our teammates made contact and had good "at bats" even if they struck or fouled out. No longer was it 1-2-3.

In the top of the sixth, I gave up one hit. The second batter I faced hit into a double play and their cleanup hitter, a big guy named "Skeet" Cedarholm struck out. The knuckleball seemed to be working.

Chapmann replaced Morrill with a left-handed guy named Bill Wittenburg. But we'd faced Aaron Oarcaster, our lefty, in practice and so with two outs and two on, Wittenburg walked me.

By now, I had learned some from reading the set of his jaw and the squint in his eye. And looking in from first, I could tell Carmine Catalino was not about to become befuddled with a southpaw. Not with the bases loaded. After protecting the plate with four fouls, he drove one to left that scored two runs and put me on third. Then I scored on a past ball and Carmine took second. We were in striking distance for it was now 7-6. Could we possibly humble the vaunted Chapmann B&B?

Then it was over. Ryan drove one back to the pitcher. We all lined up to "high five" each other and return to our dugouts.

Bob Holland had visibly relaxed. How close was that? Lucas . . . suffering an upset from an upstart rookie team such as we were and country kids to boot? From what I had learned thus far in reading faces and expressions, his relief included a generous nod toward the Panthers, praising our composure during our first outing. Holland's hopes, we would later learn, were riding high on son Lucas and his future.

*   *   *

I tread to my bed, "wired" like Samara and Wren when they arrived at Shadeland. Yes, physically tired, showered, and ready to drift deeply.

But our first game kept swirling down the corridors of my mind. Replaying every inning, my plays in the field, the at-bats where I contributed little but walk. I scored, true, but wouldn't it have been cool to have hit one out? For a single even. That Holland kid had some stuff, "no use in talkin'," as Uncle Albert would say.

After staring at the ceiling, I tossed the bed covers aside and got up, then knelt by the east-facing window where the moon was once again full. Had it been two months or more since I last looked upon the grumpy hills so far away? I cracked the windows open. Crickets, now, had replaced the peepers and I wondered where had the little frogs of a few weeks ago moved. The trees had leafed. And were expecting to grow, then bear seeds or nuts in the days ahead. It seemed a fruitful time.

The Panthers too shared that anticipation, I knew. We wanted to be a good team, one to reckon with. We wanted to grow into our capabilities and stretch them as well.

As I look back on our first season of Little League baseball, I ponder what "chemistry" (to use a current expression) brought us together. We had no heritage as our fathers hadn't really played as a team, anyway, on our level. There was no history in our immediate area. Yes, Chapmann, the county seat, had been at Little League since the 1950s. Other towns and communities of the area were on record in one form or another—grown, declined, combined. But Chapmann Little League remained the epicenter with eight teams sponsored by car dealerships, fraternal groups, drugstores. "They got their money and the power," said Jules Alphonse of his interpretation, "but we gots th' heart."

"Yes, indeed, Jules. You said a mouthful. When you play with heart, boys, win or lose, you leave the field with your self respect."

In retrospect, I think my cousin Nathe was one of those who, as a coach, seized the "teachable moment." Here too, a term from a later era but whether he was familiar with the concept or not, Nathe seemed adept. And innovative.

During one of our evening conversations, I'd learned he'd help sponsor and coach a Little League team in Sacramento, but "only for a few games. That was the month I got fired—when the nephew needed my job. Our team was nicknamed the 'yogurts' because the manager had the boys doing yoga during practice and pre-game. Anyway, the experience never left me and I decided I'd try again . . . when I wasn't trying to find a job or make a living."

Games were usually scheduled for a Tuesday and Friday. Practices were Wednesday morning and Saturdays, all day, if there wasn't a game scheduled. Nathe also liked separate practices devoted to just the infield, outfield, and pitchers and catchers.

We liked the individual attention, though it meant a commitment for both player and parent. Nathe arranged the transportation, often in the T&C with the top down and a treat for those needing a ride. Then, there'd be lunch at The Shack or sandwiches on the porch at Summers Run Farm or out in its big old barn.

The barn, as mentioned, had been converted into an indoor practice area when the weather was inclement. Two batting cages and two pitchers mounds were in place and saw frequent use even when the sun shone. We'd rotate, some Panthers on the field, others up in the cages. While things were never routine with Nathe, we were never in the dark as to the meaning of the workouts and their goals.

Bert Westermann often showed up to help us pitchers. There were six of us now. "Air Rifle" Andrews was our ace with "Scoop" Oarcaster our southpaw. I came in when there was a double play situation and threw the knuckler. Trent Smythe was starting to get the feel of the mound and Mister Mac encouraged "Lute" Ludlow, our left fielder, to try his hand . "Backup for the backups," said Nathe, "That's why the Japanese do well at Williamsport—deep pitching staff."

Tim Hathaway became our most interesting pitcher-player. I knew a couple parents looked askance at a deaf player, afraid he'd get hurt, get someone hurt or worse, cost us a game or games. I eavesdropped. I heard a little grumbling.

But both Nathe and Mister Mac liked the idea of another leftie on the mound and between the three of us—Mac, Bert Westermann, and myself as signer and lip reading provider, Tim caught on and caught up with idea. In his first appearance, he gave a good account of himself. Mister Mac found Tim amusing. "He starts his delivery out there like a wet dishrag," he told Nathe and me. "That's why he's foolin' 'em—they can't see his release point."

Tim, being slightly built, could not put much punch behind a blistering heater. Sportswriter Ned Farren from the *Chapmann Tribune* gave the Panthers a full-page write up and called Tim, a "diminutive junkballer," for that's what he threw largely, a sinker and then a looping curve that he could break inside or out. Tim and I both were working on our fastballs, ringing the gongs. We agreed we might need the heater in our mix.

Thinking back on those days, the hours and sessions we spent together as Panthers seemed to implant a welding effect. There arose a kind of organic symbiosis where we began melding into an entity. Call it more than a team. Call it more than the confidence gained.

Call it some term more acceptable than pride. When the Panthers started winning, Nathe and Mister Mac cautioned us: "Now don't go swelling up like a poisoned pup, thinking how good y' are," said Mac, "or I'll come out there and slap y' silly." Whenever we were threatened with being "slapped silly," we'd look for the giveaway smirk. It never failed to appear. Away from our coaches, we began using the term ourselves, threatening each other with getting slapped silly for some infraction or violation of boyhood codes.

During and through it all, there seemed to bubble a kind of chemical process, as if all the surgings of growing toward manhood had united us, simmering, knowing we hadn't yet left kiddish things behind. Nevertheless, we had all opened the door and were peering toward the vast realm of teen age and adulthood. The Panthers were becoming bigger boys united around a game, yes.

But like the budding leaves in the silvery moonlight, we'd only begun to realize we were basking in a time we'd never know again. A pause, and then these games and our time together would come to an end. A time, when once gone, would be gone forever, never to fill our hearts as it would in the weeks and months ahead.

"For when this has ended, boys, and your time on this field we built together is over," cautioned Nathe, "it's over. Cherish each and every moment here. They shall never return."

Call it awareness. Call it a shedding the cocoon of selfishness and the insulation of childhood. Call it standing on the remnants of where we'd been, sheltered and centered on our selves.

For whatever was growing among us as we developed the skills we needed to play this game, we knew another element climbed deep within. One could simply call it youthful camaraderie but it seemed more, looking back as I do now. It seemed more than some frivolous parade, a series of escapades on our way through being pals, chums, friends toward the road to manhood.

Call it veiled affection and one we boys wouldn't dare express. Call it being humane. Call it learning acceptance, decency, tolerance, respect, forgiveness. Call it hoping the best would happen for Tim, the deaf Panther from the Fountain House Home; for Aaron who'd lost his father just when the dad could now applaud the son; for Trent Smythe whose life at home seemed grim and joyless; for Kevin Wingate who bounced about in almost comic chaos and uncertainty. Call it concern for Jeff Linch, not a Panther, but a kid my age growing older and aware he was surrounded by extremes and imbalance. Call it learning the importance of good will.

Once, I'd overhead Nathe quote a line from a film, "we are spiritual beings on an earthly journey." I decided then that good will and empathy for all those with whom we travel on the road, such seemed best for the long term. Not the shortest or the most comfortable of journeys, but the route of good will held the promise we'd all arrive at our destination with the fewest scars or regrets.

Boys who play baseball together learn more than just mechanics and teamwork.

*   *   *

The play-by-play of my first evening on our new field floated down to where it would be swept up and stored somewhere. Overshadowing the events of those hours now past, Nathe's prayer remained. It framed this game and the season for us all, I hoped. My teammates and I hadn't the language or sophistication to express our reaction. I hoped he sensed mine. For when he prayed as we were about to take the field we had built, I felt something sweep over me. And within the range of my brief experience, I knew we had accomplished something worthwhile here and, regardless of the outcome of the contest before us, we would accomplish more to come.

When Nathe had us huddle, take a knee on the Summers lawn, his mellow baritone said: "These young men—and we're thankful for each one—have devoted their minds and skills to being the best they can be at this hour. They support their teammates and they play this game with daring and honesty. We know you favor the stirrings of the human spirit when it tries to do its best. We like to think it pleasures you and we look forward to bringing honor to such and each other on this day. Amen."

"And thank you, Lord, for this ball field what Mr. Nathe and Mister Mac gave us. Amen," added Jules.

"And Mr. Alphonse and Uncle Albert who helped," I coughed. And Moms, Aunt Margy, Mrs. "Mac", and Gram Bea I added silently. I needed to voice something as I felt the team looked to me for leadership, close as I was to Nathe and Mister Mac. I tried to sign most of it for Tim, or repeat for lip reading. He nodded, cocked his head, and grew very thoughtful as we left the lawn and walked onto our field, home of the Panthers.

I stood and opened the windows wider. The ancient moonlit hills were still thick with trees, likely rustling in a breeze wending its way up the lane and sweeping the curtains into the room. I crawled back into my bed, feeling blessed.

*   *   *

CHAPTER 31

The Four Horsemen of the Outfield

Nathe and I paid a call on the Alphonse home the morning after the game. "I want to thank Lydia and the girls for singing the National Anthem—didn't get a chance last night," he said.

"Mrs. Alphonse gave y' the chills. The guitars were great too." Lydia Alphonse had been singing in a trio with the Bradshaw girls who supported her contralto solos with their twin guitars. I appreciated the music, but I also found the Chapmann team standing along the foul line distracting. *Which one of those guys could hit a home run tonight?*

"Aunt Margy says this trio they've got going now is the rage, singing everywhere. Weddings, receptions, at the nursing home an' the like. Going to be at the county fair this year. She's booked them for 'An Evening at Shadeland.'"

"I heard, indeed," said Nathe as we pulled into Griffin Hollow and the shady drive of the Alphonse home. "Maybe your mother can team up with them sometime. Marguerite wants to have at least three 'Evenings' this summer, maybe into the fall sometime. Did y'know, Claude, I heard your mom sing 'Over the Rainbow' once?"

"Oh? Not in person, I guess."

"Nope. Marguerite had a cassette from some event down there in Kentucky. Very nice. An a cappella performance. Stunning even on a so-so tape." I had not thought of my mother singing at Shadeland someday. I'm sure Moms would take to the idea.

The Kinkades honored music. My Aunt Marguerite arranged little recitals for students from the college and performances on the grounds or in the main living room of Shadeland. She told me, "There's some talent in this neck of the woods." Ticket prices were nominal, just enough to cover the buffet and pay the musicians decently. Aunt Margy herself was an accomplished flautist and had formed "Fair the Winds," a woodwind quartet. "Occasionally, we're a quintet if we can find a pianist or french horn player. Depends on the piece."

"An Evening at Shadeland" was well received I'd been told. Folks from the college, neighbors, and summer visitors enjoyed not only the music but the grounds, what was blooming presently, the change of seasons come fall, the sunsets through the trees.

*   *   *

The twins came hopping off the Alphonse porch as we uncoiled ourselves from the car. "Hope we can pop in unannounced," Nathe asked of them.

"Sure you'uns can," Jules assured us. "Everyone's home on account of we got maintenance chores today. Trucks need servicing an' th' like. You are welcome."

"Yes, come to the porch," called Mrs. Alphonse. "I've got coffee time ready. Iced tea, being it's nearly summer. Or lemonade." Mrs. A. graciously accepted Nathe's gratitude for her rendition of "The Star Spangled Banner."

"The Bradshaw girls and I are finally getting together. They want to branch out from bluegrass and we're exploring more folk, gospel, an' such like together. They're so much fun to work with and they are musicians, even if they're self taught."

"You'uns should hear Mama do hymns. There's not a note she can't hit, high, low, and everythin' in between."

"Oh, my," Lydia laughed as we boys huddled over a box of baseball cards. "Jules, our chatterbox. I hope, Nathean, he doesn't wear you and the team out."

"Every team needs an emotional center and mouthpiece," said Nathe. "He sums up the matter every time. That boy, I'm a-thinking, will make a fine lawyer some day. Unless, Jules," he called to him, "you decide to play for the Pirates, that is."

"Right now, it's the Pirates for me. Gus is going to play for the Indians. We'll meet in the World Series."

"How twins can be so different. Now, we have to drag everything out of August, wouldn't y' know."

Mid-morning and the air remained cool under the maples. Lawrence and "Papa" James joined us, brushing off road dust and truck grime and proclaiming how uncivilized they must look. Nathe again thanked James for liming the field, "and the job behind the plate, Lawrence, why you looked like a veteran. It's hoped we won't suffer that embarrassment twice. I talked to the league president earlier this morning, and he explained there was a mix-up and some of it's due to being short-handed."

"Well, I truly did enjoy it, Mister Nathe. Surprised me how much. I'm reconsidering the umpire business as we speak."

"That's right," James said, "Lawrence and the rest of us have been puzzling over how managing th' team is going to work out. He's going to go back to school for a spell, part-time, and I've got this contract with th' township that's going to test us all while th' weather holds. I don't know."

"Yes, I think it might be such that I'll need to relinquish the management, maybe just umpire when I can. Seems like Mister Mac and you are doing all the work anyway with the boys—I can't get free, things as they are and what's coming up."

"Well, hey," said Nathe. "You might be just the ticket if the league's needing more umps. Banks and I can handle it."

"You know, I have been gaining knowledge. I knew the rules but not some of the fine points and I wouldn't mind being an expert on Little League. Might be some opportunity there. I kinda like being. . . ."

"Authoritative." Nathe supplied the right term and Lawrence blessed us all with that winning grin.

"Yes, exactly, that's why I've been studying the rules assiduously."

"Well, indeed, and from my perspective, Lawrence, you're a natural. Plus it appears you study the dictionary as well. One doesn't hear the word 'assiduously' very often."

Lawrence laughed and told us he tries to add a word to his list daily and to use that word until it becomes second nature and familiar.

"Furthermore, Lawrence, you're a diplomat. Reminds me of a director I worked with once on a *Gunsmoke* appearance. He was very respectful, called everyone mister or miss, but was very explicit as to the overall effect he wanted. He allowed us to suggest the details and how to plan the walk through. Good kind to work for. You understood 'im and you wanted to please the guy."

"That's fascinating, yessir."

"Even big name actors will take clear directions because if the picture flops, they want the director to take the blame. Stars just want to make sure their lighting's right and they like the dialogue so they look good up there on the screen. Actors respect a director who doesn't waffle. Same with managers and coaches—they'll respect the ump who knows his stuff and can back it up."

"Yes, I can understand, take command, run the game."

"Right. Whatever you decide, Lawrence, will work for us." Nathe stood to leave. "Mac and I both like your confidence behind the plate. You can run the show out there. Just be thinking how to handle some of the parents after the game. That's what I do," he laughed.

"Well, thank you, sir. That is flattering. And good advice."

"There's just one thing," said Jules. "Don't you think that one call strike on me was just a tiny bit wide." Jules raised his thumb and index finger to illustrate the margin.

Lawrence squeezed his brother's digits tighter. "Umm, could have been, perhaps, but just a little less than tiny," said Lawrence. We were blessed once again with the smile. It wasn't fawning, just assuredly diplomatic backed by the clear message "there'd be no point in arguing the call, sir."

*   *   *

Nathe and I crossed the road to thank the Bradshaw sisters, but they and Mr. Bradshaw were gone for the day, it appeared. Jules and Gus met us at the car where we had a discussion of practices and drills.

"Mr. Nathe . . . will we be doing some more of that home run derby drill?" asked Jules. "That is the coolest thing. I gotta catch Gus. He's three points ahead of me."

"And I think Gus is our team leader so far."

Recently, Nathe introduced us to a version of "move up" where everyone got a chance to swing at softly pitched balls such as one might encounter in a home run derby.

But we couldn't drive anything deep. There were flags and a spray-painted line to observe. Hit a fly beyond those boundaries and one forfeited an at-bat. We each had three at-bats in a round. Anyone placing his hits beyond the reach of the fielders, in or out, scored a point, minding, of course, the orange line drawn about two-thirds of the distance to the outfield fence.

For us, it became dynamite practice instilling good batting technique—keeping our heads down, following the pitch, and watching the ball hit the bat. As solid fundamentals started taking shape, we began, later in the season, to place our hits with some predictability. As in, pulling the ball or hitting to the opposite field.

For the infielders, it could become fast-paced enough, they were in constant motion. For us outfielders, it taught a lot about ball angle, judging height and trajectory, and throwing to our respective cutoff men with accuracy and quick-out-of-the glove recovery. Plus the importance of backing up our infield. Of course, it was always a kick to scoop up a shoestring catch.

My Grandmother Bea, Samara, and Wren would watch the Panthers' version of home run derby and marvel. "You look like a bunch of ants out there, everyone scurrying about," said Gram Bea. "I wonder if it's something like cricket, that drill of Nathe's. We'll have to ask your Cousin Faye. She's lived in England most of her life."

Aunt Marguerite had to laugh. "Yes, she's more Brit than Pennsylvanian by now, but she wrote once: 'Just when I think I grasp the basics of this thing called cricket, I go to a match and find I'm as befuddled as when I began. I'm glad there's baseball. Now there's something that's forthright and logical. Nonetheless, I will make some changes when I assume the position of Commissioner of Baseball, rest assured.'

"You will meet Cousin Fanylla Summers Tattersall some day soon, Clauders. Be forewarned. We'll school you all we can."

"Oh, Claude, don't be alarmed. We all dearly love her but she is on stage all the time, be aware. A career actress since the age of five or younger, I was told. She's responsible for Nathe's career in film, you know."

"Oh?" I didn't.

"Yes, and she's a very distant cousin related by the most roundabout of connections. The family tree is so frail by that point it's just a little twig. Yes, Cousin Faye put Nathe in a play at Chautauqua at the age of seven and that was it. He loved it, the audience loved him, and so did a movie director. The one who cast him in *Wagon Train to Sunrise*."

*　　*　　*

227

Practice after our game included javelin drill for us outfielders; more tennis ball toss teaching us to turn away from a pitch heading for our nose; and skull sessions with Nathe's big magnetic boards depicting infield and outfield positioning and where to throw the ball in this situation or that.

We'd called on the Murfitt woodworkers to build us several down-sized javelins from ash, and then Nathe recruited a high school track star to teach us technique. Nathe's theory: it would strengthen our arms, shoulder, hips and back giving us power when throwing from the left and right corners of the outfield especially. He painted a column of targets on the lawn for us to hit. Armed as Roman Lancers we were, and Nathe labeled us the Four Horseman of the Outfield: Luther, Tim, Trent, and myself.

The name stuck, for we swore an oath: "We Are the Gods of Left, Center, and Right. No Baseballs Shall Ever Pass Through Our Domain," we intoned in our most ominous and thunderous baritones. Tim couldn't hear our declaration but joined in when I signed. He had a natural laugh for never having heard one.

*   *   *

I didn't see him at first. The car parked behind the house should have been a clue, but then vehicles "to-ing and fro-ing" were common at Shadeland. I'd been told "to-ing and fro-ing" was coined by Cousin Faye. She also called automobiles of any type or size, "machines."

This "machine" said rental on the bumper. Then I saw the big hat behind some shrubbery, an expensive silver belly matching the color of the car. I stumbled in on Bryan Van Strassel and Beth, likely having a life-changing discussion. We shook hands. He dressed the part. Successful Agri-businessman of the Future. Speaking of domains, money and power seemed written all over him. Boots, buckle, and bluster. A confidence derived from having more than enough and enough to want even more. I excused myself, grateful for the phone call. "It's your mother, Claude," said Gram.

"Claude, hon, this is Moms. Guess what happened last night? At the fanciest supper club in town?"

"Uh, you were asked to go up and sing with the band."

"I was asked to become Mrs. Vic Delveccio, babe. I'm engaged!"

*   *   *

CHAPTER 32

The Short Game

Every year, marriage ceremonies were conducted on the grounds of Shadeland. I had hoped my mother would plan hers in what the Kinkades called the Front Room during the Chrstmas holidays with boughs of evergreen tied in red or gold ribbons. Or outside along the Weeping Wall where the swallows sallied forth, swooping over the brook that fed into Summers Run. Perhaps in autumn, when the vines of the Wall turn crimson and golden maple leaves float on the frosty water of the springs.

Or on the patio. Perhaps she'd choose under the colonnade that joined the main home to the old carriage house. However, at this point, it appeared the setting would be Las Vegas where the Delveccios could invite the family's network of business associates and its hundreds of friends. I'd likely be saying "I do" when asked "who gives this woman to married?" somewhere amidst the palm trees of Las Vegas. I hoped it would be in church rather than the fanciest supper club in town. Mom assured me the Delveccios were devout.

Beth and Bryan had been married, I understood, in a church. Aunt Marguerite told me her daughter wept some on her wedding day. "She confided a few years latcr . . . it was because she knew she'd made a mistake. But it's easy for a young girl's head to get turned by all that wealth and family position. . . . I notice . . . Bryan has taken on more of his father's personality."

"Oh? Like how?"

"The Van Strassel self-importance. It's easy for a young man's head to get turned when flattered and courted by senators and the governor. He was under stress, assuredly, and uncomfortable here. That's when folks lash out. How did he strike you, Clauders?"

"Well . . . when I first met him, I felt . . . kind of inferior. Never felt such before like I was being. . . ."

"Dismissed?"

"Yes'm. Like I was an old dog who wandered in. Then he asked, 'Ya'll another cousin who hides out in all this old woodwork around here?'"

"Mmmm." Aunt Margy nodded her understanding.

"Then Beth explained there aren't that many cousins really and why I was here and when she said 'Gulf War', he looked kinda sheepish bein' rude."

"Good."

"Then, this morning—it was the strangest thing."

"How so, son?"

"He was about to get in the car and he sent Wren to find me. Then, he sent the kids off and acted like he couldn't quite leave 'em behind. Watched them for a long time until they ran out of sight. Then he shook my hand and says to me, 'Sorry if I seemed abrupt last night. Been a bur under my saddle these days.'

"And I said it was fine and for him to have a good trip home. And then he said, 'Yeah, goin' home, such as it is.' And he looked around some and asked me: 'Will ya'll be around here for some time? I mean, bein' Blake's son an' all, maybe living here for a few years till you go off to college?' I said there was a good chance of it."

"Then he said something about this place growing on a person—'all this old rock and ivy and maple trees. Not much of this greenery down in Texas.' Then he said something like, 'Sorry about your dad an' all. Heard he was a good man. Too bad him and my old man never met—he mighta learned some things.' And I didn't quite get if he met my dad or his—about learning things."

"Hmmm. . . . Interesting, that. I'll wager the father has some ringers with his sons, all those acres and business to oversee, not to mention their love of money. Beth says Granddad Van Strassel calls Wren and Samara, 'Bethany's kids.' That tells y' something. So, then he drove off?"

"Not really. He told me to not screw up what I had here and then he kinda got choked up I think and took a deep breath. He said I seemed like a good sort and that he was sorry to have to ask this, but would I look after his children. 'Whatever happens,' he said, 'they're my children too.'"

"I said I would. That I'd be honored to."

"Clauders . . . Good for you."

"Then he threw his hat in the back and jumped in the car and didn't look my way again or say another word. Left like he was late for something."

"Yes, poor kid, him. It's a heartbreak all around. For me too. You want your flesh and blood to be happy with their mate, regardless of what you think of him or his family." Aunt Marguerite then fitted her flute back in its velvet case for she'd been practicing much of the morning.

"It's too bad he can't break away from down there, cut the cord, and find something up here. Still, the marriage . . . seems shot at this point." Shaking her head, she closed the lid, snapped the latch, and looked up at me. "Her kids need their father, but Beth's not going back to Texas. I know my daughter and I know the set of her jaw."

*   *   *

Being charged with keeping a watchful eye on Wren and Samara sobered me. I'd never had so much as a pet and now here a responsibility clearly more weighty than my oath as one of the Four Horseman of the Outfield. That both Wren and Samara were explorers seemed evident to all. Rules had already been laid down about different hazards and the boundaries.

I predicted Samara would not likely climb up the barn roof to see the copper rooster there, but I couldn't put it past Wren. Of him, Bethany told us: "There was not a rock or a bug in Texas, I swear, that he didn't turn over or have some question for me. I've become an amateur entomologist and geologist."

* * *

When Aunt Marguerite asked me my thoughts of Mom's engagement, I told her of both my surprise and my scuttled hopes of matchmaking my mother and Cousin Nathe.

She looked at me with a measure of regret and empathy. "Perhaps I shouldn't say this, Claude, but there are no secrets in this family. You are not the only one around here who nurtured the idea of Nathe and Daisy."

She leaned back in the wicker rocker, and it squawked like the night I first heard the chorus of a million Pennsylvania peepers. "As the song says, 'Wouldn't it be loverly?'

"But . . . we all just want your mom to be happy with Vic. Lord knows she deserves it. We keep an old war bond poster in the attic. It says: 'Those who stay at home serve as well.' I'm glad I didn't lose my husband to war. And I don't think there's another woman up there in Connecticut. He's married to his career, like Brother Blake. Tell Daisy of our deepest love and best wishes, won't you, dear? I'll drop her a note today."

"Yes, ma'am. That means a lot. She might be back for a game, if we make it into the playoffs. I'll talk her into singing a number for a Shadeland Evening, all right?"

"Now that would be loverly."

* * *

233

Our next practice drilled us on bunting and our next game we put such into practice. By now, Tim Hathaway had become relaxed with all of us. Especially when our coaches tapped him to pitch. He reveled. Plus his mischievous side came to light.

With the first bunt he laid down that morning, he burned his way to third instead of first. His second bunt strolled along the first base line wavering between fair and foul. Our fielders were watching it shade foul, but Tim scooped up the ball himself and threw to Gus covering first, putting himself out, then rolling on the ground, laughing. We all joined in, Mister Mac and Nathe, no exception.

Mac scowled at Nathe and said they'd both violated the first rule of coaching. "Never let 'em see you laugh, Kiddo. Don't even crack a smile even if you're dying to." Nathe grinned and then he laughed out loud. "Seems to me, Banks, you laughed first."

*   *   *

We traveled into Chapmann for our second game and our first at The Chapmann Youth Sports Complex. There were two tennis courts, a playground, and four diamonds arranged around a snack bar hub. A girl's softball game was in progress as we arrived with Mary Anne Bucci on the mound, we noticed.

We also noticed Bob Holland was engaged in a spirited discussion with the Chapmann Bread and Bakery manager and coach. Much hand gesturing and head shaking on the part of Holland while the coaches were looking on somberly and trying to offer a justification why Lucas Holland didn't pitch in their game.

"Dollars to doughnuts—no pun intended—" Mister Mac growled around his toothpick, "Bob's taking them to task for not letting Lucas shut down the rally. If I know Bob." The Eagles—reputed to have some of the best sluggers in the Chapmann section—scored seven runs in the fifth, according to the scoreboard, and beat Holland's team. Spoiled the dream of a perfect season for Chapmann Bread and Bakery.

We faced a seasoned team sponsored by Worthe Drugstore. Mister Mac had scouted the team earlier and right out of the box, we began putting bunts down the third base side.

"Their third baseman is a southpaw. So's the pitcher we're facing. He's decent in the control department but slow getting off the mound and at that clumsy stage. Wears a size 12 shoe, I'm bettin' on it." Now, Mac's theory being, a bunt laid down where only the third basemen or a left-handed pitcher had the best shot at fielding presented a problem for Worthe.

Unlike a right hander, a leftie needed to rotate most of his body to get himself set for his throw to first. This consumed enough precious time, a runner might beat it out unless the peg was perfect and fast enough to make up for the extra motion. "Kids rush their throw, it goes sailing into right field, and the batter might get to second if he's speedy. Or, someone comes home."

Two good bunts and a wild throw to first base and we had men on second and third. No outs. Gus singled and a run scored. Runners on first and third. Our clean-up batter was Kevin Wingate who had a home run written all over him, if unproven at this stage. The conventional wisdom said Kevin would be signaled to hit away, drive one to the outfield at least. But to the surprise of everyone, especially Worthe Drug, Kevin laid a beautiful drag bunt down the first base line.

Confusion reigned. Hesitation spiked. Gus took second and our speedster Tim Hathaway scored. Two runs in and one out. I then bunted down between the mound and first. Out by a step but Gus took third. Next, a wild pitch and Gus scored. Three to zero and two out. Mac called for a bunt again, unheard of, but he'd warned us he wanted everyone to bunt at least once in this game, in a real-life situation. This time the catcher scooped it and fired to first in time, then kicking his facemask in obvious anger.

Mister Mac told Nathe: "The short game gave us a jump, now we'll see what they can do with our leftie." Aaron Oarcaster pitched for five innings. I came in for a double play situation in the sixth, got it, and we took home our first victory over a Chapmann team, 6-3.

I was riding with Nathe to The Shack for a team party and pizza supper but he was delayed. Bob Holland had collared him. I later learned Holland wanted to yank Lucas from the Bread and Bakery team and place him on ours. "After all," Holland was reputed to have said: "We live in the township. And you guys are short a player or two, I heard."

* * *

Then, two mornings after our game in Chapmann—like Gram Bea and my father's trip up the barn to see the rooster—I experienced "the fright of my life."

Nathe, Tim, and I were riding home with Aunt Marguerite in the Oldsmobile. As we pulled into Shadeland, we saw a figure loping up the drive.

"Dear Lord, what now?" said Aunt Margy and sped up. We pulled abreast of P. M. Murphy in a state.

"It's the little one!" he shouted and waved us on. "She's in the pasture with the bull!"

* * *

CHAPTER 33

A Bushel and A Peck

Dread. That steel ball lodged in one's stomach. I remember it from dealing with our times of waiting and wondering. I recall telling my mother, "Moms, Dad could be just around the corner coming up the walk any minute now." How we jumped when the phone rang.

How my mother's voice and expression would sag in relief when the caller was Grandmother Ronnie or Marguerite from "P. A." Then, how she would turn her face to the ceiling after the pleasantries from long distance were over, and let the disappointment cloud her features one more time. No, it wasn't her Blake on the line.

No word yet, no news, nothing to report. Classified. We'll be in touch. Yes, we know, Mrs. Kinkade. Thank you for calling. I would listen in. Like Nathe's grandmother listening in on "the Bell", I became a shameless eavesdropper. In case of bad news, I didn't want Mom to repeat it to me. I wanted to hear anything dreadful first hand.

Now we spilled out of the Olds, its alarm bell ringing, *Door Ajar, Door Ajar, Door Ajar.* Now we rushed to the fence and scrambled through the thick grass, tall enough to snare our ankles and cause us to stumble. Now I signed "bull" to Tim as he ran aside me. Then "little girl" as we searched the meadow and ran looking for Standing Ovation, yelling, hoping. Now running with the steel ball rolling and punching its way, caroming around my innards, hard enough to be all the more painful.

Then we heard a woman's voice and stopped as a bunch. *"I love you a bushel and peck, a bushel and a peck and a hug around the neck. . . ."* Here came Gram Bea, with a smiling Samara bouncing away, riding piggyback, smiling and hugging indeed. *"A hug around the neck and a barrel and a heap."* Gram angled her way up the slope toward us. *"A barrel and a heap and I'm talking in my sleep. Y' bet yer pretty neck I do.'"* She deposited her great-granddaughter on the ground at our feet and straightened her blouse, smiling as brightly as the little girl beside her. By now, P. M. Murphy, Bethany, and Wren had arrived on our scene.

Aunt Marguerite sank to the grass and shook her head. Bethany gathered up Samara and Wren reproached his little sister. Gram explained Samara wanted to feed flowers to the bull.

"Oh," Bethany gasped, "the Ferdinand book."

"Yes, she'd picked a nice big bouquet and held it right under his nose. He was still resting in the shade and didn't see any need for getting up for such a little mite—"

"'Mara!' scolded Wren. "You coulda got yourself killed!"

"So, I eased my way to within a few feet. He wrapped his tongue around the flowers, kindly, and then I coaxed her to come to me."

"He's black an' he's just like Fer'nand and he was hungry and he likes flowers."

"Well, dear, he's not really hungry. He has plenty to eat up here. See all this grass?"

"Mahter, you're squeezing me too much. But he liked the flowers I gave him."

Bethany let her daughter slide to the ground and had a moment, shuddering and wiping her eyes. Then she knelt and explained the bull in the book was make-believe.

"Honey, it's best you not bother this bull any more. He's okay. He doesn't need too many of these flowers. They might make him sick, y' see. Like ice cream."

"Yes," said Marguerite. "Your mother's right, sweetheart. It's best you not go near Mr. Logan's bull—"

"Remember seein' bulls on television, 'Mar? It doesn't matter if you're a cowboy or a clown, they'll throw y' up in the air and then stomp you flat. Geez."

Hand in hand or arm in arm for some of us, we turned and worked our way back across the meadow to the fence and the impatient Oldsmobile, insisting someone tend to these open doors and this infernal chiming. My Aunt Marguerite stopped at the fence and it seemed her turn to wipe her eyes and then laugh.

"Well, we've just had another brush with the rooster, everyone."

"Oh, I'd say," said my grandmother Bea. "Another fright on the farm."

"And you're the hero of this one, Mom. How's your back, lugging that kid?"

"She wasn't heavy."

"And you too, Philip, thank goodness you sounded the alarm."

"Well," he coughed. "I did little. I was up in my tower and looking for those eagles that have been seen about. I spotted this blue object floating across the grass, and I thought at first it was one of those accursed plastic bags that get set adrift."

Aunt Marguerite insisted P. M. Murphy join us for lunch. "It's been far too long since you've sat at our table. This house doesn't want you to stay a stranger any longer."

"Well, I'm hardly dressed—"

"No one has dressed in this house for dinner," she laughed, "in years, let alone lunch. Do join us. We need to catch up. We don't see enough of you these days. Besides, Philip, we need to celebrate our good fortune today." Gram Bea took him by the arm in silent agreement.

"Well, perhaps, this time," said Mr. Philip M. Murphy. "All's well that ends well, we can say of it."

"Then Uncle Albert would say," I piped up, "'And this ended pretty darn well, folks.'" I felt moved to help Mr. Murphy feel more at ease now that I'd been relieved of the steel ball and its poison. Nathe laughed and he, Tim, and I high-fived each other. "Yes, yes, indeed. Dad will say that very thing when he gets the full report tonight."

With little Cousin Samara returned to the fold unharmed, I became generous to all, buoyed by good will, and relieved my responsibility to watch over the Van Strassel children had not turned tragic.

*   *   *

Such a spectrum of personalities and histories gathered at Aunt Marguerite's table for lunch. A former movie star, a deaf boy and orphan, four generations of Kinkade women, two sons bereft of a father, and the neighborhood recluse. We were all a bit buoyant as I now recall that memorable afternoon.

Nathe said a little prayer of gratitude for our good fortune this morning and asked for blessings on each one "seated at this table today." Tim and I prayed with our eyes wide open as I signed for him. Then he turned to the plate in front of him, deep in thought.

I'd taken a leaf from the book of Lawrence Alphonse and pledged to add a new word to my vocabulary each day. I decided to start in the middle with "M" and work the dictionary both directions from there. In the course of this venture, I had come upon the word "magnanimous" and ranked it highly as a very good word and trait, a trait I also pledged to install somewhere within my being.

I felt magnanimous right now. Certainly worlds better than feeling sick with dread just less than an hour ago. I looked around the table at each one assembled there in lively conversation, all relieved, all glad for each other's company, and I said to myself: *This is my family.*

No, not every one was blood kin, but Tim had become a friend like family and I began learning as he spoke what a quiet, generous, and yes, magnanimous soul was this Parsimonius Mysterious Murphy. For today he spoke of his youth and a frugal childhood where he was raised under the cloud of the Great Depression and the "scourge of war."

"Folks ask me why I continue to wear these green army fatigues. 'We thought you hated war, being a conscientious objector and such,' they tell me.

"Well, for one reason," he laughed, "they're cheap. But in the larger realm, my attire reminds me daily of the men and boys we lost trying to save Korea. As they would slip away from us, mine was often the last human face they saw." His expression sank visibly, as soulful as Tim's had been a moment ago. I was signing furiously for him as I wanted Tim to catch every bit of the table conversation now and the turn it had taken with P. M.'s description of his life and times.

I didn't need to be told. I could read such on the faces of my aunt, Gram Bea, and Nathe that we were being escorted down a passage, hidden deep in the soul of a compassionate man, who they'd known for decades, whose scars were still healing.

"Color, race, religion, Jew or gentile," he told us, "none of that mattered as I held their hand in hopes the chaplain would arrive soon to help them on their way. How many sightless eyes have I closed."

An awkward moment might have opened but remained closed when Nathe spoke: "Philip, do you remember a conversation you and I had nearly thirty years ago? Across the fence over at the farm?"

"Yes, how well I do. I was gathering wild asparagus for us both. You joined me." Mr. Murphy laughed pleasantly, "as mellow as a cello," a quality one wouldn't expect from a large-framed man, a sinewy and hard-twisted, angular fellow full of bones and firm muscularity. One pegged him a basso profundo.

"That's right. We had a good harvest that day."

"Yes, in both greens and thought. There I was, a voice raised against the world's violence and greed and you were at my side, a famous young man at this point so full of promise and poised to influence millions with your appearances on the screen."

"I hope, Phil," said Aunt Marguerite, "you weren't starstruck. Quite out of character for you."

He laughed and shook that lionish head. "Well, I was struck that here we two were engaged in the most common of tasks, harvesting our dinner. I a hermit and Nathean, a public persona with his name on everyone's lips. Yes, struck by the contrast and what different paths we had trod and were treading. Isn't it remarkable? Two lives beginning within a rifle shot of each other and yet what divergent courses life had dictated for us."

"I was between pictures, I remember, and you said how pleased you were with my 'last effort.'"

"*Redemption.*"

"Yes, *Finding Redemption.* On 'New Leaf Farm'. You told me how refreshing to see so little violence and so few guns. In contrast to some of my other stuff," Nathe laughed.

I found the rise and fall of P. M.'s voice hypnotic. How the cadence and tone rose and fell as if he were a tenor, warming up before a concert. So lulled and mesmerized as if I were riding the gentle swells in a little boat on a pleasant country lake.

"Yes." He leaned forward and folded his bony hands under his chin. "Memories from that film are vivid to me yet today. I felt moved, profoundly. Especially with the minister who came on stage now and then. How he reminded me of the old Scots reverend I sat under as a boy. He had no idea how I loved that man. A simple country preacher, a Presbyterian but not so steeped in doctrine he couldn't minister to Jew and gentile alike. He explained the mysteries of life and God as the core of the natural world around us. I think of him yet today as he was a beekeeper and botanist when he wasn't in his study or the pulpit."

I'd become so caught up with P. M.'s narrative, I'd forgotten to sign until Tim tugged at my shirtsleeve. I gave him the basics, promising I would fill in the details later.

* * *

We arose from our time together, P. M. excusing himself and thanking Marguerite and Bea for such a fine lunch. "Far more luxurious than my simple fare," he said of it. He promised he would supply my aunt's fruit and vegetable stand with "my wares, such as they are."

"Well, Philip, your buckwheat honey is for the gods. As well as the clover. I hope you have more hives this year. Everything sold out within the week. It's honey in the comb, boys. Nothing quite like it. And do think about drying more herbs this year. Herbs have become the rage."

"I shall. I'm like your father. I love harvesting things but do not relish the selling."

"Yes," said Gram Bea. "I called David the Sentimental Stockman. He so enjoyed seeing his animals thrive but hated market day even though it meant dollars in the bank. If he could have his way, he would have kept everything until we were swimming in critters."

We ambled out to the porch. And we were all surprised and flattered when P. M. invited Tim and me over to visit his bird tower. "Come by later this afternoon if you can spare the time. Viewings are better then. I'll have things redd up a bit."

"We will. Thank you, sir."

P. M. smiled broadly and started down the steps when Nathe reminded him. "Philip . . . this has been a 'Day of Pleasant Bread'."

Mr. Murphy laughed roundly, the tenor of it echoing down the colonnade. "How true! I hadn't thought of such until now. From the film—"

"Yes, indeed. And do you know where that line came from originally? Reverend Wooduff. I remember him saying such to my grandmother after dinner one Sunday."

"Really? You met my hero, the Reverend Clyde Woodruff?"

"Only twice was I in his presence. Sunday dinner and once at the eleven o'clock service when he announced from the pulpit something like: 'And in our midst this morning is a young man you all know. Nathean Summers is here, fresh from *Where The Sun Now Stands*.' I felt so honored. As much as if not more than all the other accolades and honors that came our way for that picture—"

"And well deserved."

"Well, thanks. Hometown crowd meant more. I remember the 'bread' line especially because it was the first suggestion I ever made on a script. The director looked at me as if I had two heads and said, 'Brilliant m' boy. We'll incorporate it. Perhaps, you *do* have a future.'"

Both men laughed. Nathe told P. M. the Reverend Woodruff had retired by that time. "As much as they let ministers retire. I can see why he was a model for you."

"Oh, my, of a certainty. Good ol' Ruff. Of the old school. Just a few of us relics left. Well, must be off as I have guests coming. I shall laugh all the way home."

Nathe watched him stride down the drive, then leaned against the porch column, as naturally as if the cameras were on him and the scene begun.

*　　*　　*

I asked Tim if he wanted a tour of Shadeland. He nodded with that characteristic intensity and the little "mmm" that meant "yes" or "I understand." Wren asked, "All right if I come too?" I signed him, "sure" and we all laughed. I seemed to be installing signing as second nature. "Yes, indeed, I'm a-thinking so," as Cousin Nathe would say.

"I'm supposed to ask before I come tagging along," Wren told us. "And to not be a pest."

"You're not a pest," I, the Snot-nosed Adolescent, assured him.

"Well, tell me if I am."

We coursed through the house. The Homestead Room where we lunched, then the main dining room, the little kitchen, the big kitchen, the new wing reserved for guests, then upstairs to The Montana Room, and finally my bedroom.

Tim asked: "Was this your father's room when he lived here?"

I said yes and he signed back: "That makes it special." Then: "Do you ever feel him nearby? Standing in the corner maybe? Or at the foot of your bed?"

I considered how to frame my answer and finally came up with, "not yet."

Tim uttered "mmm." Then he signed, "Maybe someday, when he knows you are living here now."

*　　*　　*

CHAPTER 34

A Day of Pleasant Bread

Within a week of our arriving at Shadeland, I began working my way toward the question. I really didn't know Aunt Marguerite and Gram Bea all that well, yet, and I didn't want to raise the memory of my dad in some inappropriate, perhaps even insensitive manner. They were still grieving as were my mother and I. I began asking obliquely how the home was built over the years.

"Well, the first house on these grounds was stone and log . . . two stories with two little bedrooms up and kitchen and living area down. Rather unusual for 1820. You can still see one wall in the Homestead. Then, a stone wall and rooms were built all around the first place. Then the north wing was added about 1860, and it itself was expanded in 1900. Then, ten years ago, we added the big kitchen and the guest bedrooms. . . . You want to know which room was his, don't you, dear?" asked Aunt Marguerite.

"Yes, ma'am. I do."

"You're in it."

*   *   *

I searched my father's room for any artifact. Perhaps his initials written on the wallpaper, something carved on a bedpost; the broken blade from a pen knife lodged in a crack of the flooring; a .22 shell fallen from his pocket; the scrap from a homework assignment; a baseball card he'd left in a book long forgotten.

Thus far, nothing. That Tim predicted I might some day feel his presence gave me hope. My deaf friend had a sense of things. To Tim, it remained inescapable: I now slept in the bed that once was his. Surely, where my father dreamed would open a channel for his son.

I judged Mr. P. M. Murphy recognized Tim's resident wisdom gained from a world of silence. That Tim's hearing loss was near total meant something to a man who'd witnessed more loss and carnage than many. A man to whom handicaps or injuries were compelling. According to the Kinkades and Uncle Albert as well, Mr. Murphy could rehabilitate damaged creatures, especially those with broken wings.

I'd heard of his interest in birds, their diet and habitat, their benefits to us all, and the migratory habits of some. According to Uncle Albert, the *Chapmann Tribune* had approached P. M. more than once about writing a weekly column on the area's bird life and population. P. M. told Albert: "It's flattering, but I have little truck with meetings, schedules, or deadlines. Perhaps, in my dotage, I'll consider it."

I signed this information to Tim on our way down the lane to P. M.'s hideaway including the warning signs posted as one turned into his shady drive. When we arrived, the signs had been removed. "That's funny," I signed to Tim.

P. M. met us halfway up the lane in a much more animated and congenial frame of mind than my first encounter. No specter hiding in the dark shadows of The Enchanted Forest, this man who strode our way and escorted us toward his domain in a clearly energized state.

"Hear the wrens greeting you boys—oh, well, forgive me. I wish young Tim could hear such articulation. Wrens feed on spiders, you know. Tolerant as I am, I'm not fond of the genus arachnida—spiders, scorpions, mites, and ticks. Perhaps, in my dotage, I'll find a place in my heart for them as well," he laughed. I joined in. Poor Tim seemed bewildered at this juncture.

But soon, P. M. put us at ease as we ascended his first tower. To our amazement, we found spotting scopes, telescopes of impressive dimension and a giant lens mounted on a sturdy tripod attached to an expensive 35 mm camera. All costly, all heavy duty, all serious stuff for viewing and recording. No amateur birdwatcher, this guy. We were thirty feet above the ground.

We each took a position behind a lens, Tim signing he could see Fountain House Home through the afternoon's haze. P. M. seemed pleased with Tim's fascination as we tried out the different scopes and found even the camera could bring us in close enough to where a family of Eastern Bluebirds filled the frame.

"Look here, my friends." P. M. rifled through a file of 5 x 7 prints of bluebirds feeding their young, prints so sharp and distinct one could marvel at the clarity and detail of the veins of each feather. "I have a remote camera mounted in the box with a flash. When I think there's a frenzy of activity, I click the shutter. The flash fires and I record the progress each day. I have close to a hundred shots of this family. Soon they'll fledge and the parents will begin feeding the birds on the ground or in the trees while teaching them to fly.

"Bluebirds have the most remarkable eyesight—eyes no bigger than a BB, yet they can spot a beetle twenty feet away. And so acrobatic, almost as agile as swallows."

I signed furiously in rhythm with Tim's brisk nodding and "mmm's." Then he asked me what 'fledge' meant and I passed the question on to P. M.

"Well, good question, my friend. It's when the parents coax the young to leave the nest and try life on their own. With most species, the young are inexperienced and must be taught how to feed, survive the predators, and become independent enough to face the world."

*   *   *

Tim signed it was 5:30 PM and told us he must leave to sign in and answer the dinner bell at Fountain House. He shook Mr. Murphy's hand in both of his and clearly said, "thank you," his first words of the day. Then Tim signed, "you are a great teacher." When I relayed the compliment to Mr. Murphy, he seemed speechless. We bid him good bye and left the study, the bird towers, the laboratory and workshop, the herbal drying hooks and flats, the apiary, the cabinets of bird prints, glass cases of carefully preserved butterflies and moths, the collection of nests, birdhouses, bat houses, and birdbaths behind. We'd entered the world of P. M. Murphy and left in a daze. Tim and I remained wordless until we reached the point where we would part company.

Then, I saw Standing Ovation hugging the fence up the lane toward Fountain House Road and I rode with Tim to there. We left our bikes in the grass and climbed the ditch bank to where we could look the old boy in the eye. I had but a solitary molasses cube in my pocket, for I'd taken to treating Mr. Ovation whenever I could break away from Wren and win the bull's recognition. I stuck it in his mouth and he dropped his head to grind away on my paltry offering.

We scratched the curly hair between those eyes as huge and black as billiard balls and rubbed the basketball-sized hump of his neck. Tim signed "wow" and "I would not want to meet him in the open without a fence between us." Yes, up close, one could truly appreciate the power of the beast. Such, I could attest from my encounter months ago in the Run. I then thought of Samara feeding flowers to Ovation and I shuddered.

Tim said he wanted to draw his portrait soon and asked if he would be around here tomorrow. I said I thought so as Aunt Marguerite had borrowed the bull from Mr. Logan to breed the Shorthorns of Shadeland.

Tim then jumped on his bike after re-securing the bird prints, art paper, and box of colored pencils P. M. Murphy had presented to him. P. M. seemed enthralled with Tim's rough sketches of what he'd seen on the towers and elsewhere. "Here," said P. M. of the pencils, "these have been gathering dust for years, and the prints will give you points of reference."

We waved and I pedaled my way toward Shadeland and my own supper. It had indeed been "A Day of Pleasant Bread".

*   *   *

CHAPTER 35

The Embarrassing Home Run

"Okay . . . here's the situation. We're gonna start Trent on the mound, then we'll bring in Lute. If the thing starts getting away from us, we'll call on you lefties or Ben or Claude to quench the fire. You fielders will have fun out there tonight—could be a slugfest."

And such it became. Our opponents, a county team from the little burg of Hambridge Springs, could hit all right. They tagged Trent for three runs in the first but we got them retired without any errors.

Mister Mac greeted us at the dugout with, "All right, good gloves out there, good ball smarts. Like what I see."

Trent Smythe slid past him on the verge of tears. "Sorry 'bout all those hits, coach."

Mac squared him around and laid both those big paws on Trent's shoulders. "Kiddo, you're doing just what we hoped. You're in the zone, throwing very few balls, no wild pitches. Just keep chuckin' like y' are. If they hit it, hey, you got eight guys out there to help us out."

Trent nodded, brushed his eye, and found a batting helmet. He hit the first delivery thrown by the Hambridge pitcher for a single. "That'll take the sting out of it," said Mac.

Our next two batters were thrown out and then Kevin Wingate homered. I batted fifth and sent a towering foul out to the left fielder. Inning over; score 3-2.

On it went with each side gathering two or three runs per its half of the inning. When Trent left the mound after the third, the game had become tied 8-8. Luther Ludlow took over in the fourth and gave up two runs.

When it came my turn to bat in the fifth, I straightened out my foul of the first inning and drove one over the left-center fence, scoring three runs. My first-ever hit for extra bases. Hambridge failed to score in the top of the sixth, and the game ended on a score of 11-10, our favor. Both teams lined up, high fived, and told each other, "good game."

Nathe asked the parents to stay afterwards so he and Mister Mac could field any questions and "just have a general meeting about anything on someone's mind." We Panthers stood around to listen.

Mister Mac led off with: "The last two games have accomplished just what we wanted. We gave your boys the chance to see how small ball works, namely bunting and producing runs with good base running and by playing against the other team's shortcomings or mistakes, what I call 'the short game.'

"Tonight, we took a chance on letting our backup pitchers start and told them to throw to the mitt and don't worry about the hits. Game could have been a blowout because these Hambridge kids hit as well as some of those town kids in Chapmann. But we had solid play in the field, our bats were hot, and the two boys who pitched tonight turned in a great performance."

Mac then turned to where they stood and tipped his hat to Luther and Trent. Everyone applauded.

"I'm of the school, at this level of the sport, that win or lose is well down the list. Winning comes later in the season or much later when these guys move on to the bigger leagues. Right now, we're here to build a love of the game, instill confidence, and give them the basics on how to play and improve. Frankly, I really don't care how we come out at the end of season. I know that sounds goofy to some of you, perhaps, but I'm not a win-at-all-costs guy. We could have lost both of these games, and it wouldn't matter to me as long as the boys got a feel for the field and learned to trust themselves and each of their teammates. That is what's important at this level, come right down to it." Nathe then addressed parental behavior.

"We appreciate we don't, thus far, have any parents coaching from the stands. A little personal anecdote: I helped coach a team one summer in Sacramento, and we had a mother who was a former softball champ, and she could not resist yelling at her son on what to do now, what to do next. She had a voice that carried to center field and it was 'swing level' or 'Chad-babe, throw the breaker'.

"Finally, we had to have a group meeting like this. We didn't single her out or any of the other parents who did this sort of thing, and there were a number. However, we did tell the group their sons would not play if this sort of behavior continued. It worked, for the most part.

"Just a comment on the composition of our team. We do not have a big strapping twelve-year-old six-footer, weighing 180 pounds on the mound. I'm kind of thankful for that. Teams tend to get unbalanced when everything rests on a kid who probably belongs in an older league. He's trying to strike out the side each inning because he's learned he can do so.

"The team gets tied down to this kid winning the game single-handedly. The outfield isn't getting much action so they fall asleep out there. The infield doesn't get much chance to sharpen their play and hone the strategies for different situations when there are runners on base. So much for the big star syndrome. It leads to imbalance.

"So . . . we Panthers are not the biggest guys around and we don't have several players in reserve—we've barely enough, eleven players. There'll be some games when we're down to ten, maybe nine, given an injury, illness, or a family vacation or such.

"That being said—that we're a modest team in stature and short on numbers—I feel, I believe, judging from the level of play we've seen these first few games, that we can give the boys a good season and make some memories out here they'll cherish all their lives, win or lose.

"Mac and I strongly believe one can over-manage the game at this level. There's a point where you simply sit back and let the boys play. Yes, there will be blunders, errors, mistakes in the field or running the bases, bad judgment, swinging at a bad pitch—all that. But, this is the league where you learn.

"They're not going to be playing like Roberto Clemente in a couple years. Takes time and love of this game to play it that well. Getting savvy about baseball comes later. Let 'em play now and learn from the goof-ups. Let them play now and enjoy their teammates and being out here under a baseball sky or the lights and to take home the joys that come with baseball. If so many of us didn't like this game, why have we been playing it for more than a hundred years? Why did your dad play and mine?

"So, folks, now it's our sons' turn to play.

"Let's simply let them try themselves on for size. See how they fit. They'll have good games, even great games, and some of their games will be so-so. It's kind of like life, wouldn't y' say?"

* * *

I was privy to the reason behind this meeting. After my second turn at bat, Mister Mac motioned me to his side on the bench and had me sit away from earshot of the rest of the team.

"You know Bob Holland, don't y'?"

"Yessir."

"How 'bout you slippin' outside and take a tour around the stands, see if he showed up tonight. I have reason to think he's here."

I returned to the dugout and reported both he and Lucas were watching the game.

"Good," said Mac. "Thanks. Nathe . . . I think we'd better call that meeting after the game."

Nathe simply answered, "Gotcha."

*   *   *

Later, upon reflection, I realized the rationale behind the parents' meeting. It outlined expectations for us all. And it cued Bob Holland on what he might expect if he continued to petition the league to move his son Lucas from the Chapmann Bread and Bakery to the Panthers. I also guessed Lucas, truth be known, might not be that keen to move to a new club. Perhaps he had deep loyalties within his old one. Just a guess. Perhaps his somber expression told me baseball was becoming a chore.

I wondered: would I want my father living his dreams through me, smoothing my way, building my resume', challenging the rules, browbeating the coaches, upbraiding officials? Would I want a Van Strassel childhood with its parental rancor, demands, and approval withheld until I met expectations? Or a Bob Holland fussing about? I might not be "up to snuff" as we say out in Summers Run Country.

Dad may learn I'm not as dedicated he thinks I should be. Or as talented as he remembers he was once. What then? Would there be room for my dreams in his grand scheme or just his?

Perhaps Uncle Albert said it best: "Well, Lucas may be the best hurler in the county at his age. But when he's 14 and playing on the big field with the big guys—all of whom may have the same idea—then's when he takes a good hard look in the mirror.

"Richard Strauss once told me: 'Yes, Albert, the screen test may be brilliant, but it's the solo performance, standing alone in front of the cameras and the crew and all those dollars

255

clipping along that separates the actors from the pretenders. You love your good days when you can do no wrong but you grow from the bad.' I'd be surprised if we hear from Bob Holland again."

As it turned out, we didn't.

* * *

Tim had gained permission from the Fountain House staff to sleep over at Shadeland the night after the game. He'd brought some of his bird prints to show the family and especially P. M. Murphy the next morning. He'd rendered the American Avocet, an Eastern Bluebird pair, the Whip-Poor-Will, a Blue Jay with wings spread, and the Chipping Sparrow. And finally, the star of the show, several studies of Standing Ovation. As we admired them, Tim drew a quick sketch of Wren and the Radio Flyer wagon with Samara in the bed and then as requested again, a little pony's head.

While Tim worked away, Nathe sat back "ruminating" as he seemed prone to do. Marguerite looked up from her study of the prints and smiled his way, passing the prints on to Gram and Uncle Albert for another "gander."

"You're getting a bee in your bonnet, Cousin. Would you care to share?"

"Not yet," he laughed, caught in his reverie. I waited for his trademark expression. And it came.

"I'm . . . just a-thinkin'. You're the one around here who gets a bee in her bonnet, Marguerite."

"Not lately. I've turned such over to you. I swear you've come up with more projects and ideas. Here you are. Spokesman for this, chairman of that, baseball coach. What's next? For the man who said he was flattered to be asked but taking his time re-entering life around here, it appears you might be building a hive full of bees."

"Just an idea. I'll tell y' later."

I signed this all to Tim the best I could, unable to manufacture the nuances of their exchange. I didn't tell Tim but I felt certain it involved him.

*   *   *

We spread our bags and canvas on the lawn. Nathe and Uncle Albert had gone home to Summers Run Farm. Wren and Samara had been tucked in. Shadeland appeared to be shutting down for the night. Lamps were turned off and soon only a guitar pick of a moon shown down upon us.

First, we discussed his art and how good everyone found it. Then, of course, the game. He told me hitting a home run must be so cool and he wished he had the power to do it.

"You will. Just a square contact and follow-through."

"What did Mister Mac say to you out there, after the game? And Mrs. Mac too."

"Oh, he asked me how I liked the feel of hitting a homer, and I said I did not think I wanted to do it again because it made the pitcher feel bad, I knew. And I asked Mrs. Mac if she did not think so too.

"Then I said, 'besides, there you are, running around the bases all by yourself, folks looking at you, shouting and such—too embarrassing.'"

Tim signed: "I can guess what Mister Mac said when he heard that."

"Right. He pulled me up by my ear and said: 'I hear anymore talk like that and I will come out there and slap you silly.'"

Tim laughed, propped himself up on his elbow and asked, "then what?"

"Mrs. Mac took him by the arm and winked at me and said good night. I heard Mister Mac muttering something about embarrassing and said it was the first time he had ever heard such but it sounded like a Blake Kinkade remark."

257

Tim lay back down and signed. "Wish I could have heard that. The guys would have laughed their heads off."

Then he raised back up. "Do you think Lucas Holland is going to play for us?"

"Do not think so. I would be surprised if we hear from Bob Holland again."

He lay back down. "I hope not. He would want Lucas to pitch all the time. Might be a big problem. I would not want Bob Holland for a dad."

I had to ask Tim to repeat as the moon's glow seemed fickle tonight and gauzy.

He signed again and added: "Better to be without a dad than one you did not like."

Then Tim asked if I had thought anymore about seeing my dad or feeling his presence in my room. "Even out on the ball field tonight. I would love to have a parent there. Guess you too. Your mom, maybe soon. Maybe the spirit of your dad since he played there once long ago." I had to lean up on my elbows to catch the signs Tim was sending my way furiously.

"Do you ever think about your dad coming up the drive toward you and the house? I imagine that some. Some guy walking up toward Fountain House with his jacket off, looped over his shoulder. He looks like some movie star, Nathe maybe. Turns out to be my dad and he has been looking for me for years. Ever think of such a thing?"

I signed back that yes, I did. "Or he gets off a plane and we run across the tarmac and meet each other. We did that in real life a couple times."

"Nice," he signed. Then he lay quietly for a spell. I rolled to my back and we both watched the clouds moving across the moon or the moon moving through the clouds. Then he reached over and tugged the sleeve of my shirt.

I looked his way and he signed: "Do you ever hope your dad is found? Maybe he has been captured all this time and released?"

258

He rolled toward me to read my answer in the silvery moonlight, brighter now that the clouds had floated on. I signed: "No. Too much to hope for. I wish it could be so, but it is just a wish that will never come true."

"Yes, it is hard to have a wish that will not come true. If your dad will never come home, do you have another wish of some kind?" I mulled it over.

Several things came to mind: Nathe and my mother falling in love or sensing my dad's presence somewhere at Shadeland or on the banks of Summers Run. Finally, I signed "no" and asked Tim if he did. He signed "yes" and rolled to his back. I watched his pale fingers form the letters.

"I w-o-u-l-d l-i-k-e t-o h-e-a-r a b-i-r-d s-i-n-g."

*   *   *

CHAPTER 36

This Matter of Adoption

As I look back on these years and events I'm recording, I remain impressed how quickly our moods and circumstances changed. We were mere boys, tossed as we were, on a makeshift raft. We created some of the turbulence of our pond by our own horseplay. Some from paddling urgently to shore in front of an approaching storm. Some from the wake of others roaring by and heedless of our comfort or safety. Decisions, judgments, choices, expectations. Influences, families, origins, situations and setbacks. *Life*

Tim and I were fresh from basking in the pleasure P. M. Murphy took in Tim's "promising" artwork, "so skillfully executed." Now, just minutes from there at Fountain House Home, we were looking at its debris. Several of the drawings were smudged and spoiled beyond recovery.

A big kid named Doyle passed by Tim's bunk and asked of his work, what are these things, sumpthin' from a little kid's coloring book? He spilled his drink on the lot and left us surveying the wreckage, his companion laughing behind him. How I wished I were the six-foot-three, 275-pounder my cousin Nathe had bloodied on the baseball diamond years ago. Doyle and I would have had "words" right then. I boiled, feeling my father's indignation over bullying rising in my veins as well. I held my tongue, deciding confrontation might make things worse for Tim.

"I can do them over again," Tim signed, "even better this time now that I know more about birds and how to draw them. You can sit on Robert's bunk. He is nice. Doyle is okay most of the time, but if he thinks you are avoiding him and not paying enough attention, he picks on you. He turned eighteen and graduated from high school. That means he will be leaving here soon. That is when they kick you out of here. I will not be sad to see him go."

Tim showed me around the institution: the communal showers, the stainless steel kitchen like Aunt Marguerite's big one only more impersonal, the lounge and television room, the game room, the dining room, and the offices.

"They interview folks who want to adopt one of us in there. Babies do not stay around long. Everyone wants a baby or a toddler like Samara. Older kids, not so much.

"I hated coming here. There were no foster homes available so they sent me here. I had been living with my grandmother, but she got kind of goofy and could not manage. It is better now. I like Reverend and Mrs. Vanderhoff. He is funny, kind of silly and those guys make fun of him behind his back. But I think he does a good job. The state is closing orphanages, I guess. Will not license any new ones. Everyone is supposed to go to a foster home but if there are none out there, you come here.

"If they close Fountain House, then I will have to go somewhere else. There is a school for kids like me down near Pittsburgh. I may go there and live and learn how to get along better. Probably before I turn 18. Sometimes I wish I could leave now and be on my own. But I am only 11 and deaf. What do I know or where would I go? Or do? I am kind of like a bird. I cannot fledge yet. Not for a long time. Since I have no parents, like the birds, I will have to decide on my own. I try not to think about the things I may have to deal with some day."

*   *   *

I rode home, determination now—not a steel ball—gnawing at my gut. I was going to get Tim Hathaway out of there. Into my new home at Shadeland or over at Summers Run Farm and Cousin Nathe's.

Before I left Fountain House, Tim signed, "Home, Sweet Home." I grinned weakly in reply. I had a sweet home and by darn, there's no reason I couldn't share it. And do something about this. Maybe Nathe would consider being a foster parent for Tim. But then, perhaps he had to be married to qualify. I'll bet only married folks with families of their own become foster parents, I told myself.

Aunt Margy will know the rules. She's on the advisory board of Fountain House Home.

She was frosting a cake when I broached the subject and my plans for Tim. I waded through the idea, recognizing that Shadeland was filling up with all of us . . . and the fact that Summers Run Farm had room but Nathe wasn't married . . . but then she and Dr. Seaborn *were* married. . . . Then there's my grandparents Ronnie and C. J. and Grandma Ronnie signs—but maybe the state would say they're too old and too nomadic without a permanent address, just a mailing service that forwarded things. On I went, the pros and cons of it all.

"You've been thinking about this, haven't you, Clauders?"

"Yes, ma'am. All the way home."

"Well . . . Nathe's not the only one with a bee in his bonnet around these parts. You just brought it to light. Still, might be too early to bring it up. Perhaps I should be cagey like Nathe the other night."

She became silent, hiding behind that sly, knowing glint in her eye I'd begun to recognize in the few months I'd known, her. She was teasing me.

"Aunt Margy, if you don't tell me, I'll take a swipe of frosting off this cake and blame it on Wren."

She laughed, that wonderful contralto echoing around the little kitchen. "Here are the beaters. I saved them for someone who happened by. Take a seat, Claude.

"There may be an answer for Tim. Don't get your hopes up. Adoption comes with a dozen hoops an' such. And as I said the other day, there are no secrets in this house. But there are some things we treat with utmost care . . . and sensitivity. I know you will keep this in strictest confidence."

"Yes, ma'am." I laid the beaters aside and folded my arms on the butcher block surface between us. I wanted to catch every tidbit, anything as small as the cake crumbs sprinkled here and there.

"There's been some talk . . . about this. A seed's been planted. Nanners and I have known each other since college. I was her big sister in our sorority. And she's become acquainted with Tim."

"And Nanners is?. . ."

"Mrs. Mac, your teacher last term. Nancy. I'm the only one around here who calls her 'Nanners'."

"Whoa." I leaned back until I nearly tipped my stool over.

"Now, the fact is, McIntyres have been on the list at Fountain House for a while and nearly had a couple come their way. One was a darling little girl who was taken in by her aunt from Santa Fe. Then they were on a list for a boy, but he was placed within the family as well. The agency gives preference, usually, to a family member.

"Now, and this is very personal, Nancy has suffered two miscarriages and a stillbirth. It's been the sorrow of her life that she hasn't been able to give her and Banks a child. Therefore, they've considered adoption off and on, over the years.

"The state agent told us Tim would be nearly impossible to place. He has no family of record other than a grandmother with problems of her own. He's nearly a teenager and those wanting children often specify no one over eight or nine years of age or absolutely no teens. And of course, being deaf opens a whole new set of concerns and regulations. The fact Tim's deaf doesn't deter her or Banks in the least for that matter.

"But the state is a nervous nellie when it comes to placing kids with handicaps. Very stringent regulations, inspections, interviews, and the like.

"So, Mister Mac is okay with Tim an' all."

"Let's put it this way. Their file has always been open, but now it's tagged for Tim Hathaway and the wheels are starting to turn."

"Wow. Good news, Aunt Marg, very good news."

"No promises, son. There's the state and all that folderol. But yes, let's pray and be hopeful."

I jumped from my seat and began licking the beaters with relish. "I'll take these down to get the mail. It hadn't come when I checked."

I turned to leave through the butler's alcove and the door that led outside into the bright afternoon sun. Then I had another thought: "There any reason you called Mrs. Mac 'Nanners' other than her being Nancy?"

"She was 'Nanners' to everyone on the floor because she'd been elected social chairman and very much the source on proper etiquette an' such. She schooled us all the time about being up to snuff. And, she became 'Nanners Miss Manners' up and down the hall."

Marguerite raised her finger and pointed that steely gray-eyed gaze my direction. "If you ever breathe a word of this to anyone, I will come over there and slap you silly."

"Not a word, Aunt Marg. I haven't been slapped silly yet and I don't intend to be." Then she called me back.

"There is another matter. The Chapmann humane shelter always has dogs, speaking of adoption," she said, wiping her hands on her checkered apron. "I . . . wouldn't have an objection to a dog—well mannered, mind you—and to be kept

. . . outside of course. A boy should likely have a dog to tag along after him."

I took a healthy lick of devil's food batter. "I don't need a dog for that, Aunt Margy. I have Wren."

*　　*　　*

CHAPTER 37

On the Oregon Trail

Like P. M. Murphy of a few days ago, it seemed my turn to laugh my way down a lane. How quickly things could change. My friend Tim might find a home. And nearby, not in Erie, Pittsburgh, or Cleveland. Aunt Marguerite cautioned me to not mention the matter to Tim. Or Mister Mac.

"Nancy has interviewed and is getting the particulars on adopting a handicapped child. Banks is letting her gather the preliminaries. We'll just have to wait and see."

I pictured the file of Tim Hathaway being plucked from a bank of metal drawers and carried to some desk by hands that dance over a keyboard and insert new dates and update material. Then to another inbox and yet another, a third. As it made its way up each step of the system, the file grew fatter and its priority flagged higher.

*   *   *

My mother phoned: "Granddad C. J. and Ronnie are in Ohio, hon. They'll be there tomorrow night, they think." I took this as a warning. I knew what my grandparents might ask of me.

"Moms, I can't go on any trips with them. We'll be starting toward the playoffs pretty soon, just a few more games."

"Honey, they've been looking forward to seeing you for so long. Surely the Pirates—"

"Panthers."

"Panthers. Surely they can spare you for a week or so. Mom and Dad are going to park the rig at the Finger Lakes and fish—you'll have a great time. Oh, and guess what I heard last night. Like I told you? Well, it's official.

"Come September, I'm singing every night with the Barry Blanton Orchestra! They're on Toni Rossi's albums. Like I said, their vocalist is off for two months, health troubles of some kind, and I'm doing her numbers. Oh, wow, babe. I sign the contract tomorrow. What do you think of your Moms now, huh?"

"That's great, really is, but I hope Gramps and Ronnie don't have any ideas about me leaving the farm—"

"Oh, sorry, babe, I gotta git. Judy's here and we're going to lunch. I'll call tomorrow. Bye."

The dial tone began humming in my ear. "Good-bye, Moms."

*   *   *

I knew the subject had to come up. Yet, I didn't want to burden Aunt Marguerite with my agony over Granddad C. J. and Ronnie until the timing seemed right. But she brought it up at breakfast the day of their impending arrival.

I told her: "I love 'em, sure I do. What kid wouldn't? But they think if I live here, I'll forget about them and Mom. They've always liked Nevada for the boating and the BX at the base where they can grocery shop. They might sell the RV and buy a big double wide. They sent some stuff about the house and this fancy mobile court where there's a pool and a golf course. They're excited about all of us living out there. C. J. says I can play baseball all year long in the winter leagues. But I love it here."

"You're troubled, Clauders. Why don't you go visit with Nathe this morning before they get here? He knows something about separation and living apart. I've done my share but he did it for years, off and on, as a boy your age. I'm sure you've thought of that."

"Yes'm. I have. A lot. I wonder if Nathe was ever wakeful about such." She touched my arm and said separations were often a fact of our lives these distracted days and sleepless nights.

*   *   *

I parked my bike and found Nathe on the porch with the *Tribune* and yesterday's mail. I told him I hoped I wasn't intruding.

"This is your second home, Claude. 'You're as welcome as the flowers on Mocking Bird Hill', goes the old song. Your grandparents are coming over for grilled salmon tonight. Pop and I owe Marguerite a dozen dinners.

"We'll discuss the fishing trip and the games coming up. And, if it they mention it, your future. Hope that's all right with you."

"Yessir, it's time to do such." I could tell Marguerite had cued in my cousin Nathe. Which was fine. *Cards on the table.*

"Help yourself to the fridge. There's orange juice. Honey in the comb. A loaf of man-made bread over there. Baked it myself."

"I guess you know they want me to live and travel with them until Vic and Mom get married."

"Do you want to try that for a spell?"

"Nossir. I don't. But they'll feel bad if I don't go with them, I know. I'd sooner stay here until after the wedding and maybe later." I told Nathe I felt like a fledgling bird, nothing but a lot of fret and worry for the adults in my life, feeding and housing me. Not knowing if I should leave the nest or where to light if I do while trying to balance my hopes and wants with their expectations.

"Then, down the road, suppose it doesn't work out between Mom and Vic. They call the wedding off or they get divorced.

Then what do we do? Come back to P. A.? Am I being . . . snot-nosed about any of this?" I asked him. "I don't want to be like a little kid throwing a tantrum, being—what's that word Uncle Albert uses? Ob-something?"

"Obstreperous. Means defiant or sullen, bad-tempered."

"Yes. I don't want to be a pouty toddler about this and I don't wanna be a crabby teenager either. I wanna do the right thing for everyone in my life right now."

"Son, it just pains me to see you agonize over it. But, you're the only Jarrett grandchild and that makes you someone they'll fight for. They don't want to lose you anymore than Gram Bea does. I'm sure you won't forget your grandparents on either side."

"No. No sir. Definitely shall not happen. They all mean too much to me. But if Granddad C. J. and Ronnie pressure me, I'm going to have to go, I think."

"Well, your mom has the stronger claim, but like I said out at the lake, the Kinkades think of you as their flesh and blood and branded by Blake David Kinkade." Nathe folded the paper and stood to watch Uncle Albert and his new lawnmower, a riding rotary. "Dad not only shed his mutton chops but he traded in the old reel mowers. Said they made him look like a relic." Albert waved and pirouetted around a locust tree, something Nathe said he couldn't do with the gang of reels.

"Look at that. Mowing the lawn in a herringbone sport coat. The consummate country gentlemen. Well, it is unseasonably cool this morning." Nathe smiled my way. "Some day, I want to be just like my dad. Son, let's go in the apple room and have a little chat. This new mower is a tad louder than the old one."

Wallpaper along one wall in the "apple room" was a study in varieties: Winesap, McIntosh, Northern Spy, Gravenstein, Granny Smith, Yellow Transparent. I tried to determine the paper's pattern and asked if Nathe had ever counted the number of different apples arrayed there.

"Twenty. I love that paper. Remember the apple grafting scene at the end of *Oregon Trail*?"

"Yes, when Jacob found his new home in the territory. I read it in the book too."

"Good." Nathe poured himself another cup of coffee and sat down on the leather club chair.

"I wanted to talk with you this morning about that very scene. George Nye was the actor there. Wonderful old guy and he actually knew how to cut a graft and splice too. But he had a great line, remember? 'Blood ties and kin are powerful, Jacob, but you should live where your heart wants you to.' Might be something for us all to think on."

"Yessir. It fits. I don't want to hurt C. J. and Ronnie, but I'm just getting settled in here and I like being a farm boy."

Nathe shoved a stack of books aside he'd been studying on the sofa. He motioned me to sit down.

"I've been troubled myself, lately. I probably spoke out of turn when we camped by the lake that day. About the conspiracy to keep you here in P. A. It's not our place, really. Marguerite is in a stew about all this as well. She says you've become her anchor over there: helping with the little ones, working with Holzers on the garden and the orchard, and keeping up the lawn." The shade of "rumination" passed again over his face. I wondered if my dad ever wore such an expression. A long pause. Finally, Nathe sighed.

"Claude. You might have to make a tough call here in the days ahead."

"Like, I might have to go off and see the rooster, then?"

He nodded. "In this case, Pennsylvania or Nevada. It's coming to a head now that your mom's engaged and the wedding's taking shape."

"What do you think I should do, Cousin? I lay awake about this."

"All of us here . . . don't want any hard feelings about where you should live. Your aunt and I hope . . . your grandfolks will see how you like it here and fit in so well, and that will be that. We can't say much more at this point." He smiled and said, "Decisions," and thumbed the pages of a book beside him, and for a long moment, the churring of the paper became the only sound in the room. It, and the ticking of the old monstrous school clock on the wall surrounded by the twenty apples. *Time, the unseen but ever-present element governing our lives.*

"Blood ties are strong and a mother's is the strongest."

"But . . . Aunt Margy is my only aunt. Gram Bea is my dad's mother."

"True. Did you ever learn to play chess?"

"Yessir. A bit."

"Okay. Your mom's the queen and the rest of us are just bishops, knights, and rooks."

"And I'm the pawn."

"So it seems to be, son. Indeed." He grinned in sympathy. "No one wants you to be batted around like a pawn between the families. It might come down to the old Biblical story about the wise king cutting the baby in half. Remember it? Two mothers were claiming this infant and the one gave it up, rather than see it destroyed."

"Yes, such crossed my mind lately."

We listened to the mower skirting the house and the apple room now and discussed the final episode from *Children of the Oregon Trail*. Then, Nathe began talking about the Panthers and coaching.

"I think coaching has shown me I could have been a good father."

I looked at him warily. When he didn't offer more, I said, "But, there's Temple."

"Yes, I have a daughter." Though the morning rays had climbed above the trees and were brightening the room, Nathe's expression remained cloudy.

"If she's truly mine." He looked at me, frowning and biting his lip. "And I really do not want to know the truth about Temple.

"She was a loving, chirpy little sprite, like Samara, and I thought back then if she wasn't mine, I couldn't bear to know the truth. Because . . . I was afraid I might love her less. I couldn't face learning that I could be that petty. That's one reason, I didn't want to know if she had a different father and was the product of betrayal.

"Now, she bears my name for what it's worth out there. Only a few remember Nathean Summers anymore in Hollywood. That's why Sherylinn, her mother, insisted on naming her Temple, so it would jog folks to think, 'Shirley Temple.'

"I have never asked Sher if I was the father. If I did, she'd lie, and so she hides Temple from me because she knows the truth and doesn't want to admit she was unfaithful. Then she would come up with something crazy, lash out at me saying if Temple were a boy, I would have been a better father.

"When I told her it didn't matter—boy or girl—and that she wanted a show business career for our child more than a father, she all but agreed. She argued she could manage Temple's career without interference from a guy who'd soured out on the film business. I became just a name she could use along with Shirley Temple's. I started my new career, publishing, and let them pursue their careers making the rounds and doing commercials. It . . . just seemed less warfare, and if Temple grows into a successful and happy young woman, then why would I not want such for her?

"Now . . . I wonder how to fill my voids and empty spaces. I don't want to marry again unless I meet my soul mate, like the girl Peter Benedict lost. As to being a father, well maybe it's my lot to be a good dugout dad, watching the Alphonses, the Catalinos, the Gamoskis, the real dads on the field, take their sons home after the game."

*   *   *

CHAPTER 38

Planning and Providence

"Someone's not happy with me." Nathe handed me his most recent editorial from the *Chapmann Tribune*.

Nathe had been the subject of a couple long articles in recent editions and had been writing lately for the *Tribune* about community planning, growth, and something called land ethos. Someone disagreed and had clipped his piece from the paper and sent it back him.

Scrawled across most of it were the words: "Say, mister High and Mighty. We don't care how you did it in Hollywood. Plan and zone yourself all you like but not us, thank you very much. Hollis Linch."

"Does it sound like war?" I asked. "Maybe getting the ol'.30-30 out and loaded?"

"No," Nathe laughed, "it's a verbal shootout. Some folks want to live back in the Fifties. Even the Thirties for that matter. At least he signed it. Most don't."

*   *   *

Monday evening, folks poured into the fellowship room of Meadow Brook Community Church. Some were prompted by curiosity and to see Nathe in person, surely, but many came burdened with the challenges facing the township and the health of Summers Run in the years ahead. My job was to load the slide projector and pass out the spiral-bound book that

Nathe and the committee had created over the months past. The *Chapmann Tribune* sent a reporter to interview anyone with views for its ongoing series: *The Approaching Storm: Progress, Change, and Preservation in Pymatuning County.*

Nathe presented an impressive pictorial of the region from both the air and ground. None of the weedy areas or those featuring run-down homes and farms were from our area, he assured them, but "others needing attention elsewhere, Fairfield and Marchand Counties mostly. And here are some before and after pictures. What a dramatic difference as you can see, thanks to citizen action." For me, there were two telling moments.

When Nathe stepped away from the lectern and said: "Now. . . we know . . . these issues are unsettling and raise matters we'd rather ignore. But my cousin Marguerite has a wonderful expression when it's dinner time over there. She says, 'Let's all gather at the table.' And so, let's conclude our time together tonight by doing just that. Let us gather at the table."

Naturally, earlier, I'd added my aunt's call to my collection of how families meet for the last meal of the day. Of course, of them all, hers remains my favorite. But how appropriate to hear it announced in public and how meaningful for this meeting tonight.

My second moment for the night came at the door when I was passing out *A Comprehensive Growth, Recovery, and Planning Manual for Pickett Township and Surrounding Areas.* Hollis Linch, his visage stern and mouth drawn into a pout, brushed by me without so much as a "no, thank you." His son Jeff took a book and we made eye contact.

*   *   *

That next evening, as I took the mound for my third inning, I looked toward the Kinkades and my maternal grandparents watching me. So far, I had held the hard-hitting Eagles scoreless. The knuckler had them buffaloed for now.

Granddad C. J. pumped a vigorous thumbs up. Earlier, when Mister Mac and Nathe gave me the ball at the game's outset, they told me: "Good luck, Clemente. This ball will laugh at these guys when it goes by."

Fourth inning, down they went again on a single, a double play, and a strikeout. Now it was our turn at the plate. Jules Alphonse donned his batting helmet and said: "I think these Eagles are getting plucked tonight. I see tail feathers falling all over the place."

We'd faced one of their best pitchers and the Eagles had several. We were chatting in the dugout about his release point and by now we had a sense of his speed and where he might be vulnerable. Our bats woke up and we scored three runs. Could it be? A little country mouse could scamper past the Screamin' Eagles as they called themselves?

Fifth inning and my first sign of trouble. After the first Eagle grounded out, the second reached first on an error and I gave up a blooper single that fell into short left field. Mister Mac came to the mound and told me and Carmine: "Claude, if you feel you need the heater and feel good about throwing it, this might be the place."

Up now came the number three batter and their cleanup man, the very ones who stared at us insolently during warm ups. I threw the heater and got ahead in the count on both. Then a combination of the knuckler, a couple off-speed pitches, and another fast ball, and they both whiffed. This time my gramps stood and pumped both thumbs up, danced a little jig, and applauded. No question he and I belonged to each other. We were of the knuckleball fraternity.

We faced a new pitcher in the fifth but we stuck to the fundamentals we'd learned in the batting barn and Nathe's version of home run derby. We added two more runs and were threatening with a third when it happened.

I stood on second base with a double. Tim's job was to bunt me over to third. He laid down a beautiful drag bunt along the first base side and tore down the line to beat it out. He had done so before in this very situation but this time, such was not to be.

I often think back on those scenes so vivid. I reflect upon their mystery today as I record their impact. In doing so, I remain convinced there is a power we humans call Providence and It does intervene at times during our earthly journey. Whether it does so upon petition, capriciously, or as part of a grand design, I am not prepared to say. All I can offer is this: there are those events and occasions when we of the genus mankind can do little but pause and wonder before we move on.

In the course of his furious flight toward first base, Tim's helmet came ajar and whether he knocked it away or it bounced loose of its own accord, no one can be sure. I had my own task at hand, namely to reach third and tear for the plate should the throw to first go awry. Mister Mac, coaching third, gave me the sign to come in standing ready to point my feet homeward should he send me. I didn't see Tim fall.

Folks later described the pitcher's throw to first as a rocket and how they cringed when they saw the ball fly skyward from its contact with back of Tim's skull. When I turned to see where the play stood now, I found Tim in a heap on the first base bag.

Mister Mac waved me to come with him and we tore across the mound. The umpire, correctly, grabbed me and shouted, "all players back, all players stand back!"

"This kid's deaf," barked Mac, retrieving me, "and he's our signer."

"All right, all right. Everyone else, stay back. Give us some room here."

By the time Mac, Nathe, and I knelt by Tim's side, he had rolled off the bag and was looking straight into the sky.

He looked so gone.

I bit my lip for I felt the tears welling. Was I looking into the sightless eyes of my friend? I thrust my hands directly in front of his face and signed and voiced as well: "Lie still. Lie very still. Do not move." I wiped my tears for Tim's face was now a blur.

He had not stirred.

I took hold of Tim's jaw so he wouldn't turn right or left, while my Grandmother Ronnie ran up and stood over us and signed away. I told her to sign ambulance and to tell Tim to remain still, that help was on the way. Mac called out for Nancy. Tim looked listless.

He began to fade.

My grandmother signed away. She bent over him and I felt her hair brush mine as she signed: "Do not move your head." Then she asked me, "Does he read, Claude?"

"Yes," I told her. "A bit" I looked into those dark eyes urging them silently to not go sightless. Ronnie knelt even closer to where Tim could see only three faces I'm sure: hers, mine in the middle, and Mac's. Tim's eyes seemed to narrow, and I wondered if he were dropping away from us now with no way to slow the slide.

Then I heard Mister Mac say: "Jack, good. Move back a little, Claude. We got an EMT here." I eased away from Tim and released his jaw. Then I saw those eyes squinting into the hint of an approaching grin. Jack, the emergency tech, had crawled to where he could gingerly test for Tim's pulse. Tim did as he was told, lying still as death. But it was the eyes.

No longer sightless, no longer listless. His gaze, moving from my grandmother, to me, and finally resting on Mac standing behind the EMT and looking down. The grin broadened into a full-on smile. Tim raised his arm and pointed toward his coach and said, "I . . . hear . . . yhou."

*   *   *

277

CHAPTER 39

Chase Around Brown

That summer, when I last saw Tim Hathaway in a Panthers uniform he was practically out of it. Before the big game with the Eagles, we'd assembled on the Chapmann practice field to work on some last minute drills, including bunting. Tim laid one down the first base line just as he would later in the game.

As he started toward first base, his pants slipped to his knees and the more he struggled, the more they continued their trip downward to his ankles. To the bag he hopped finally as if he were in a sack race on the Fourth of July, falling over the base, then rolling on the ground, helpless while the rest of us likewise dissolved into puddles of boyish laughter around the diamond. Nathe called practice over at this point, and we trooped up the hill in high spirits ready to give the Eagles a game they couldn't forget. Later, at the hospital, I found Tim's head bandaged and his neck in traction.

Little League Baseball for "Halfway" Hathaway was over for 1992, at least. Good news, though, he seemed to have recovered seventy percent of his hearing in his left ear. The attending physician thought he might be a candidate for a transplant for the right ear. "Had this boy had some parental attention years ago, he might have been spared all this." The specialists and auditory techs called him "a case you remember."

"It is something they take from a dead guy," Tim signed of the procedure. "That thing that looks like a seashell? They take yours out and stick his in."

*   *   *

I wish I could give a glowing report of a season finale, one where we Panthers marched through the state and regionals and all the way to Williamsport. Our victory over the Eagles that memorable night became essentially our last.

The Gamoski family had saved four years for a trip through the Canadian Rockies, Glacier, and other Western points celebrating graduations and anniversaries all along the route at this time, this very summer. So there went Ryan. With Tim in the dugout but not permitted to play, we were down to nine players.

We lost our first game in tournament play to Chapmann Bread & Bakery with Lucas Holland on the mound. This time, we knocked him out in extra innings. We lost 5-4.

"We still have a chance," we told each other. However, we were jarred from our dreams of stardom by a cruel turn much more grave than Tim's injury.

For our next game, we faced elimination against the Eagles in Chapmann, screaming this time for revenge. We were confident until Nathe had us huddle in the dugout. Mister Mac stood leaning against the doorway. Uncharacteristic for him as he was usually pacing about and taking care of things. Nathe was rolling a baseball in his hand long before he spoke. He had our attention. Finally, he looked up.

"Boys, Mister Mac and I . . . are leaving it up to you if you want to play tonight. Trent Smythe's little sister has been missing for more than a day and a night now. You likely haven't heard, but they found her body this afternoon in an abandoned refrigerator.

"Trent will not be with us tonight. That leaves the eight of us." Nathe sighed and looked each one of us in the eye, those of us who weren't staring at our shoes or the sand in front of us. "The Eagles want us to forfeit so they'll have a rest. In fact, Lawrence is looking up the rules about an automatic forfeit right now."

Said Jules Alphonse: "Seems like the 'Trentster' might appreciate if we honor the family by playing and playing our best, just the eight of us. And not just walking off the field," he said. "I don't know how I'd feel if I was him, Mr. Nathe. Maybe we ought to think about this an' all the sadness when we salute the flag tonight."

"I don't want to sound selfish, but I'd rather not turn in my uniform without playing one final game," I said, "It's a sad day when you turn in your uniform anyway. I'd rather play one more game for Trent and his folks. Otherwise, tonight is doubly sad, I think." When I turned in my Kaintucks uniform last year, I felt blue for a week. Baseball was over. Now this.

"I feel that way," offered the usually quiet Luther. Aaron nodded and I could feel my teammates agreeing though nothing was said.

"I think we should play, end up the season with a game," said Aaron. "Who knows, we might win."

Lawrence Alphonse had plate duties that evening and when he spoke with Mister Mac, it didn't look good. Mac stepped into the dugout.

"Guys, there's a rule we have to have nine men on the field," he said.

"Could we borrow one from Worthe Drug or Greendale?" I asked. "They've got some players hanging around."

"'Fraid not, Claude. Already asked about that. The Eagles said they'd protest, since it's not our regular roster."

*   *   *

There we left it. No pizza at The Shack after the game. None of Uncle Albert's homemade ice cream on the porch at Summers Run Farm. We would next gather for a funeral to bring the final curtain down on what the *Tribune* sportswriter called *"an unusually bittersweet season. The star that shone for the Pickett Township Panthers sputtered out last night in Chapmann, the team losing by forfeiture to the Chapmann Eagles. Strangers—not just parents and neighbors—started driving out to Summers Run Field for a nostalgic Little League baseball experience. Once there, they witnessed play by a scrappy bunch of farm kids and took them to their hearts. Situated near the banks of its namesake, Summers Run Field was beautifully resurrected from an old diamond and equipped with lights for night time contests. . . ."*

*   *   *

Several days after the funeral and respects were paid, I followed Trent Smythe to the family utility room where he gave me his uniform, freshly washed and folded. "I take care of it myself. My folks are from out in eastern Montana and don't care much for baseball. Football's big and rodeo out there."

I put Trent's uniform in a poke and he escorted me through the garage. "Watch your step out here. There's always motor oil or such on the floor."

We waded through the ATVs, the snow machines, the trailers, the horse tack, the saddles, the bass boat, the pontoons scattered about, and the motor bikes, the trail bikes, the dirt bikes that bore names like Scavenger, Avenger, and Li'l Darlin' painted in pink. "That bike was my sister's."

He looked over the array surrounding us before he hoisted the door by hand. "Opener's broke. All this stuff belongs to my folks, would y' believe? All the things they need to 'chase around' with their friends on the weekends. That's why they never come to any Saturday games. Out chasin' around. My dad's name is Brownell—Brown for short. 'Chase Around Brown,' I call 'im, 'cause he's always talking about 'chasin'" around with so-and-so. Chasin' around the lake, up in the woods."

We stepped out into a shadow-less day. I offered my hand and before I could utter anything weak or awkward, Trent said for us to not feel sorry for him. That he'd get along.

"The only thing I'm sorry about is that Shadee never got to see me play. I would have liked that. I liked her because she liked me. I'll miss her a lot. We were pals."

I nodded, gave him a little wave, and turned to go.

"You know something?" he called to me. "Shadee might be better off where she is now than livin' here. My sister got herself preggers again, some guy in Hannelsburg. She's not going to give this one up, I hear. I wanted . . . something better for Shadee."

"Right." *What did I know of such things?* "Well, okay, Trent. We'll see you at school." I stepped around the horse trailer in the drive. It reminded me. "Uh, thanks for being a Horseman."

"Yeah, that was cool. We were pretty good. I won't be coming back to Little League next season. Too old. Well, see y'."

I walked off toward my bike, straddled it, patted the family dog, and prepared to leave. Then Trent called to me again.

"You know who I feel sorry for? Jeff Linch. It's not going to be easy for him, facing the kids at school this year. I'd move if it was me." *Boys on a raft.*

Trent put his foot on the hitch of the horse trailer and brushed the dust from his pant leg. "I don't bear him any grudge an' I'll tell him such. Not his fault. Jeff says you're a good friend of his."

The body of Shandell "Shadee" Smythe was found on the farm of Hollis Linch.

*   *   *

CHAPTER 40

Harry the Ferguson

Jeff Linch invited me over to his place to shoot rats. No need to bring a gun, he assured me. "I got a couple .22s here with scopes." I biked into the Linch yard to be met by a swirling quartet of dogs.

"Back all you dogs!" Jeff commanded. "They's harmless, just curious. Here's yours." He handed me a Remington pump. I didn't mention the .22 of my dad's. I thought Jeff might resent comparing his serviceable rifles against the heirloom craftsmanship of the Winchester. He strode off carrying a Ruger semi-automatic rifle.

"Had any gun training about being safe an' all?" he asked over his shoulder.

"Yes, my cousin Nathe has shown me a lot about guns and safe handling."

"Good. We don't need no more tragedies around here. I read your dad's book about savin' the land and such. Made sense and purty clear. My dad said it was high falutin' but he din't read it. We'll go up on the old railroad bed and shoot down into the gully. I use subsonics on a still day. They don't make as much noise." I followed my new friend, my trepidation easing. *This doesn't seem as dangerous or as strange as I feared.*

I had almost backed out. My memory of an imaginary Jeff Linch glaring at me in front of Shadeland still haunted.

This afternoon, another episode I would not mention to my mother.

"Roger, he married my sister, he lives over there and he shoots a .22 Hornet. It gets out quite a bit farther but it makes more bang and scares 'em into hiding."

*   *   *

We spent the afternoon harvesting rats, three for me and six for Jeff. "They've holed up for now. Purty good day, really. Let's go back and get us a drink." We returned to the house to be met by the four Linch dogs.

"They's mutts mostly. Sometimes I take 'em with me to root them rats out, but then y' got to be more watchful 'cause they'll get in the line of fire, runnin' about. You ever drink from an old hand pump like this? I'd take y' into the house to cool off but I'm ashamed of it."

We sat in the shade of a lilac hedge, drank the very frosty water, and then I mentioned I should be getting home.

"Yeah, I gotta put these guns up 'cause I got some chores. Before y' go, I got a favor to ask."

"Okay. Anything I'm able, Jeff."

He looked at me surprised that I should utter his name.

"Well . . . I'm gonna be cleaning up the place and I might need some help."

Jeff explained he planned on pulling all the appliances from their graves and shipping the lot to Miller Bros. Salvage. He showed me the muscular yellow bucket loader and the hay racks he would be putting to the task. Then the fences he was going to pull down, the sheds he planned to "torch", the dead cars he and the Millers would be loading.

"We're gonna leave the stuff out back. It don't show from the road anyways. Somebody might want 'em someday 'cause they's antiques.

"I can run the loader better than Pap these days so I'm not afraid of it. It's all set to go and so am I. I got the date circled on the calendar. Gonna be a day to remember for me 'cause I can't stand the sight of it any longer after what's happened here.

"I might need someone to set the choker on some of this—not much to it—just hookin' chains. We gotta drag everything up in the yard 'cause Millers won't send their forklift down into the weeds. Th' first thing that's goin' outa here is that refrigerator where they found her."

He asked if I could bring Harry the Ferguson. "Be handy if you'uns could spare it for a day. Hook the hay rack on it and speed things along by quite a bit. We'll see that it ain't hurt none." I told him I'd ask.

Then, I said thanks for the day, that I enjoyed it, and retrieved my bike from the dogs showing renewed interest in my departure.

"Thanks for comin' over. Purty good day. Looks like you got a good eye. Uh, I got another matter on my mind."

"Okay."

He hooked his thumbs in the hip pocket of his jeans, scraped the dirt with the toe of his boot and looked away. "Well, uh, come the first day of school . . . I'd be obliged if you and me was seen as friends and talkin' to one another." He then faced me, daring me to be repelled by his request.

"Sure. Be glad to."

"Such might help on the account of you bein' liked an' all and you'uns being a family that's respected around hereabouts. Kids over there think we're white trash, and this situation we just had here ain't gonna help matters."

*   *   *

I explained my mission to Nathe and Jeff's request. He cautioned me about always hooking to the drawbar and avoiding slopes and ditches. Then we affixed a rear view mirror to the Ferguson's cowling. "We'll be sending sweet corn to Marguerite's soon and driving on the lane. A mirror's handy to see what's coming up behind. Startles y' sometimes when a car passes a tractor and you didn't know it was there."

The mirror was one of those convex types common on the passenger side where "Objects in mirror are closer than they appear" was etched along the bottom.

"Mirror and appear," said Nathe. "Rhymes. Wonder if that was deliberate?" Then we mounted two more flashers on the roll bar. "These can be seen by oncoming traffic better, too." It was fun working with Nathe, drilling the holes, snaking the wiring, making a good thing better. Talking while we worked together.

I found it of interest. The precautions we take with guns and tractors. Are we as careful with each other?

* * *

The day I worked at Jeff Linch's. Perhaps it's a theme topic with its title written in all upper case letters. It became a boy's delight.

For we dragged, piled, yanked things free, pushed stuff into heaps, loaded, hauled, smashed, torched, and leveled. The next day when the two Miller Bros. semis pulled in to load the appliances, the vehicles, the metal cabinets, and the household junk that wouldn't burn, Jeff told me: "I'll catch holy red hell for this but Roger and Linda will back me up. Linda's on the fishing trip they take to Alaska ever couple years. I told Mam and Pap I wasn't goin' this year.

"Pap said 'suit yerself. But I gotta get outa here and free my mind. All this snoopin' around and inquiry and such and folks clamberin' about and making threats and insinuations. I'm sick to death of it, and when I get back I'm gonna tell them supervisors and the county to lay off and let a man be.'

"'If you're gonna stay here then, boy, you mind an' feed them turkeys so they'll keep comin' up to the house and don't go off nowhere's else.'"

Jeff laughed. "That's the way he talks. Like a hillbilly. I'm not feedin' his wild turkeys. They get into everything and make a purty mess."

"You're bold, Jeffers," I told him. "I guess Hollis will be mad at us too." I meant Nathe, myself, and Harry the Ferguson.

"Well, Roger'll be back before then. He's on a run to Florida. He's an over-the-road trucker haulin' fruit an' vegetables. Roger said if Hollis were to lay a hand on me for this, that he'd step in and there'd be more than words.

"Roger wants to retire in a few years and he said he wanted this junk to be long gone when he did. 'Looks like a buryin' ground out there in the moonlight,' he says, 'and I'm tired of these rats and skunks tryin' to get in my chicken coop. You do what needs to be done here.'

"Roger's been at Pap for years and the weeds were getting taller and the buildings fallin' down. But if I myself clean the place up, then that'll keep the peace between Pap and Mam and Roger and Linda. It'll be my doin', not theirs, and my fault, y' see."

When I left the Linch place that evening, Jeff had begun attacking the weeds with the loader. He would pull the bucket backwards and drag them into windrows, mixing weeds with the ashes of the canoe-shaped shed and other dismal derelicts of outbuildings begging for a swift and merciful end. All would be burned.

Miller Bros. Salvage hauled three loads out and would return in the morning for the last of it. Jeff Linch told me: "I grew some today."

*   *   *

287

CHAPTER 41

The Crevices of Memory

The neighborhood grapevine reported, upon his return from Alaska, Hollis Linch immediately called the township supervisor, then the various county agencies raging about the violation of his property. When he learned his son had leveled the place, he pinned a note to Jeff's bicycle in the yard.

It read: "Ok Boy. You have had your say. Now I have had mine."

He then entered the house, built fires in its corners and with the flames licking their way up the walls, he stepped into the living room where he shot himself.

Mam Linch is reputed to have described her husband as so distraught by the death of Shadee Smythe and all the attendant publicity, outcry, and investigation . . . "he just had to get away an', we took that fishing trip to get his mind off things for a spell. He was not himself up there, I could tell, fussin' and ailin', not sleepin' good 'tall. I just had a notion it would all come to a bad end."

The notes left behind. I added the last communications of Roland Shanahan, mercurial motion picture director, and now Hollis Linch to my realm of experience.

*   *   *

My mother suggests I keep a journal. My coach urges me to cherish every moment.

288

For these past six months of my life, I have become a resident of a world known as Summers Run. I ford its waters. I snooze in the cooling shade it offers. I climb the rocks where it reveals a hint of its geological design. I marvel at its hills in the moonlight and in the afternoon, I harvest hickory nuts from its slopes and the loganberries hidden in the little patches it perfected for them alone. My father Blake did likewise and I look for him within these places.

Back when I was of the age of Wren, my dad and I spent a rare week exploring his boyhood home. It "pleasures" me now to recall how startled we were when a ruffed grouse exploded from behind a fallen oak. He laughed, caught quite unguarded and relishing the moment. Not long ago, I retraced the steps we'd left behind on that day.

As we did then, I lay on the edge of the hemlock ravine . . . you know the place . . . just beyond the lower meadow where the brook winds its way down to Summers Run. Boylike, I think I might hear his voice here. Or the echo of his laughter. Perhaps there'll be a face in the clouds overhead, a shadow slipping past, or a sudden gust rustling the hair off my brow.

Instead, he sends me a woodcock, hopping its way through the evergreen boughs, unaware of my motionless presence.

The community of Summers Run provides raucous blue jays to wake you to its misty mornings. Or crows squabbling in the hayfield. At dusk, though, the Run knows one needs a bobolink or the whip-poor-will to settle us down and into the night.

Wren, whose curiosity may become legendary, is certain he and I can find a whip-poor-will if "we're stealthy enough." P. M. Murphy then tells him, "now there's the 'will of the wisp'. I think I saw one once, but alas, it was nearly nightfall. Perhaps, young Wren, you will be blessed. Your eyes are much younger than mine."

When I tell Wren of the elusive peepers filling the air in the evenings of early spring, he is confident their secrets will be revealed to the two of us as well.

I'm sure Wren will also learn Summers Run is a place of seasons, not dates marked on the calendars. Oh, to be certain, folks hereabouts take note of frosts and phases of the moon, but they also believe there is a tempo to our times in this place.

As elsewhere, life here too speeds along with major events filling its passing: the anniversaries, weddings, the births and deaths, the games won and lost, the adventures of a very small boy climbing to the top of the barn.

I may climb the barn for my father, one of these days. One of these days when Wren is not around to copy me. If I do so, I will tell my dad I touched the rooster there.

On the other hand, life here also can crawl along within the rhythms of the day and its common tasks. Such causes me to wonder if it is the little things of life that endure and are the most remembered. The knowing look, the wistful smile, the absent-minded whistle, a favorite saying or a quote, the sounds of a hundred things, the texture of a dozen, the aroma of a handful.

While the large and grand fill the canyons of our minds and blend together, it seems to me the small and quiet lodge in the deepest crevices of our memory. There they stand alone. Why such remain so crisp puzzles me yet.

Accordingly, I look forward to when my friend Tim hears his first whip-poor-will. A pleasure equal to hearing the cheers sent my way, rounding the bases after a home run. The canyon-crevice sort of thing found in life.

Tim calls. He says he has been practicing on the phones of the Home, that the staff indulge him. I invite him over to listen to Aunt Marguerite practice on the flute. He sits enthralled as she plays "Gently Passing" for an audience of three boys. And he brings a letter, addressed to Mr. Timothy Hathaway, informing him his art work, *Standing Ovation*, has been received and that a decision will be forthcoming.

Yes, decisions are always forthcoming, thanks to time and its persistent passing.

It appears decisions regarding his adoption by the McIntyres have moved through the preliminaries and the bulk of the processing decreed by the state of Pennsylvania. According to Aunt Marguerite, what remains are essentially formalities and then Tim will be moving soon to his new home.

Meanwhile, as Tim is leaving his days as an orphan behind, my future whereabouts seem less than settled. My mother assures me if I move to Las Vegas as she plans, I can spend my summers in P. A. if I choose. "Or, your granddad tells me, you could play baseball out here all year long. He says you have potential."

Since the Panthers' season had been cut short, my grandparents decide to renew their plans to camp in the Finger Lake country. On their way back to Nevada in September, they will pass through Summers Run and then "we'll talk."

School will be underway by that time. Perhaps I'll enjoy a season of Decision Delayed. The motion to move Claude to Las Vegas: *Tabled.*

Soon, The Four Horseman of the Outfield will ride again in 7th grade. I wonder if I shall ask them to admit a fifth rider, Jeff Linch. With the possible exception of Luther Ludlow, we all bear wounds and scars. I hope Trent will approve and Jeff will be admitted.

Most importantly, there remains my cousin Nathe, the coach who can sense a teachable moment whether on the baseball diamond or in The Apple Room of Summers Run Farm. Often, a Panther will slip and refer to him as Claude's dad. When Nathe stands off a ways hitting flies to us in the outfield or guiding my cast, hand in glove, with a fly rod and line, I needn't squint to imagine him as Blake Kinkade.

Nathe wants me to know about my father, about himself, and about life. He is becoming my anchor.

Like the woodcock flitting its way along the hemlocks and into the willows—only the length of a heartbeat away—Nathe was sent to me, rather than a vision, a shadow, or a voice.

*   *   *

At this time of year, the families gather on a woodlot we share. From here, we haul in the winter's wood cut several seasons ago and nicely cured, ready to burn brightly in The Homestead Room or at Uncle Albert's.

We are loading the wagon for its final trip down the trail when Aunt Marguerite lays her coffee mug aside and honors the family's tradition of singing:

Now the day is o'er
Night is drawing nigh;
Shadows of the evening
Steal across the sky.

I did not know this hymn. Bethany joins her mother, though, and Gram Bea, Albert, and Nathe. Wren and I look on and Samara clings to Beth, a bit bewildered over the strange behavior of this family she'd been born into. The families then start walking down the hollow behind me while I lead with the tractor. I watch them in the mirror. Gram Bea, a great-grandkid holding each hand, and everyone singing together.

Now the darkness gathers,
Stars begin to peep,
Birds and beasts and flowers
Soon will be asleep.

I wonder if Winter Wood Day should be counted as a canyon event or crevice moment. I finally decide it qualifies as both.

Once we arrive at Summers Run Road, I turn on the flashers and the rest of the party loads into the Oldsmobile or Albert's pickup, heading for Summers Run Farm and "Brunswick Stew, folks, like it or lump it. Been a-simmering all the day long."

Nathe says he wants to ride with the load and for me to take the long road home, that he needs to film a sunset down by the covered bridge.

"Guess we'll be late for dinner," I tell him.

"Better late for dinner, son, than late for a sunset."

With Harry the Ferguson humming along beneath me and the hymn still on my mind, I drive toward the evening, passing the farms I now know as my neighbors. Harvey Logan stands at his mailbox leafing through what he finds there. Looking up, he laughs, slapping his thighs as we pass, and in the mirror I see Nathe salute as if he were the Grand Marshall of a Summers Run parade.

I watch him enjoy the passage of the countryside he'd learned to treasure as a boy. A man cherishing every moment of his return to boyhood and its memories and joy. The message etched in the glass—Objects in mirror are closer than they appear—becomes more than just a statement now. For Nathe and I are drawing closer, ever closer than we appear.

He is the man my father sent to take his place. And I am becoming . . . the son he never had.

*   *   *

LaVergne, TN USA
17 June 2010
186428LV00001B/4/P